PRAISE FOR A

D0440798

Herb of Grace

"Senft is a talented author and her research on various herbs is a welcome surprise to readers. The story incorporates facts about herbs, what each of them can be used for and what will happen if used incorrectly. This sweet romance has a believable storyline with a lot of heart." —*RT Book Reviews*

"With a complex mix of both younger and older characters and a complex story line, this book is truly a success."
—Brodart Books & Library Services

"[A] genuine must read for those who love Amish fiction. Readers will not be able to put this book down until finished, it is just that great and filled with rich characterization. *Herb of Grace* is a five star recommended book."
—AmishReader.blogspot.com

The Wounded Heart

"This relatable story, which launches Senft's Amish Quilt series, shows that while waiting to see God's plan can be difficult, remembering to put Jesus first, others next and yourself last ("JOY") is necessary." —*RT Book Reviews*

"With this quaint, gentle read, Senft's promising series is off to a good start and will make a nice alternative for Jerry S. Eicher readers who want to try a new author."

—*Library Journal*

"Senft perfectly captures the Amish setting of the novel. Amelia is an endearing character, and there were a few laugh-out-loud moments for me that I wasn't even expecting. Although this is the first book I have read by the author, she has been added to my 'must read' list. If you are a fan of Amish fiction, then plan on reading *The Wounded Heart* soon!"

—Christian Fiction Addiction

The Hidden Life

"I absolutely loved *The Hidden Life*! Nothing is as enjoyable as feeling the same way the characters do throughout the story and believing that you are mixed into the same world.... *The Hidden Life* is full of conflict, romance, and drama! Overall I felt Adina captured the Amish way of life with fine detail. Be prepared to become an even bigger fan of Adina's after you read this book and you will be eagerly anticipating the next installment *The Tempted Soul* just like me!" —Destination Amish

The Tempted Soul

"I do declare that Adina has saved the best story for last. I loved this book! Saying that it is a heartfelt story just doesn't seem like it does the book justice." —Destination Amish

BALM *of* GILEAD

Also by Adina Senft

The Healing Grace Novels

Herb of Grace
Keys of Heaven

The Amish Quilt Series

The Wounded Heart
The Hidden Life
The Tempted Soul

Available from FaithWords wherever books are sold.

BALM *of* GILEAD

A HEALING GRACE NOVEL

ADINA SENFT

New York Boston Nashville

This book is a work of fiction. Names, characters, places, and incidents are the product of the author's imagination or are used fictitiously. Any resemblance to actual events, locales, or persons, living or dead, is coincidental. Though the herbal recipes and cures in this book are based on traditional herbal practices, please consult your doctor before using them to treat any ailments.

Copyright © 2015 by Shelley Bates

All rights reserved. In accordance with the U.S. Copyright Act of 1976, the scanning, uploading, and electronic sharing of any part of this book without the permission of the publisher constitute unlawful piracy and theft of the author's intellectual property. If you would like to use material from the book (other than for review purposes), prior written permission must be obtained by contacting the publisher at permissions@hbgusa.com. Thank you for your support of the author's rights.

FaithWords
Hachette Book Group
1290 Avenue of the Americas
New York, NY 10104

www.faithwords.com

Printed in the United States of America

RRD-C

First Edition: July 2015
10 9 8 7 6 5 4 3 2

FaithWords is a division of Hachette Book Group, Inc.
The FaithWords name and logo are trademarks of Hachette Book Group, Inc.

The Hachette Speakers Bureau provides a wide range of authors for speaking events. To find out more, go to www.hachettespeakersbureau.com or call (866) 376-6591.

The publisher is not responsible for websites (or their content) that are not owned by the publisher.

Library of Congress Cataloging-in-Publication Data has been applied for.

ISBN: 978-1-455-54867-5

For friends of the plain people everywhere

ACKNOWLEDGMENTS

My thanks to herbalist Paula Grainger, who is so generous with her expertise and willing to help heal my imaginary people. Thanks also to my amazing team at FaithWords—Christina Boys, Katie Connors, Virginia Hensley, and Julee Brand—for making these books not only beautiful, but the best they can be. And thanks always to Jeff for his unstinting support, and for his willingness to pack up the pickup and head off on the next research adventure.

Author's Note

In the ancient world, a tree known as Balm of Gilead, or the Mecca balsam, provided healing balsamic oils. In the new world, a species of poplar tree possesses similar properties and is also known as Balm of Gilead. Its fragrant, sticky buds are harvested and infused with oil to make a salve for the treatment of skin conditions.

In plant lore, poplars are considered to be protective trees, which may be why the Amish and *Englisch* alike plant them as windbreaks in fields and along roads. There is also a belief among ancient peoples that in the whisper of the poplar tree's leaves, you can hear the still, small voice of God.

Is there no balm in Gilead; is there no physician there? Why then is not the health of the daughter of my people recovered?

—Jeremiah 8:22, KJV

BALM *of* GILEAD

Chapter 1

An Amish woman's year, Sarah Yoder always thought, was governed not so much by the twelve-month paper calendar on the kitchen wall than by the hand of God. Instead of crossing off squares, a woman lived by the rhythm of the preaching on every other Sunday, and by the cycle of the blossoms and fruit in garden and orchard.

Because of the wet spring and hot summer they'd had this year in Whinburg Township, the gardens had gone crazy—and still were, here at the tail end of September with its chilly nights and crisp blue days. A branch on one of the old Spartans in Jacob and Corinne Yoder's apple orchard had actually broken from the weight of its apples, so the word had gone out and sisters' day had been moved up to deal with the emergency.

Autumn was Sarah's favorite season. Every one held its blessings, it was true—winter for the rest the plants took under their blanket of snow and for the lamplit evenings spent with family and friends when there was no work to be done in the fields, spring for the tender greens and shy flowers and the seeds going into the soil, summer for the long days of growing and canning and putting by. But there was something about autumn that Sarah loved more than any of these.

Maybe it was the sense of the earth giving back all that the work of her hands had put into it. Maybe it was the pantry with its rows and rows of jewel-toned jars full of canned fruit, pickles, and vegetables. Or maybe it was just the quiet in the air now that the fieldwork was coming to a close—air that was still enough that she could smell burning leaves and hear the shouts of the little scholars going into the one-room schoolhouse for their afternoon lessons on the other side of the county road.

Her younger son, Caleb, had had a brief—very brief—moment of nostalgia for those innocent days he'd left behind, earlier at breakfast. As he tucked away ham and eggs and biscuits and strawberry jam, he'd said, "It's hard to believe my scholar days are gone for good, Mamm. I don't even have to keep my work journal anymore. Can I have another piece of ham?"

She'd forked a piece onto his plate and tried not to smile. An eighty-year-old man couldn't have reminisced any better about the days of yore. "Are you looking forward to your first day of work with Jon Hostetler?"

His mouth full, Caleb nodded vigorously. With a mighty swallow, he said, "Daadi Jacob says I'm to keep humble and do as I'm told, and before I know it, I'll be running a work crew and maybe even my own outfit."

Sarah stifled a pang at the thought of how quickly those words came out of a man's mouth. The years would run by just as quickly and her boy, almost fifteen now, would be working and marrying and going to his own home, one he would probably build with his own hands.

Which was just as it should be, if God willed it.

But for now, she would value every moment with him, even the ones where she swore she would wad up the dishcloth and stuff it in his mouth to keep him from talking her ear off. There would come a day, she knew, when she would give anything to hear him talking, even if it was about something mystifying, like how he helped Henry Byler over on the next place fire his pieces of pottery in the kiln.

But then, the whole subject of Henry Byler was mystifying, and one best avoided if a woman were to keep peace in her heart.

Her walk across the fields on the path that she, Caleb, and her older son, Simon, had worn into the soil brought her to her in-laws' place for sisters' day. Already she could hear the voices of women raised in encouragement, exclamation, and laughter. Picking up her pace, Sarah cut through the backyard and walked around the laurel hedge into the orchard.

Half a dozen women and a few young men stood on ladders, their dresses and shirts in purple, brick, and green making them look like brightly colored birds in the trees.

"Sarah!" Corinne, her late husband's mother, was filling a basket next to the poor abused Spartan, which thankfully was old enough and low enough that she didn't need to climb up on a ladder. In her early sixties, Corinne still had the sunny smile of a girl as she waved, the breeze catching at her purple dress. "Choose any tree you like. We're determined to lighten the load on the branches by at least half, and make as much applesauce as we possibly can by dinnertime."

"And pie," called Corinne's youngest daughter, Amanda, who at twenty-one was the only child still at home. "Not to mention tarts, strudel, and *Schnitz.*"

Yes, Amanda was still at home…but not for lack of

matchmaking attempts by her whole family. Sarah, Corinne, and her other sisters-in-law, Miriam and Barbara, were going to have to put their heads together and see if they couldn't improve their results in that department.

Ja, it was true that God had His plan for Amanda, and He would reveal the special someone He had in mind for her in His own good time. But plans could be helped along, couldn't they? Didn't the Scripture say that all things worked together for good to them that loved God, and were called according to His purpose?

If the Bible said it, then it was so.

"What did you bring?" Corinne called. "Whatever it is, I hope there's lots—this is hungry work."

Sarah lifted the plastic container. "Pumpkin cupcakes with cream cheese frosting."

Amanda whooped. "My favorite!"

"I'll just put them in the house and be right back." It only took a minute to drop the container on the counter with those of the other women, and hurry back out. She chose a tree, and Jake Byler tilted one of the ladders against a thick branch. Sarah picked up a basket and balanced it on one hip as she climbed, then settled to the work of picking.

"This one's full, Jake—take it, please, and hand me up another." With one hand, he passed a basket up to his mother, Barbara Byler, in the next tree while she let down her full one to his shoulder. As her boy loaded it on the children's wagon that was usually hitched to a pony, Barbara smiled through the leaves at Sarah. "I got a letter from Joe this morning—did you get one from Simon?"

"No—what did he say? Are they coming home?" Oh, she hoped so. Her elder boy had left unexpectedly in the spring to go and work at a dude ranch in Colorado—spreading his wings, as the *Youngie* did during *Rumspringe*, their season of running around. But no one in Willow Creek had expected him to fly all the way to Colorado, much less take his best friend, Joe Byler, with him. Both of them were steady boys, thoughtful, hardworking. Not the kind who would try something so outlandish, and most especially not against their parents' wishes.

There had been a time or two when Sarah had wondered if she would ever see her boy again. He might be another woman's child, but when she'd married his father, Michael, he had become her own son in every way, so that it hadn't mattered that she hadn't borne him herself. His absence left a void in her heart that only his return would fill.

"They are," Barbara said, a note in her voice telling Sarah that she was *this close* to jumping up and down on her ladder and cheering. "When they went to town to mail the letter, he said they were going to see about the bus schedule, and that would tell them what train to get." She lowered her voice. "I don't mind telling you that I won't feel easy until Joe is back in his own bed and I can see him with my own eyes."

"Do you think they'll stay home now?" Sarah voiced her own thoughts on the matter for the first time. "Do you think this travel bug is out of their systems for good?"

Barbara was about the only person she could ask such a question of, because no one else in Willow Creek had had their sons go much farther than Whinburg or Strasburg. Well, unless you counted Timothy Yost a generation ago, but his father had thrown him out of the house in the middle of such an ugly situation that it had taken both men more than twenty years to be reconciled.

Sarah could safely say that that would never happen between herself and Simon, even though he was a passionate young man who thought and felt much more than he ever said.

"I think Joe is about done with *Rumspringe*," Barbara told her. "He didn't come out and say it in a letter, but from a question or two he asked about some of the other young folks, I got the feeling he wants to settle down and start baptism classes."

"Ah." Sarah let out a long sigh. "That does sound *gut*. I'm glad to hear it."

"What about Simon? What does he say?"

"Oh, you know him. If nothing else, at least this summer I've found out what kind of a correspondent he is. By which I mean—not a very good one."

Barbara laughed and let a couple of apples roll into her basket, making a hollow sound on the laths. "That's a boy for you. Come on. First one to fill her basket gets one of those cupcakes."

Later that afternoon, in the kitchen, Sarah made sure Barbara got one, because it was a simple fact that her large, square hands were better at coaxing the fruit off their branches than Sarah's own were. When she came back, she found Miriam, her sister-in-law, leaning against the counter breathing in the scent of the coffee in her cup as though it were the finest perfume.

"*Ischt gut*," Miriam said, seeing that Sarah had caught her. She offered her the cup. When Sarah looked surprised, she shook her head. "I love the smell of it, but that's it for me. The doctor says no more than two cups a day. That's going to mean some big changes."

"I'd say so. Is it your heart?"

Miriam nodded sadly, watching Sarah pour a little cream into the cup and taste it. "Cut down the coffee and sugar, and eat more vegetables, and this rapid heartbeat problem will look after itself."

"Would you like me to make you a tea to drink? I have a recipe that calms the body and the mind. I would love it if you'd let me."

"I can't put you to that trouble, Sarah."

But Sarah knew that Miriam would be the first person to put herself to the trouble of helping just about anyone else. "It's no trouble. You've done so much for me and the boys— please let me do this little thing for you."

After a second's hesitation, Miriam finally nodded. "I have to be smart about this, don't I? Mamm's father and Dat's mother both died of heart disease, so it's in the family. But if *der Herr* wills it, then—"

"We wait on His will," Sarah said softly, "but in the meantime, we're good stewards of the temples He gave us for His spirit to dwell in. And if the doctor tells you to take care of your heart, then you do that and no fussing."

Miriam's smile was real this time. "So bossy."

"I know."

They both laughed, and across the room, their mother-in-law, Corinne, looked up, love for the two of them softening her face. Not for the first time, Sarah thanked the *gut Gott* in Heaven for the family to which He'd brought her. Though she'd lost Michael nearly six years ago, his family was her family, as loving and close as if she'd been born to it.

Once again, her mind flew across the creek and over the hill that divided her five acres from the place that now belonged to Henry Byler. Henry, alone on his late aunt's shabby farm, bravely trying to make a living with his hands and re-

sisting with every cell of his being the call of God to return
to the church and community where he belonged.

But she must not think of him. That was Ginny
Hochstetler's place now. He had chosen his future when he'd
asked Ginny to be his wife, and all the wishing in the world
wouldn't unmake that choice.

CHAPTER 2

"I f we're having a Christmas wedding, we need to make some decisions now. Time's a-wasting."

Henry's bride-to-be, dressed this morning in pumpkin-colored jeans and a harvest yellow sequined T-shirt that said PLANT KINDNESS—HARVEST HAPPINESS, plunked a stack of invitation samples on the kitchen table at the bed-and-breakfast she owned, the Rose Arbor Inn. Two couples and a single had reservations and would be arriving this afternoon for the autumn weekend, but for now, the cozy kitchen belonged just to the two of them.

"Tell me what you like," Henry suggested, pushing his whisker-clean dessert bowl to one side. Among her many other stellar qualities, Ginny made the best apple crumble on the planet—and believed in serving it for breakfast, after eggs and sausage.

"I only brought home the ones I liked. You're the artist—you get to narrow down the field."

Henry couldn't see the connection between wedding invitations and the bowls and plates he made, but it was clear that bringing this up wouldn't help the situation. So he bent his attention to the samples.

"I suppose the first question to ask is, how many are we

going to need?" He set aside a parchment-colored one with a design someone believed to be Art Nouveau.

"There are thirty in my immediate family, including kids," Ginny said, "but that's only four households. We should count address labels for the invitations, not people. The guest list is separate."

"Is that what you did the first time?"

"Are you kidding? When I was married the first time, I converted to the Mennonite faith for my husband. His church was a pretty liberal one, true, but I only sent one invitation to Philly—to my parents. The church filled up the rest of the meetinghouse. This time I aim to have a blowout, right here at the Inn."

He couldn't resist that smile—with those chocolate eyes, café au lait skin, and spiraled hair tied up in a yellow bandanna, she was the kind of joyous woman who made it impossible not to grin back. Of course she would want a blowout. She'd left the church, divorced her husband, and now she could indulge herself in any way she wanted without having to worry about degrees of plainness and what people would think.

Not for her the solemn hymns and the preaching about the married couples in the Bible, beginning with Adam and Eve. Not for her a blue dress and a white organdy *Kapp* and apron that she would wear only twice—on her wedding day and in her coffin.

He would marry Ginny Hochstetler and close the door forever on a future that could hold even the possibility of those things. For either of them.

"What about this one? Yellow is your favorite color." At least it was interesting, the way it was folded. Almost like origami.

"Hello? Christmas wedding?"

"Ginny, I don't know anyone less likely to conform to a traditional color palette than you. Does it come in other colors?"

"Red, green, white, and pale blue with snowflakes."

"Blue with snowflakes it is."

"Done. That was easy." She swept the samples together and stuffed them back in the stationer's envelope. "Are you going to be like this about new cars and wallpaper, too?"

"I leave wallpaper in your capable hands, and the likelihood of my being able to afford a new car is pretty low." He caught sight of the corner of a catalog in the stack of mail. "Wait—is that the D.W. Frith fall catalog? When did it come? I haven't seen mine yet."

"We're not done, Henry."

"I just need one second."

He flipped through the glossy pages. The autumn and spring editions of the catalog were the East Coast department store's biggest of the retail year. Dave Petersen, the vice president of procurement who handled him, had said that after the success of the video featuring him and his studio out in the barn on their website, a full-page spread in the fall edition was almost a given. Had they...? Was it...?

And there it was. Ginny came around the table to look over his shoulder with such calm that he knew she'd already seen it. "They did a nice job," she said with masterful understatement.

Hadn't they just. His pieces were laid out on a cherry sideboard in what he could only assume was the kind of home environment that the people who got this catalog either owned or aspired to. His Iris vase held an autumn arrangement of chrysanthemums that matched the green, gold, and purple glazes perfectly. How many trips by how many production assistants to New York florists had that taken? A batter bowl sat on a serving charger and held nothing more than a hand-carved mixing spoon set at an artistic angle. Four place settings of his water-glaze plates with a rolled-up napkin in a ring set on each were arranged as though a buffet were just waiting for its guests, along with glasses and sterling silver.

If he hadn't formed and fired these pieces himself, he would hardly have recognized them.

"Well?" Ginny prompted him. "Are you happy with it?"

He hardly knew how to respond. On the one hand, his artistic soul was completely wowed by the production values. He was no shopper, but even he could see it would take some real willpower for a customer to resist whipping out the plastic and buying as many pieces as the credit limit would allow.

"*Handmade on an Amish farm by potter*—honestly, how many times do I have to tell them I'm not Amish?—*Glaze recipe handed down through the generations*—all one of them. *Available only as shown, by special order.* At least that part is true."

"Skip to the bottom," Ginny suggested.

"Set of four…two sizes…*a hundred and forty dollars a plate?*" Henry felt as though someone had given him a good hard shove in the solar plexus.

"Look what they're asking for the batter bowl."

"Four hundred dollars. For one bowl." Henry sat back. "No one is going to buy these. Or if they do, they won't use them. Who is going to bang a spoon on the side of a four-hundred-dollar batter bowl?"

"I would," Ginny said. "And do. I like the batter bowl you made me."

"That was entirely worth the price of a kiss." He covered the hand that lay on his shoulder with his, and craned to look up at her. "But not four hundred dollars."

"Didn't you talk about the price the pieces would retail for with Dave Petersen?"

"They hadn't set them yet when he told me what they needed for the layout. They wanted to build the demand—and now I see why."

"Well, all I can say is I hope you're getting a nice chunk of it."

"Maybe I should ask for more."

But Ginny only smiled, squeezed his shoulder, and went back to her chair, where she pulled out a pad of lined yellow paper. He did his best to drag his attention off the catalog and concentrate, but it wasn't easy. How could a man live up to that kind of price tag? What if people thought his pieces weren't worth it? What if they went online and said the kinds of things that the newspaper art critics had said back in Denver, years ago?

He was really putting himself out there, allowing himself to be blandished by the praise of Dave Petersen and the marketing team. He shouldn't have listened. He should have stayed small, stayed humble, given people the value they paid for and no more.

Just like an Amish man.

"Henry? Did you hear me?"

"Sorry, honey. What?"

"I know you've got sticker shock, but I need you with me, here. How many should we expect on your side of the family?"

"I'll invite all of them, but they won't come."

"It's the right time of year—wedding season. And train fare from Ohio isn't so bad in the winter."

"They won't come, Ginny."

"Because you're marrying a black, divorced refugee from the Mennonite church?"

"If she were still alive, my mother would love you, refugee or not. But my brothers and sisters won't come all that way for a worldly wedding."

"If you were marrying an Amish woman, would they?"

"Oh, yes. But they can't be seen to support what they view as sin, you see."

"I can't say I do. This is the first time I've ever heard of marriage being a sin. Usually it's the lack of it that's the problem."

He had to admit that from that point of view, she was right. But then there was his family's point of view, which, like his father, was bound strictly to the letter of the law.

"What about our Amish friends here? Do you think they'll see it that way?"

"Paul and Barbara will come, don't worry. It's just the ones back home that won't."

"And Sarah and Caleb? And Priscilla's family, and Katie Schrock's?"

The thought of Sarah Yoder attending his wedding... watching him with those gray eyes that saw more than he wanted them to...judging him and finding him wanting... oh no. With any luck, there would be so many weddings among the *Gmee* that week that she'd have to send her regrets. An Amish bride invited the entire church, as well as relatives from out of town. In some communities, there were multiple weddings every Tuesday and Thursday from

November until February, and people had to run from one to another in order to attend the ones they'd been invited to on the same day.

"You're going to Katie's wedding, so I'm sure her family will be happy to come to yours," Henry said. "You've been good to Priscilla, too."

In the leftmost column on her pad, Ginny began a rapid list of names, and in less than five minutes, had reached the bottom line and flipped the paper over. "Is everyone going to fit in the Inn?" Henry inquired. These people would be his future family, and her friends would be his friends. But there sure were a lot of them—and this was only the first cut. "Maybe I should get on the phone and start booking rooms in town."

"We'll need to," Ginny said absently, her pen busily marching down the second page. "Mama and Daddy can stay here, and Sienna and her family, since they're coming from California, and Grammy, because she's eighty-six, but everyone else will need to be put up at the motels." She looked up. "And did I tell you I'm going to Philadelphia to look for a dress?"

"Not until now."

"You don't mind, do you?" She looked honestly concerned that he might.

"Of course not. I don't think you'd find anything suitable in Willow Creek...or Whinburg...or even Lancaster."

"There isn't even a dress shop in either of the first two. I could make it, I suppose, but it's much more fun to make a weekend of it with Mama and my sisters. We never got a chance to before." Her gaze held his. "I don't suppose you got a chance to, either. Before."

It was just like Ginny to bring it up as if it were perfectly normal—that subject that he'd never confided to anyone. Well, except Sarah, and that didn't count.

"Allison and I were only engaged for a couple of weeks before the accident," he said. "We hadn't even set a date yet, never mind thought about guest lists and dresses and where people were going to stay." He braced himself, waiting for that debilitating stab of pain in his heart that always accompanied any thought of Allison—the accident—the drunk driver that had killed a happy future as surely as he'd killed a vibrant, bright twenty-eight-year-old, who by now might have been a partner in the law firm where she'd been hired right after passing the bar.

But the pain had softened into memory, it seemed. He could still see the sparkle in her eyes, but he could also remember the joke that had prompted it. He could focus on the loss and the injustice of it, or, as Ginny had told him not so long ago, he could focus on the happiness Allison had left in her wake like the scent of perfume.

Ginny believed in happiness. And now he would, too.

Henry got up, came around the table, and tilted her face up to his for a kiss that meant business.

"What was that for?" she said a little breathlessly, straightening her bandanna and looking as though she was trying to remember what she'd been doing.

"I can never appreciate you too much," he told her. "You amaze me."

"You just hold that thought, Henry Byler. When we've been married for twenty years, I'll remind you of this moment."

He kissed her again, just because he could. "When we've been married for twenty years, you still won't need to."

Chapter 3

Priscilla Mast had often been struck by the differences between men and women. Oh, not the obvious ones—men working out in fields and factories, women working in home and garden. Men growing beards when they were married, women changing the color of the *Kapp*. Men driving, women riding alongside. Men speaking in church, women keeping silence. Those were the obvious things. But there were subtler things that became more obvious the older she got.

For instance, if she had been planning to travel a long distance to return to people who cared about her, she would have found out train schedules and bus schedules, decided on them, bought a ticket, and been able to write and tell her family that she would be arriving on this day at this time in this place. Her family could count down the days, hours, and finally minutes until they could see her again. They would know the train or bus to meet. They would actually be able to look forward to it.

But boys? Could they really be as oblivious as this to the simple pleasure of looking forward to something?

Dear Pris,

Well, the folks here have given us notice that the snow will be flying soon, and they'll be closing the ranch to visitors. There will be some more at Christmas—visitors, not snow, but there will probably be lots of that, too—but other than a couple to pull some kids around the ranch in a sleigh, they won't be needing many horses. So, they're not going to need me and Simon after Sunday.

So I guess that means we're coming home. I hope that's good news. It is to me. I'll see you soon, I hope.

> Best,
> Joe

Boys, honestly.

Pris folded up the letter and tucked it into the pocket in the side seam of her dress, under her black bib apron. Then she tapped into order the rest of the mail she'd pulled out of the mailbox at the end of the drive, and walked down to the house. It didn't hold anything else very interesting, except for a new issue of *Die Botschaft*, and a letter for Mamm from each of Priscilla's aunts, who lived in Lititz and New Hope and who corresponded with her faithfully every week.

She would just have to look forward to Joe and Simon's return in a general sense. At least this way, when they finally did turn up, it would be like walking into the kitchen and having everyone yell "Surprise!" on her birthday. Not that anyone had ever done that, because it was impossible to keep a secret of any kind in their family, but she imagined it would be something similar.

She handed the mail to Mamm and leaned against the door of the oven, which felt delightfully warm against her legs after the crisp air outside. It smelled heavenly in the kitchen. "I think roasted pork with apples and onions and potatoes and noodles is my favorite meal in the world."

Mamm glanced up from her letters and smiled. "Mine, too, except for the chicken roast at weddings. And if I could make a meal out of pecan pie, I probably would."

"Is the applesauce done yet?" Priscilla checked the big pot simmering on the stove, and the scent of hot cinnamon wafted into the room. "Mm. If I could bottle this scent and sell it in February, I could make a fortune."

"You're not doing too badly as it is," Mamm said absently, half her attention on whatever mishap her next oldest sister, who was notoriously clumsy and absentminded, had written to tell her about. It always sounded hilarious when she wrote about it, but Pris was pretty sure things like falling off the kitchen ladder or slipping in a cow pie weren't all that funny when they actually happened to you.

Pris left her to her letter and climbed the stairs to her room, where, since Dat had brought home a nice pneumatic sewing machine for Mamm, the old treadle sewing machine had been set up just for her use. Her room over the porch was tiny to begin with, but Dat had built shelves for her fabric, and when the bureau had been moved into Katie and Saranne's room, he had made boxes with drawers that slid under the bed, leaving just enough room for the sewing machine.

She was a real businesswoman now.

And since Pris was working two jobs, Mamm had divided the bulk of her chores between Katie and Saranne, with some of the easier ones going to the twins, who were almost seven. This had the double benefit of more responsibility for the younger ones and a little free time for Pris. As soon as they helped clean up after breakfast and Saranne and the twins left for school, Mamm and Katie would hang out the clothes on the line, or bake, or sew, depending on what day it was. Monday was usually wash day in their district, and Mamm baked on Wednesdays and Saturdays. Tuesdays were sewing, Thursdays were her quilting circle, and Friday was the day she went to town if she needed bulk goods or a pair of shoes.

Pris worked as a *Maud* at the Rose Arbor Inn on Mondays, Wednesdays, and Fridays, and even though she could have quit and focused solely on her second business, she didn't. For one thing, tourists only came during the summer, and what would she do with herself in the cold months? And for another, she liked it at the Inn, and Ginny had to be the easiest and most fun person to work for in all of Whinburg Township. And now that she was getting married to Henry, she seemed to be the happiest, as well.

Katie must have heard her go upstairs, because she left off cleaning the bathroom and followed her up the steps and into her room. "Are you sewing?"

"*Ja*. Evie Troyer says she's down to half a dozen pot holders, so I have to get busy."

"Want some help?"

"The piecing goes fast. I'm not worried about that. But if you and Saranne help me with the quilting and binding tonight, I'll pay you a quarter for every one you finish."

"A dollar for four? Do you know how much work is in those things?"

All too well. "All right, then, a dollar per pair."

"Done."

Grinning at clinching a deal so easily, Katie leaned companionably on the door frame while Pris organized today's pieces. Since Evie, the bishop's wife, had first broached the idea of selling Pris's pot holders at her stall in the Amish Market, Pris had honed her process to optimum efficiency. Her special pot holders, which were seven-inch pieced squares whose strips and triangles formed the shape of a chicken, had become a favorite among the tourists. Back in June, when she'd had her bright idea, Evie had predicted they'd go for ten dollars apiece, and Pris had laughed.

Well, she wasn't laughing now—or if she was, it was for a good reason. While the money she made as a *Maud* had to go to Dat to help with the household expenses, he had told her that anything she made with her pot holders was her own to keep. For the first time in her life, she had money to spend, and she didn't have to do anything slightly on the shady side to get it.

As if she had been thinking the same thing, Katie said, "I'm sure glad you never went to work at the Hex Barn like you wanted to."

"So am I." The Hex Barn was madly popular among the tourists, but it stocked things like *Amish-Made Whoopie Pies!* that came in a big box from an *Englisch* bakery in Lancaster, and pot holders and table runners that said right on them they were made in Indonesia. "Dat was right, though it took me a long time to admit it. Imagine if I'd gone to work there, out front where the tourists could see me."

"It would be like saying you approved of the nonsense they sell."

"How could anyone say with a straight face that those quilts are sewn by local Amish women when I know for a fact they're quilted by Filipino ladies thousands of miles away?"

"How do you know that?"

"Simon told me once. He worked on the receiving dock, remember? Boxes of those quilts would come in, all wrapped in plastic."

"But the Mennonite ladies do piece them."

"They shouldn't say *Amish* on them, then. It's the principle."

Katie was silent for a moment, then looked at Pris from under her lashes. "I haven't heard you mention Simon's name all summer, except to read it out loud in one of Joe's letters."

"I have no reason to." And she didn't. That was all over now—a young girl's crush—over before it had even begun. "He's Joe's friend—our friend. That's all."

"I'll be glad when they're home again," Katie mused. "Jake Byler has gotten really wild. I never realized what a good influence Joe was on him until Joe went to Colorado. Did you hear that he got caught driving someone's car without a license?"

"Jake did?" Even for him, that was pretty wild. "What happened? Why would he do such a crazy thing?"

"Trying to impress some *Englisch* girl. I guess the sheriff took him down to the station and the girl drove away in the car. I hope she gave it back to whoever it belonged to."

"Maybe it was hers."

Katie shrugged. "If it had been mine, I wouldn't be dating Jake anymore."

"Me, either. I thought he would have learned some sense after that field caught fire in the spring."

"That wasn't his fault—he helped put it out, didn't he?"

Pris nodded, her foot working with a steady rhythm as the fabric fed itself under the needle. First strips, then triangles, then put it all together and on to the next one.

"I wonder if they've changed," Katie said.

What? "Who?"

"Joe and Simon, silly. Living among rough men on a dude ranch? Only getting to church three times all summer?"

"Church was a hundred miles away by bus, Katie." Pris clipped the threads and lined up the triangles that formed the chicken's comb. "I don't think we can blame them for that. Besides, doesn't the Bible say that where two or three are gathered together in His name, *der Herr* will be there, too?"

"*Ja,* but... on a dude ranch?"

"Even there. God made those mountains and the land the ranch sits on, didn't He? And anyway, Joe says the owners are nice people. I don't think the boys will have changed—but they'll have some interesting stories to tell."

Katie didn't look convinced as she went away to finish the bathroom and then deal with the kitchen floor, which had to be washed every other day, what with Dat and the boys tramping in from barn and fields. Even though they took their boots off in the mudroom, dirt still came sneaking in.

Priscilla tried to focus on keeping her seams a perfect quarter-inch wide, but her mind wandered. She'd never given any thought to whether the boys would have changed during their time away. But really, how could they help it? Seeing half the country, seeing the mountains, meeting new people, and living a completely different life... well, it would be odd if they hadn't changed.

Maybe Simon will appreciate you more now. Maybe absence has made the heart grow fonder.

Ach, neh. She would not go there. The very thought made her disloyal to Joe, and she was Joe's girl. If she'd had a buggy whip for her brain, she'd have used it to bring her unruly thoughts back into line. But since she didn't, she assembled strips and triangles like a person possessed.

Even Mamm was astonished at the pile of pot holders she had ready for the girls to quilt and bind by suppertime.

CHAPTER 4

When Sarah had been a teenager and getting together with the other *Youngie* for a Sunday evening singing, they'd enjoyed a pretty diverse list of songs. There were the ones from the *Ausbund*, of course, that they'd been singing all their lives. But once in a while someone would have an *Englisch* hymn in their homemade songbook, or a popular song from the radio, and they'd all learn it that evening. Whether or not they got the tune absolutely right wasn't the point—the point was doing something all together. Maybe it pushed the boundaries just a little bit—the way Pris had once told her they sang a popular song about country roads—but there was no real harm in it.

One of the *Englisch* hymns always seemed to come back to Sarah in the autumn, when every man in the settlement raced against time to get the harvest in before the rain started, and every woman's canner boiled nonstop as she preserved for the winter the bounty of vegetables and fruit that God had provided.

The hymn asked what the harvest would be. A person might make her choices in the joy of spring or the heat of summer, but every choice had its harvest. Every decision bore its fruit. Sarah had often thought how hard it was to see clearly in the heat of the moment—to make the kinds of choices that would produce fruit to sustain a person through the hard times.

She set her basket on the soil in the garden she had planted in squares and triangles and borders, like a living quilt, and regarded the drooping string on the pea trellises. Since the peas were long over, it was time for them to come down so she could get in some winter vegetables.

She had one of the four teepee-shaped trellises down and wrapped in a bundle and was unstringing the second when someone yoo-hooed from the slope of the hill between her place and that of her in-laws.

Amanda Yoder waved as she made her way through the long grass that Sarah kept unmowed so that the wild plants could grow and produce leaves and flowers for her herbal cures. "You're deep in thought this morning," Amanda said when she was close. "I called you twice. Anything in particular going on in that blond head of yours?"

Sarah smiled as Amanda began unstringing the third trellis as if she'd come over for that purpose. It was so like her to see what needed to be done and do it. "I was thinking about an *Englisch* hymn we used to sing about the harvest. It comes into my mind at this time of year." She sang a few lines and Amanda nodded. "I've heard that one, too. I think Malinda Kanagy has it in her songbook. It's a very good question, isn't it—what will the harvest be?"

"A little too good, considering the kind of summer I had." Sarah's mouth formed a rueful moue as she snipped the string off the poles and added it to the growing ball in her other hand. "Benny Peachey may have forgiven me for trying to make his *Aendi* leave their farm, but I don't think it's been thrown into the sea of forgetfulness quite yet."

"He's just a boy," Amanda said. "Something like that has to be looked at with the eyes of an adult. He'll come around when he gets older."

"Maybe. Their lives haven't changed much since that cell tower went in, though I did see when we were there for church the other week that Linda has a new propane-powered washing machine and a refrigerator, too, instead of an icebox."

"You know what I saw when I was there?" Amanda handed her the string and Sarah wound it onto the ball. "I saw how settled Crist Peachey has become. As though he'd finally found the place where God meant him to be, and as far as he was concerned, it was the best place in the world."

"Is it true he actually filed for a patent on that solar cell he and Arlon invented?"

"I don't know about things like that," Amanda admitted. "Dat would, though."

"Trust me to see the washing machine and you to see the change in Crist."

"We all have our gifts." Amanda grinned at her and moved to the last trellis. "I didn't come to talk about our brothers and sisters, though. I came to bring you a letter."

Sarah put the string in her pocket and began to pull up the long, thin bamboo poles of the trellis. "A letter came to your place for me? That's odd."

"It's from Silas." Amanda pulled it out of her pocket and handed it over.

"What on earth? Silas Lapp?" Sure enough, there was her name at her in-laws' address, written in a black, spiky hand. She looked up. "Do I really want to know what it says?"

Amanda smiled, but her gaze did not quite meet Sarah's. "I don't know if you do, but I sure do."

All right, then. If he had sent the letter to Yoders', then clearly he had no objection to Amanda's knowing he was writing to Sarah. Which was sad and a pretty hard knock to any hopes that Sarah may have had on the subject of those two.

Dear Sarah,

Please excuse this letter going to Jacob's—I do not know your address and did not want to make a scene by calling to ask for it. I hope you are well and that Caleb is also well. You will be expecting your eldest boy home soon, too. I hope he has enjoyed his time in Colorado—seeing that country was one of the greatest experiences of my life.

I know it has been a couple of months since we saw one another, but I find myself thinking of you often. I wonder if you would like to add one more to your list of correspondents. I cannot say I'm an interesting writer, but I am a faithful one. While you may not be so interested in hearing about the daily activities of the cell tower in my field, I am most interested in hearing about the herbs and cures you compile from yours.

I hope you will not think me forward. Instead, I hope you will consider me—

Your friend,
Silas

Sarah had to read the letter twice—three times—before she really believed that what she read was what he meant. Finally, she simply handed it over to Amanda and could tell what part she had come to by the gradual closing of her face.

It was like watching a convulvus flower close with the fading of the light.

The letter bent as Amanda handed it back. "Don't look like that, Sarah. It was pretty much what I was expecting. I haven't had any hopes in that direction since he left."

"But I did. Somehow, I wanted him to get a revelation about what a good wife you'd make, and come back to court you."

Amanda shook her head. "I had my chance, but obviously it wasn't God's will. I just have to possess my soul in patience until He reveals my future husband to me." Her clear blue gaze met Sarah's. "So what are you going to do?"

Ignore it.

Write him back and say yes, she would enjoy a correspondence, with no expectations of anything else.

Write him back and tell him she would enjoy getting to know him better and when might his next visit be?

Write him back and confess that she had feelings for someone else and—

Stop that!

"I don't know," she finally said. When she looked down at the ball of string in her hands, she saw that she'd wound her fingers right into it. With a sigh, she unraveled it and rewound it properly. Her hands knew her thoughts better than she did—why else would they get themselves into such a tangle?

"Do you really not know how you feel about him?" Amanda asked. "He's such a nice man, and well able to provide for you. I know Mamm and Dat worry about you sometimes."

"They don't need to," Sarah said quickly, more than willing to abandon the subject, even if it meant talking about her finances. "I've actually managed to pay back some of the money I owed them and even get a little ahead this month. I never would have suspected that I could make a living giving people cures."

"God would not have prompted Ruth Lehman to call you to a *Dokterfraa*'s work if He did not think it would support you," Amanda pointed out.

That was true, but it had been a mighty leap of faith to step out on His promise, all the same.

Amanda wasn't finished. "Doesn't it worry you, Sarah? That God put Silas in your path—delivered him right to your door, practically—and you turned him down when he obviously followed God's prompting and asked to court you?"

Here was something Sarah hadn't considered—and she should have. "It was such a mess in June, what with that runaway *Englisch* boy, Eric, and Henry, and the Peacheys...oh, Amanda...Silas was just one more thing to deal with. And as I said, I was hoping he would notice you, not me. I couldn't get away fast enough, in case there was still a chance that he might come to his senses."

"And now that he wants a second chance—or maybe I should say, now that *der Herr* is giving you a second chance?"

Sarah bent to put the ball of string in her basket. She was never sure whether it was a gift or a curse that Amanda's gaze demanded so much honesty of the person she was speaking to. "You think I should encourage him, don't you?" she asked as she straightened.

"I think you should pray about it before you write back. That's what got you into trouble before, remember—not praying."

Goodness. Amanda was like a mirror that God held up to show her all her faults. The only difference between Amanda and a real mirror was that Amanda loved her and pointed out the truth only because she wanted Sarah to be both right with the Lord and happy.

There was certainly no denying that Sarah had blundered on ahead in June like a horse with the bit between its teeth, instead of waiting to feel the gentle touch of the rein guiding her in the way she should go. She had given Linda Peachey bad advice and come dangerously close to dividing a woman from her husband's family. Granted, she'd done it with the best of motives and had been honestly anxious to see if her cures could help, but that was selfish thinking. If she'd waited on the Lord, she might have found out before it was too late that He already had plans for Linda, and His plans were much grander than Sarah's. And much less likely to result in others' being hurt and offended.

"You're absolutely right," she admitted to her young sister-in-law. "I'll pray about it, and I won't put pen to paper until I have peace about what kind of reply I should make."

Amanda picked up the bundle of bamboo rods and Sarah picked up her basket. They made their way to the barn across the grass, three of her hens escorting them as though they hoped there might be a handful of corn in it for them.

Yes, she would pray. Though deep inside, Sarah was a little afraid of what the answer might be.

❀

Hi Caleb,

Thanks for sending the jar of your mom's jam. I had it on my toast and those blackberries were just as good as the ones we ate while we were picking. I wish I could send you something but my mom doesn't make jam.

I wanted to tell you that I got into the fine arts high school. It started two weeks ago. I have to take a train to get to it but Dad said that if I could cross three states to run away I shouldn't have any trouble with a 30-minute train ride. Then I walk to the school. They liked my lamp and my sketches for the next thing I want to make, and my homeroom teacher really likes my idea journal. They weren't so happy about my grades from middle school though. I'm kind of on probation until I get As and Bs.

But like Henry says, when you really want something, you have to be willing to work for it. I really want this, so I guess that means I have to take geometry and suck up the homework. But since a plate is a circle and a box is a bunch of rectangles, at least geometry will help me with pottery, right?

I never did get to go and see my grandparents in California. Justin says he went to Disneyland twice. I told him I learned to drive a horse and buggy. If there's a zombie apocalypse we'll see which one saves our lives, huh?

Okay, time for English homework. We have to write a paper on Tom Sawyer. The movie was pretty good. I didn't read the book. If I get good grades this year, will your mom and Henry let me come back for the summer?

Your friend,
Eric Parker

CHAPTER 5

This late in September, the sun rode lower in the sky, which meant it reached much farther into the barn, where Henry maintained his pottery studio. At this point in the afternoon, the long rectangle of light almost touched his feet as he sat at the wheel, using both hands to gently persuade a pitcher to take shape.

This was the part of pottery that Henry loved the most. The moment when potter and clay were as close to one being as they could be, with one hand inside pressing out to encourage change, and the other outside pressing in to ensure safety and restraint. Both hands together created a graceful shape, but only if the clay was willing to be shaped. Some days, temperature and granularity and humidity all combined to make the clay cranky, and Henry's job became more about command than persuasion. But on some days, like the last clear, crisp days of September, conditions were right and the clay wanted to be made into something, leaping between his hands into the shape it wanted almost before he was ready.

This pitcher wanted to be a pitcher in no uncertain terms. The bottom had blossomed in a rich, fruitful curve, and now he had to reverse that curve and bring it back so that he could bend the spout and find the point of balance for the handle. When the wheel slowed to a stop, he stood, putting his sore hands on his hips and rolling his shoulders to get the stiffness out. Then he lifted the pitcher on its bat off the wheel and carried it over to the bench. A couple of quick movements gave him the spout he wanted, and with another hour's work with fingers and shaping tools, he sculpted the suggestion of the pumpkin shape the finished piece would have. Then he set it aside to rest while he made the handle.

Pumpkin stems were trickier than they looked. He'd spent a couple of hours in Barbara Byler's garden sketching them, much to her amusement. Hers were the closest pumpkins to his place besides Sarah Yoder's, and he wasn't going over that hill for any reason. Now his sketchbook lay open on the bench, showing the woody curve of the pumpkin stem, its prickly roughness, the nodules that pushed up here and there along the striped ribs.

Glancing often at the sketch for reference, Henry rolled a tube of clay between his wet hands, wincing at what was becoming a real annoyance. Over the summer, as his production schedule had become more intense, he'd discovered that the hard water in Whinburg Township played havoc with his hands, since he spent half the day with them buried in wet clay. The minerals in the clay dried them out enough, and the hard water amplified the problem when he washed up, to the point that he'd developed deep cracks in the skin of his finger joints and in the seam between finger and thumb.

Finally, a week or so ago, he'd been driven by the pain to the library in town, where he'd got on the Internet and ordered a box of surgical gloves. The thought of anything coming between him and the clay made him both doubtful and anxious, but other than installing an expensive water-softening system out here in the barn, he couldn't see a way around it. If the gloves worked, he would just get used to them. If they didn't, he'd have to change something—though what that might be, he didn't know. Meanwhile, he got some moisturizer at the drugstore and rubbed it into his sore hands a couple of times a day.

The pumpkin stem took shape, its curve echoing that of the body of the pitcher, arced a little forward so that there would be room for leaves on the terminus, where it attached to the body. He rolled out the leaves paper-thin, then attached them with wet clay. He suggested tendrils by carving tiny spirals here and there with a dentist's pick, and then sat back to appreciate the gift the cooperative clay had become.

"Is that a pumpkin?" came a very young man's voice from behind him.

Henry turned to see Caleb Yoder standing in the door-way—where had the sunbeam gone?—and he blinked in confusion. "Aren't you supposed to be at work?"

"I was." Caleb ambled over to look at the pitcher. "It's almost six o'clock."

Already? "Time got away on me again, I guess. Yes, it's a pumpkin. Time to let it dry now."

"What are you going to glaze it with?"

"Not sure yet. I'm torn between giving its future buyer what she expects—some variation of orange or yellow—or doing something different to be true to my art." He tried to keep a straight face as his tone made air quotes around the last four words, but when he caught Caleb's eye, the grin broke out anyway. "What do you think?"

"I think that if I put artistic ideas of what a barn should look like ahead of what the man who hired me was expecting, I wouldn't be building barns for long."

Henry had to laugh. Trust Caleb to be both honest and pragmatic without being critical. "How's it going? Do you like working for Jon Hostetler? It's been almost a week, hasn't it?"

Caleb nodded, prowling around the studio as if he thought it might have gone downhill now that he wasn't there to act as Henry's assistant. "*Ja*, I like it. I like watching something grow where there was nothing before. But if you need help here, I can come over in the evenings."

"I think we got things pretty much down to a science over the summer, Caleb. But maybe if you have a Saturday free once in a while, you can help me wedge clay. I'd give you a dollar a pound."

Caleb's eyes widened. "That's pretty generous. Sure, I'd like that."

It would give Henry's hands a break, and free up time that could be better used in actually creating pieces.

"That reminds me," Caleb said, "I got a letter from Eric." He pulled a folded-up piece of paper from his pocket and handed it to Henry. It had been typed on a computer, and on one side, Eric had inserted a digital image of himself and Caleb fishing, which Henry had taken on Eric's camera phone before the battery had run down and they had to go to town to charge it up. "He wants to know if he can come back next summer."

Henry scanned to the bottom and his face twitched briefly into a frown at seeing his and Sarah's names paired together so casually. Then he smoothed out his expression in much the same way he'd smooth away a blemish in a sheet of clay. "I don't see why not. I can't speak for your mother, of course."

"She said almost exactly the same thing. You'll be married by then, though," the boy pointed out. "You might not even be living here."

Henry breathed deeply to calm the sudden jump in adrenaline. *You'll be married by then* had sounded like the boy had meant himself and Sarah. Since when had he become so sensitive? "Maybe not *living*—it makes more sense for me to live with Ginny at the Inn, because she has to be up so early cooking breakfast for the guests. If she had to drive a couple of miles every morning, particularly during Christmas season, it wouldn't be very convenient."

Caleb nodded. "Plus, she can't just leave people on their own in her house."

"That wouldn't be very hospitable," Henry agreed. "So I'm thinking we'll rent this house, maybe to an Amish family since I never got around to running power in here. I'll keep the barn as my studio and be the guy driving back and forth."

Now it was Caleb's turn to frown as he stuffed the letter in the pocket of his broadfall pants.

"What?" Henry prompted, though he probably didn't need to. Caleb was so transparent that whatever was in his mind usually came out through his mouth whether you wanted it to or not.

"You'll have a hard time renting to an Amish family if the barn doesn't come with it," the boy finally said. "Where are they going to put their buggy and the horses?"

"Oh." Henry gazed at his studio, seeing it as it had been when he'd first moved here six months ago. The wheel sat right in the middle where the buggies had once been drawn up, and he'd converted one of the horse stalls to be an enclosed, draft-free area for the kiln. The remaining stall was storage for cartons of clay and the five-gallon buckets of glazes he'd mixed.

It had taken a lot of hard physical labor by himself, Caleb, and even Eric to get the studio into efficient working order. It would take just as much to tear it all out again—and then where would he put it? Unless he built a shed for himself in Ginny's back garden or used her boathouse, there was nowhere at the Inn for him to work.

"You could rent it to an *Englisch* family," Caleb suggested. "Once they got used to not having electricity, it would be all right."

"That, my young friend, would be a very short line of people. Well, I'm sure we'll work it out somehow. I can't give up my studio now that we've got it all shipshape, and I can't move it all to Ginny's. So whoever rents the house will have to do the compromising."

Caleb glanced outside, where twilight was thickening in the trees. "I'd better be getting home or Mamm will worry. How come you don't come for dinner anymore?"

"Because I have dinner with Ginny now."

"You could bring her."

"It's customary to have an invitation before events like that. Now, you'd best be getting home. I still need to clean up."

"Okay. Good night, Henry."

"Good night, Caleb. It's good to see you."

With a wave, the boy loped off up the hill. The track that he and Eric had worn into the grass during the summer had become a little overgrown since Henry had asked Ginny to marry him.

Which was just as well. Some things weren't meant to be kept up. Especially friendships with gray-eyed Amish widows whose very existence reminded him of everything he wanted to forget. But after Christmas, he would never need to worry about those things again.

❧

Dear Henry,

Thank you for your letter telling us of your wedding plans. I remember when you sent a similar letter on your engagement to Allison, and how Mother cried when she read it. I wonder if she would cry again now if she were alive.

I know you think you are happy—but Henry, how can you be when you are deliberately turning your back on God and closing the door on His family forever? I exhort you in love to give your life to God before it is too late. I'm sure that Geneva is wonderful and that you love her. But should you not love God more? We are to put Him first in all things, and then He will provide for us more than we could ask or think. I want that joy for you, Henry, more than anything—and so does my husband Ervin—and so did Mother and Dad before they passed.

We have been invited to help in the kitchen at two weddings here in Sugarcreek that same week, and we are expecting Ervin's two brothers and their families for Christmas, so we will not be able to travel to Pennsylvania to see you married. Lizzie and the children send their greetings, and Lizzie says to remind you that you've owed her a letter for four months.

Your loving sister,
Anne

Ginny read the letter, folded it up, and without a word, went into his arms. "Does it hurt?" she asked, turning her cheek into his shirt, her warm breath against his skin. "Because if it does, I can send them an answer."

In spite of himself, Henry smiled. "It's got nothing to do with you, and everything to do with how we were raised. And no, it doesn't hurt. It hasn't for a while now—this isn't the first letter of this kind that Anne has sent me."

"Would it make you feel better to know that my parents and my sister are raring to come for a visit, just so they can meet you?"

"Which sister? Sienna?"

"No, that's the one in California. Venezia. She's the single one, remember? The one who's the pharmaceuticals sales rep. She's still in Philly. Both Daddy and Venezia called today to see when they could come."

"I thought your dad was a pastor. How's he going to feel about a son-in-law who doesn't go to church?"

"He's pretty good about saving his sermons for people who want to hear them."

"I'm looking forward to meeting him," he said, and kissed her.

For as long as Ginny kept the Inn, he'd be living here among the Amish—among his relatives—and enduring their constant silent reproach. But if that was the price he had to pay to be with this vibrant, joyous woman and to practice the art he loved, then so be it. He'd pay it happily—and do his best to arrange the pattern of his life so that it didn't intersect too often with the rhythms of the Amish around him.

"How about I invite them down this weekend? With the

kids back in school, bookings have dropped a little, and two of the four rooms are free."

"That would be great." He gave her a squeeze and released her. "I'll look forward to it." And he took his eldest sister's letter and dropped it into the fire he'd laid and lit for Ginny in the sitting room's old-fashioned hearth. At least that way it would be good for something.

CHAPTER 6

I saiah Mast, Priscilla's father, treated off Sundays with the same solemnity as he treated church Sundays. Both were the Lord's Day, and both were to be observed with the reverence that such a day merited.

So, in the morning after breakfast and family prayers, they gathered in the front room, where Dat read a chapter from the *Martyrs' Mirror* and taught them a little, as though he were preaching a very short sermon in church. The lot had not fallen upon him, of course, so actually speaking in church was not his place, but Dat believed in being prepared. If ever *der Herr* were to choose him, there would be no doubt of his unworthiness or unfitness for the task—but at least he would be as prepared as it was possible for a man to be.

After the chapter, each member of the family took it in turn to read so many verses out of the old Bible. Every year they started fresh in Genesis, and by the end of the year, they reached the end of Revelation. Priscilla was always glad to get into the New Testament around this time of year. Everyone—particularly the twins, who were just learning English in school—found the begats and battles in the Old Testament exhausting. The New Testament was interesting, especially when Jesus was feeding the crowd with the loaves and fishes, or when Paul fell to his knees on the road to Damascus. Pris could see it as if it were happening in front of her, and the reading was consequently much livelier.

After lunch, since a person only did absolutely necessary work such as milking, or the dishes, Priscilla had some rare free time. This afternoon they were going to Mammi and Daadi Byler's for dinner at four o'clock, but the two hours between one and three were Pris's own. Her eldest brother, Christopher, had already taken the buggy over to Dan Kanagy's—he was sweet on Dan's sister Malinda, though privately Pris thought he was wasting his time. Malinda never treated him as anything more than a friend, the way she treated all the young men. While Saranne and the twins started on the twelve-hundred-piece puzzle that Saranne had been given for her birthday, Priscilla and Katie wrapped their black knitted sweaters around themselves and slipped out the door. This clear weather wouldn't last forever, and Pris wanted to savor the sunshine while she could.

"We should have caught a ride over to the Kanagys' with Chris," Katie said. "Rosanne might want to come for a walk with us."

"It's only two miles. Let's go over. I haven't seen Rosanne in ages."

"Well, between being practically grounded for three months after the fire, and then making pot holders as well as working, it's no wonder," Katie said. "If it weren't for people seeing you in church, they'd probably think you'd gone away for the summer, like Simon and Joe."

"I'd never go *that* far away," Priscilla said. "I like it right here just fine."

"But what if you meet a boy from another district and he asks you to marry him? Would you move away then?"

Priscilla snorted. "The likelihood of that happening is zero. Besides, I'm Joe's girl, and he lives right here."

"Are you going to marry him?"

"Katie, for goodness' sake. I'm not even eighteen yet. When I'm—" She stopped.

Katie looked at her curiously. "When you're what?"

"Katie. Look. Is that…"

The road took a long dip into the creek bottom, and on the top of the opposite hill, two figures came into view. One had a firm stride, as though each footstep rooted him to the earth, connecting him somehow with all that grew and lived. The other ambled, as though there was all the time in the world to get to his destination, but his long legs got him there much faster than anyone usually expected.

"It's Joe!" Priscilla exclaimed. "And Simon!"

"We'll be the first to meet them," Katie said, grabbing her hand. "Come on!"

Kapp strings flying behind them, they ran pell-mell down the hill and up the other side. Of course the boys saw them, and picked up their pace until they met under a maple that was just beginning to turn red around the edges of its leaves.

Priscilla was not a demonstrative person, but when Joe dumped his canvas duffel on the ground, snatched her up by the waist, and whirled her around, she couldn't help shrieking with glee and hugging him hard when he finally put her down. She almost thought he might have kissed her, but that would never do, right out here on the county highway, so she laughed and spun to hug Simon, who wrapped his arms around her and buried his chin in her shoulder.

Goodness.

The sensation of being held by Simon Yoder was so strange that she pushed out of his arms, and when Joe released Katie,

Pris stuck herself to Joe's side, taking them both in from that safe vantage point.

"Look at you!" she exclaimed. "So tanned, and you've both grown taller and broader."

"*Neh*," Joe said. "You just haven't seen us for a while. These are still the same pants I left in, just a little more worn."

Neither one was dressed in Sunday black, but in brown work pants and blue shirts. But despite what Joe said, Pris could see with her own eyes that they looked different. More confident somehow. They'd seen a little of the world and were now coming back to the old and familiar and taking it in with new appreciation.

"Does it feel good to be home?" Katie asked. "Because it's sure good to have you back." Then she blushed scarlet.

"It does." Simon took a deep breath. "Even the air is different here. In Colorado it's dry and you can see for miles because there's no haze. I never knew the air here was so soft."

"Smells carry farther," Joe said in his practical way. "Old Joachim Hostetler's using pig manure for fertilizer, I can tell from here."

"Don't you be talking about fertilizer when you've only been home five minutes," Pris scolded. "Surely you didn't walk all the way from the bus station in Whinburg?"

"No, we caught a ride with one of the *Youngie* who were on their way to a feed over at Kanagys'," Simon said. "Their buggy was full, but we squeezed in on the running boards. We didn't want to take a chance on no one coming out this way, and eight miles is a lot farther when you're hoofing it."

"We were on our way to Kanagys', too," Katie offered. "But we'd much rather walk home with you and hear about Colorado. Or...maybe you don't want company?"

"I do," Joe said, and squeezed Pris against his side. "I want to hear everything you didn't write in your letters."

"Me, too," Simon said. "Come on, *Maedeln*. If we walk slow, you can have us up to date by the time we get to Old Bridge Road."

So they did. There was a lot to tell—Henry and Ginny getting engaged, the *Englisch* boy running away to make pots with Henry, the Peacheys' invention and the cell tower in their field, Jake getting arrested—

Joe's arm fell away from Priscilla's waist. "What? My brother Jake? Drove a car?"

Pris nodded. "It's good you're home. He's been running wild lately and you're about the only one who can hold him in without him slipping the rein."

Joe shook his head in disbelief. "I wonder what's got into him. And Dat's still letting him live at home?"

"I think so." What would it be like to be a fly on the wall tonight while Joe tried to talk some sense into his twin?

They reached Old Bridge Road and turned left, talking and laughing until they reached Corinne and Jacob Yoder's lane. From there it was only a few hundred feet to his own lane, and Simon stood with his hand on the mailbox. "It hasn't changed at all—except, wow, Mamm's crazy garden is still going strong."

"I think it's a beautiful garden," Pris said loyally. "Your *Daadi* and Caleb turned over a whole new section for the herbs when she ran out of space, see? Behind the chicken house is all bushes and small trees now—lemon balm, elder, rosemary. It smells beautiful. I love going back there."

"I won't be surprised when I see you, then," Simon said easily. "Thanks for the escort, *Maedeln*. I'm going to go give Mamm and Caleb the surprise of their lives." He strolled off down the lane as though he'd just been visiting across the road, his duffel over his shoulder.

Katie did something expressive with her eyebrows and vanished down the next lane, where there was a shortcut to the creek and home. Joe shifted his duffel to the other shoulder and Pris stepped to his free side. "Are you coming home with me, or should I walk you to your place?"

"I don't think your folks need extra people around when it's you they'll want to see."

"But it's you *I* want to see." He took her hand.

She hardly knew what to do with honesty like that. Didn't boys beat around the bush more, and tease, and make jokes about serious subjects? And how strong and warm his hand was, calluses and all. Even if she hadn't known he'd been handling horses all summer, she'd have known he'd been doing heavy outdoor work by the strength in those hands. Her own felt soft and pale in comparison, though they worked every bit as hard in their own way.

"Come home with me, Pris," he urged. "They'll be wanting to hear all about it, and that way, you can be there to hear it, too."

It would also make a statement that even his two-year-old brother, Amos, couldn't miss if she were included in a family reunion as momentous as this. Priscilla saw at once that she was standing in a place where two ways met. She could choose to go all in now, and make it plain to his family that she was committed to being his special friend, or she could go home and put their friendship back on its old footing.

Was that what she wanted? To go back to accepting the occasional ride from him, or going with him in his courting buggy to singing on Sundays? How long would he be willing for that before he decided she wasn't as interested as he was, and broke up with her to pursue another girl? She was seventeen now, and while it was still too early to be thinking of marriage, part of her yearned to form a deeper relationship with him—especially since he'd been nothing but loyal to her no matter how far away he was. Just as she'd been loyal to him—and she'd had an opportunity or two not to be.

"All right," she said. "Let's go to your place. I can't wait to see Barbara's face when you walk in the door."

He squeezed her hand, and they turned around, heading back to the county highway. They had about half a mile to walk from the intersection to the Byler lane, and Priscilla had never been so glad for a bright, sunny day—perfect for a homecoming. A path ran along the top of the bank beside the road so that people didn't have to walk on the asphalt, and now and again when a buggy went by, someone would lean out to call, "Joe Byler! Welcome home, boy! Hallo, Priscilla!"

Which meant, of course, that it would be all over the district by suppertime that Joe was home and the first person he'd sought out even before he saw his parents was herself.

"Why didn't you tell us what train you were coming in on?" she asked him. "Any one of us would have met you at the bus station."

"I know, but then the trip home would have been all noise and talking, and we wanted to ease into it slowly, without anyone knowing we were here. It was just a stroke of luck that you and Katie were out walking."

"You don't mind my noise and talking?" she teased.

"Not one bit. You can talk all you like while I enjoy the scenery and how good it is to be home."

"Do you think you'll go back next summer?"

The shoulder that wasn't under the duffel bag lifted in a

shrug. "The pay's good. But I wouldn't go by myself. Me and Simon, we kept each other on the straight and narrow."

"Was it so difficult?"

"Not in some things—a shirt and pants are not such a big deal. We got a little ribbing about our hats when everyone else was wearing a Stetson or a Resistol. But mostly it was the things you don't think about when you're home with the *Gmee*."

"Like what?"

"Language, for one thing. It's easy to talk like the cowboys, taking the Lord's name in vain in every sentence. And drinking. Lots of that. And work—there's a fellow or two who'd be happy for me to do his work as well as my own and no thanks for it."

"Did you?"

"Not after I figured out what was going on. He tried to blame me for some stuff, too, but luckily our foreman had some brains and eyes in his head, so that didn't go very far."

"And you had to deal with this as well as the work?"

"It's dealing with people. Folks are folks, whether they're Amish or *Englisch*. Once you figure them out, it's easier, but some folks don't like to be figured out. Like that cowboy. Simon took it worse. He's got a temper on him and some pride, and they gave him quite a battle a time or two. A lot of firewood got chopped out in the shed behind the big house on those days."

"How's his foot? I saw he wasn't limping."

At this, the frown that had weighed down Joe's forehead while he'd been talking about the cowboy lifted, and a light came into his eyes that Pris had never seen before. "I tell you what, Pris, I was pretty scared after that horse stepped on him. But that care package Sarah sent was just the thing.

I followed her instructions to the letter, and even the fore-man, who's an EMT, was amazed at how well it worked. We thought he'd have blood poisoning, but after a week of the B and W salve and the dock leaves, he was well on his way to being healed, and no problems."

"I'm glad to hear it. Sarah was frantic. She said if she could have mailed herself out there, she would have."

"Simon will never say so, but he was pretty worried, too. But now he's good as new." He paused. "You know, I never did anything like that before. Like because I was there, some-body or something was different. Better."

"Really? But when you work on the farm, it's always dif-ferent and better because of what you do. That's the way God planned it."

"*Neh.* God planned that beans and corn would come up as long as there was someone to plant them. Beans don't much care who it is. But this—you should have seen his foot, Pris. Even our foreman shook his head over it. I would never have believed that such a mess could have healed up so good. Sarah might have saved him from being lame all his life."

"Sarah and *you*, you mean."

She liked that he didn't take credit for what he'd done, that no matter how far he'd traveled, *Gelassenheit* was still a guiding principle in his character. But still, she was acutely aware of how differently it could have gone without his quick thinking and obedience to Sarah's instructions.

By now they had reached the Byler lane and were walking between the tall stalks of harvested corn. Just over the rise Pris could see the roof of the house—and it was suddenly clear that someone had called the Byler telephone in the barn. Hanging out of the top gable window was one of Joe's little sisters, waving a white dish towel.

Pris laughed and pointed. "They've posted a lookout. So much for walking in without a fuss."

Joe's teeth looked very white in his tanned face as he grinned and tightened his grip on her hand. "I'm glad we had a few minutes, just by ourselves. I can face the fuss and noise now, and be glad."

Priscilla smiled back. "Me, too."

And then Joe quickened his pace, until finally, when the kitchen door burst open and his entire family spilled out onto the verandah and down the steps, he dropped both duffel and Pris's hand, and ran to meet them.

CHAPTER 7

S arah sat on her front steps, taking a few minutes to appreciate the sunshine before she and Caleb hitched up Dulcie and went for a drive. She had half a mind to head out in the direction of Peacheys' farm. Linda Peachey, to the entire family's joy, was nearly six months along in her first pregnancy, and from experience, Sarah knew that sometimes a soothing balm on the skin of the stomach at this stage might be welcome.

If that were so, then tomorrow she'd mix up a batch—a creamy base infused with calendula, lavender, and plantain that, besides the softening and soothing effect, would have the additional benefit of healing and warming the skin.

From the curve of the drive came the sound of heavy footsteps in the gravel—*crunch, crunch, crunch*. Though it was Sunday and visitors tended to arrive at any time, she wasn't expecting anyone in particular. Sarah got to her feet and shaded her eyes with one hand. Patients tended to turn up almost daily now, for which she was grateful. But on a Sunday when the Bible forbade work, it wasn't likely. On the lawn, the chickens lifted their heads in case the approaching sound should be a threat—and then scattered when the male body with the strange bulky shape over its shoulder emerged from under the trees.

"You silly old *Hinkel*, it's only me. Have you forgotten me so soon?"

Sarah caught her breath as the young man swung the duffel off his shoulder. He tossed it on the grass. "Mamm!"

"*Simon!*" She flew down the steps, across the lawn, and into his arms. "Oh, my dearest boy!" His arms went around her, hard, and she could swear there were tears on his lashes as she kissed him again and again until finally she set him away from her so she could get a good look at him. "Where did you come from? Why didn't you let me know? Did someone pick you up?"

"*Ja*, we hitched a ride with some of the *Youngie*, and then we met Pris and Katie on the road, so we walked home together." He laughed. "Mamm, stop looking at me like I'm in the doctor's office. I'm fine."

"I'll want to see that foot as soon as you take your boots off."

"Mamm, it's *gut*, I promise. I couldn't have walked the last couple of miles if it wasn't, could I?"

She hugged him again. "You're right. Oh, won't Mammi and Daadi be so happy. And as for Caleb—"

"Simon!" Caleb barreled across the yard from the barn, where he must have heard the commotion. And while Simon was usually given to shaking a man's hand or at the most, giving him a slap on the back, family was different, and his little brother was more special still. Caleb gave him as big a bear hug as he got, until they were both laughing with the joy of seeing each other again.

Sarah thought her heart would burst, and tears swam in her eyes.

Oh thank You, dear Lord, for bringing my boy back to me. Thank you for keeping him safe, and for using me to help make him well after he was hurt. Fill him with the comfort of home, I pray, and with Your love and his family's love, so that if it is Your will, he will be content to stay now.

All Sarah wanted to do was hover over Simon as he rambled around the yard and through the barn, taking in the home place with new eyes. He exclaimed over her garden, though it was past its best now. And finally, an hour later, they all climbed the stairs to his and Caleb's room and he unpacked his duffel, which was full of dirty clothes and dirtier socks. He handed Caleb something wrapped in paper and aluminum foil.

"That's a pound of fudge from Teresa, the cook at the ranch. When I couldn't walk, I told her stories about you and Mamm and the farm while I was helping her in the kitchen, so she wanted to send something home with me for you. She thought you'd like something to eat."

Caleb was already cutting into it with his pocketknife. As she tasted her piece, Sarah had to admit that Teresa had a gift for fudge, which she herself hardly ever had the time to make. How kind of her to think of a young boy so far away!

"And these are for you, Mamm. Manuel, one of the other wranglers, taught me to whittle more than just sticks."

It was a set of two large spoons carved from some golden wood—maple, maybe—and sanded and polished until they gleamed.

"Oh, Simon, they're so beautiful! You don't expect me to use them in cookie batter, do you?"

"You could put them in the salad bowl, instead of everyone using their forks."

This was a much better idea. She hugged him in sheer delight. "They remind me of the pottery Henry makes—the shape is so graceful—but it forms something useful."

Simon had been rummaging for something else in the smelly depths of the duffel, but now he lifted his head to ask his brother, "Do you still see as much of Henry as you used to, Caleb?"

But Sarah had the distinct feeling the question was directed as much at her. She ran a gentle finger along the curve of the spoon and let Caleb answer.

"Not so much since I started work with Jon Hostetler. In the mornings, I'm on the job site by six, and we clean up around five, so that doesn't leave much time for visiting. I was just there to say hi, though. He said that if I wanted, I could wedge clay on Saturdays for a dollar a pound."

"Seems fair."

"Yep. I'll probably do it, and give that money to Mamm for groceries."

This was news. "You don't have to do that, Caleb. We're doing all right."

"I know, but I want to."

Her dear, generous boy, fast growing into a responsible young man. She brushed his hair back from his forehead and hoped he could feel the gratitude in her touch.

"Did you hear he's getting married to Ginny Hochstetler at the Rose Arbor Inn?" Caleb asked his brother. "He asked her to marry him on the way home from dinner at our place a couple of months ago."

"Priscilla said something about that," Simon admitted. "What do you think, Mamm?"

Sarah calmed the hitch in her insides that the subject of

Henry always caused. It was silly, but she couldn't stop her body from reacting to the sound of his name, almost as though her spirit had tripped over something. Thank goodness it was deep inside, where no one could see it.

"I think that he is putting her ahead of God, and he'll find he's missing out on a greater happiness," she said quietly.

"Not everyone gets baptized into church," Simon pointed out. "And if he's made up his mind, why shouldn't he marry Ginny? She's nice."

"You could look at it that way," Sarah allowed. "Or you could see that his place is with the church and the family he was born into. There's still time for him to come back, and avoid a lost eternity."

"Have you said this to him?"

"*Ja*, I have, and I might as well have said it to a rock or a tree, for all the response I got. But if I hadn't done my part to offer counsel to him, I know I'd regret it."

"Mamm," Simon said, his brow wrinkling, "isn't that his cousin Paul Byler's place, not yours?"

Was he hinting that she needed to mind her own business? That she hadn't learned that lesson in the hardest way possible in the last couple of months?

"Maybe, and I hope Paul Byler fills that place. But a friend who is a true friend tells the truth when it's called for. There was an opportunity to say a word in season, and I said it." She gathered up all of Simon's dirty laundry in both arms. "Now, I know you'll want to go and say hello to the horses in the south field. While you're out there, can you bring in Dulcie and hitch her up? Caleb and I were going to go for a drive. Do you want to come with us, or have you had enough traveling for one day?"

"Where are you going?"

"I thought I'd go see Linda Peachey and see how she's getting on."

"All right. It'll be good to see Benny and Leon. I'll pull up in the yard when I get Dulcie hitched."

"And if you have a clean pair of Sunday pants and a white shirt still in your closet, you might put them on."

Sarah carried the huge ball of dirty clothes downstairs into the basement, where they could wait until washday tomorrow. Goodness, hadn't he washed his clothes all summer? She could smell horses and grass and dust and smelly feet. By tomorrow night his clothes would smell like home again, and it would be like washing the dust of a long journey off a buggy, leaving it fresh and new and ready for trips much closer to home.

When she came out of the house with a covered basket containing several packets of the tea Linda had been taking lately, Simon was sitting in the buggy, the reins looped loosely around his fingers. As Caleb climbed into the back, she hopped in on the passenger side and said, "It feels *gut* to see you in your place again, Simon."

"It feels *gut* to drive again." He flapped the reins over Dulcie's back and she started up the lane.

"I could've driven," came from the back.

"I got so used to going everywhere on horseback in Colorado that I almost went looking for a saddle when I went into the barn," Simon went on as if he hadn't heard.

They chuckled, sharing the picture. Folks in Whinburg Township didn't ride on horseback. The bishop who had had responsibility for the *Gmee* before Daniel Troyer had possessed strong opinions about the place of horses on a farm. And as for a woman pulling up her dress and exposing her legs to ride astride, well...it simply wasn't going to happen under his stewardship. Once in a while, in an emergency when someone had to go for help in a hurry, it couldn't be avoided, but as a general rule, horses were for work, not pleasure.

"I can't even think of anybody who owns a saddle around here," she mused as they clip-clopped down the road. "I think Isaiah Mast had one once, but he sold it when the old folks' farm went at auction. Speaking of the Masts, did you say that Priscilla and Katie met you and Joe out on the road?"

"*Ja*, just by chance."

"And you found them well?"

"*Ja*, they seem to be just fine. Pris looks different."

"You just haven't seen her in a while," Caleb put in from behind them. "She looks just the same."

"*Neh*, there was something about her. Something... settled."

"She's matured over the summer," Sarah said. "It's *gut* that she and Joe have been writing. She's a pretty girl and I'm sure the other boys have been taking notice. But Joe is good for her, I think. He's the one who's settled—or I hope he will be, now that he's home."

"Oh, he is," Simon said. "But I wonder if he'll..." His voice trailed off and Sarah looked at him curiously.

"If he'll what? Stay?"

"No doubt about that. I just wondered about her. And him."

"You're not making any sense," Caleb complained. "Too much talking to horses and not enough to people."

"She used to be sweet on you, earlier in the year, and before that," Sarah said, remembering how Priscilla would pop up unexpectedly, always with a good reason, but always with an eye out for a glimpse of Simon. "Did you even know?"

"Did she?" His tanned cheeks deepened in color just enough for Sarah to notice. "Do you think she still is?"

"She's with Joe," Caleb said, as if this settled the matter.

"Simon, what are you thinking?" Sarah said in a warning tone. "You don't have ideas about her, do you? Your best friend's girl?"

"No, of course not." He flapped the reins so smartly as they left the stop sign that Dulcie scooted forward and the buggy jerked before it settled into its usual rhythm. "She's a friend, always has been."

But his color heightened even further, and Sarah had a hard time keeping her gaze on the road ahead. As a student of the body and its physical manifestations, she had a little practice in listening to what skin and blood and temperature had to say, as well as the mouth.

And Simon's body was contradicting his words in the plainest way possible.

CHAPTER 8

When he got his first look at the cell tower with its experimental solar batteries in the Peacheys' unkempt field, Simon's expression was priceless. "And the phone company pays them *how* much?"

When Sarah repeated the ridiculous sum that the family was paid each month, he just shook his head in amazement. "I knew that Crist and Arlon tinkered in their barn, but no one had any idea they actually knew what they were doing."

"Come to find out, they're pretty smart," Caleb said as he swung down and took the reins to tie Dulcie to the fence. "I wonder if Benny and Leon are smart that way, too."

If they were, they hadn't given much evidence of it yet— or so Sarah thought. Those boys spent more time racketing through the woods, hunting and fishing, than they did in their father's barn. But all in God's time.

Simon and Caleb headed straight for the barn to see what kind of inventions Crist and Arlon were working on, while Sarah turned to the house. Linda let the screen door close behind her as Sarah climbed the steps. "Sarah, what a nice surprise. Is that Simon I just saw?"

Sarah couldn't help the smile that spread across her face.

"*Ja*, he arrived home this afternoon, and I'm the happiest woman in Willow Creek."

"With the exception of Barbara Byler, I think."

"You'd probably be right." The smile widened to a grin as Linda held the door for her and they went into the kitchen. "And you, *nix?*"

The other woman laughed and passed a hand over her stomach. Though her dark green dress was roomy and her cape and apron modest, Sarah's practiced eye could see the gentle rounding of her figure as her pregnancy advanced.

"I brought you some more nettle and raspberry leaf tea that you should take with your vitamins," she said. "Drink four cups a day, remember. And I wondered if you might like me to make you a nice softening cream for the skin on your stomach. As time goes on, it will stretch, and a soothing cream to rub on it will really help."

"I would," Linda said promptly. "In fact, I was going to ask you if there was something I could put on it. It's so itchy and tight." Even as she spoke, she massaged her belly, unconsciously seeking relief.

"*Gut.*" Sarah nodded in sympathy. "After I get the washing hung out tomorrow, I'll mix some up and bring it to you on my way to Ruth's on Tuesday."

"You're so good to me."

Sarah's gaze faltered. "I still feel—after my mistake in trying to encourage you to leave the farm—"

"And this will be the tenth time at least that I've told you that's in the past and forgiven—if there was anything to forgive in the first place."

Since it was Sunday, and Ella had come down to greet the visitor and put the kettle on, their conversation turned to other things—the upcoming Council Meeting, what was left to pick in their gardens, the logistics of Linda's mother coming from Strasburg over January roads when the baby was ready to be born.

Sarah didn't want to stay long because Linda needed to drink her infusion and rest, so she took the packets of tea out of her basket and set them on the table. "These ought to last you until Thanksgiving, and by then you'll need a different recipe. I'll ask Ruth what the best one might be and mix it up for you."

"*Denki*, Sarah. I appreciate it." Linda glanced at her sister-in-law, who had turned away to cough into a handkerchief. "Maybe this week Ella could talk to you about something for that cough. She sucks the candies, but it doesn't seem to help."

"I'd be happy to." Sarah smiled, and to her relief, Ella smiled back with real friendliness. So the wall that had been between them, too, was finally down. "I know just the thing. I've been picking elderberries, so I can make you a syrup. Come by any day after tomorrow and I'll have some for you." It was with a sense of relief and gratitude that Sarah went outside to find the boys. The ability to help another was a gift—just like the warmth in Ella's eyes had been for her. And the little gifts added up to a larger one—she would feel as though she could go to Council Meeting and take part in communion with a pure heart.

"I'll just go find my boys," she said to Linda from the porch. "You go and rest—if Crist and Arlon are out here, the boys will be with them."

Linda leaned on the door frame, inside the screen. "I wouldn't assume that—but if you see Crist, let him know I'm lying down. He was trying to get me to do so earlier."

The Peachey barn didn't look like any other barn in the district. The milking parlor hadn't seen a cow in years; instead, it had been scrubbed to within an inch of its life and turned into a shop. The loft above, which should have held a season's worth of hay by now, was, as far as Sarah could see, full of pieces and parts that might someday come in useful. Washing machines, lawnmower engines, even what looked like a corn augur and a whole lot of crates that could contain anything.

Having come into such unexpected success with the solar battery for the cellphone tower, the Peachey brothers were clearly deep into the next project, though Sarah's unpracticed eye couldn't tell what it might be among all the mess of machinery. What she could see was that the place was deserted except for a stray red hen that had somehow found her way inside. She picked her up and carried her out before she hurt herself on metal parts, and set her down in the grass with her flock behind a low fence.

As she straightened, she heard voices. Not the deep ones of Crist and Arlon, but more familiar tones. Aha. The boys were out in the orchard.

"I'm telling you, Yoder, she's off limits," came Benny's disembodied voice. "She and Joe were holding hands, you said so yourself. That oughta give you an idea of how things stand."

"How they stand now."

"And you aim to change them? Just walk back into town and upset everything?"

Somehow Sarah's feet stopped moving in the grass, though she'd had no intention of listening. She still couldn't see them, but the orchard was a tangle of unpruned trees and waist-high grass, branches reaching for each other and knotted trunks covered in lichen. The boys could be lying in the grass six feet away and she'd never see them. The scent of rotting windfalls mixed with the smell of leaves and the sharp tang of—Sarah glanced down—yarrow. Exactly what she needed for a tea for Ella's cough, along with the syrup. She knelt to pick some of it and put it in her basket, peering through the stalks of grass and wondering where on earth the boys could be.

"But she likes me. She has for a long time."

"And you had your chance. I had mine. And she turned both of us down when she started writing to Joe. I think you should leave well enough alone. I don't even know why we're talking about this—or about her behind her back."

"Because you've been here and I haven't. I wanted to know how things stand."

"Then you should ask Priscilla and get the cold shoulder for your trouble. What about Rosanne Kanagy? She's pretty cute—and she makes a mean blackberry pie. One of the best I ever tasted."

"There's more to a girl than her cooking."

"I dunno," came a laconic voice. Leon. "You live with one, you live with the other, seems to me."

"Nobody's living with anybody." Simon sounded a little disgusted at the young men's failure to get the point. "I'm eighteen and I'm not ready to think about marriage. I'm not even ready to think about joining church."

Sarah's heart missed a beat as her blood seemed to stand still in her veins. She got to her feet, looking more urgently through the trees. They had to be here somewhere—and not too far away, either.

"Why not?" Benny wanted to know. "I'm going to."

"You are? This fall?"

"*Neh*, in the spring. I already talked to Bishop Daniel about baptism classes." A pause. "What's the matter?"

"I just never thought." Simon's tone sounded rattled. Unsure. "You and Leon seem to be having a pretty wild *Rumspringe*."

"*Ja*, but that comes to an end eventually, or you wind up like poor old Henry Byler, all by yourself without family or church or anything."

"He has family. Right across the highway. And he's famous, from what Caleb says."

Caleb wasn't with them? Sarah came to herself with a start. Enough was enough.

"Simon!" she called. "It's time to go."

There was a crackling sound, and the scrape of old lichen being stripped off a trunk by a man's boots, and Simon slithered into view three trees away. She swallowed back the hundred questions clustered on the tip of her tongue, and merely said, "I haven't seen you up a tree in a while. Is Caleb with you?"

"*Neh*, he went to look at the tower with Crist."

Benny slid down, and on the other side, Leon swung from a branch like a monkey and dropped into the grass. Sarah smiled at them. "Hallo, boys. Find any apples?"

"One or two." Benny held one up—a half-eaten Golden Delicious whose skin was bubbled with brown russeting. "The birds have got most of what we left after we picked." His face was blank, pleasant…the kind of face that any mother of teenagers recognized.

Sarah said, "We're going now, Simon. Find Caleb, please. I'll be in the buggy."

She had done what she could. It would be up to the gentle leading of the Spirit now. And it was clear the Spirit was up to something. With an internal smile, Sarah hoped Bishop Daniel's baptism classes were ready for Benny Peachey.

CHAPTER 9

Henry was carefully lowering the pumpkin pitcher into the kiln when the telephone on the wall over by the barn door rang. Another man might have jumped at the sound in the misty stillness of the early October morning, but another man didn't have what might turn out to be four hundred dollars' worth of pottery in his hands.

He'd made sure the woodstove had been banked with a big chunk of wood in it last night, so that the barn stayed warm. Granted, the kiln heated to 1800 degrees, but he'd found it worked a lot better when it wasn't struggling against a cold environment. Besides, when the greenware came out, it would need a gentler introduction to the outside world than the crisp rime of frost he'd found on the grass this morning.

Since there was no electricity for an answering machine, the phone stopped after half a dozen rings. Henry forgot about it in last-minute adjustments to the contents of the kiln—a set of four plates, several mugs, and a batter bowl shaped like an acorn squash that suggested it might go rather well with the pumpkin pitcher—for those who could afford it. With careful movements of the separators, he moved the pieces until nothing touched and he was finally satisfied. He set up the cones that would melt when the kiln reached the temperature he wanted, and closed the lid.

The Honda generator he'd found when he moved here in the spring had turned out to be quite the workhorse, and hadn't failed him yet. As long as he kept its gas tank full, it ran like a champ to meet the huge demands of the kiln. He hadn't had to rent space in someone else's studio for the firing, which was a relief. The thought of trying to load bisque and greenware into the trunk of the car when so much was at stake with D.W. Frith gave him the willies.

He'd no sooner returned to the workbench and pulled off his surgical gloves than the phone rang again. He flexed his fingers and winced with the pain as his skin cracked and began to bleed. There had to be a solution for this—the problem only seemed to be getting worse. On the sixth ring, he finally got to the phone. Ginny was expecting her family any second, so this was probably her letting him know they'd arrived.

"Henry here."

"Am I speaking to Henry Byler, the potter?"

Not Ginny. A man, late twenties, maybe. "Yes."

"Great. Henry, you're a hard man to find. This is Matt Alvarez, with TNC."

"I'm not interested in buying anything," he said cautiously. "And it's a busy morning, so if you don't mind—"

"Wait—I'm not a phone solicitor. I'm a producer. Are you familiar with TNC? The reality channel? *Shunning Amish*?"

"Is that a television show? If it is, it doesn't make sense— the Amish don't care if people shun them."

He laughed as if Henry had cracked a joke. "It sure is— number one nationwide on Wednesday nights. It's about the ex-Amish—probably one of the most popular topics we've ever covered. We're interested in doing a segment on you."

"What?" Henry started to run a hand through his hair, then realized it was the one smeared with blood, and he lowered it. Why on earth would anyone—

"You're an interesting man, Henry. My wife showed me the video about your pottery on the Frith site earlier in the summer, and it took me a couple of months to get the green light from the network. Then about six weeks to track down someone who would talk to me—or who knew where you were. Finally I got ahold of a guy called Dave Petersen, and he told me some of your story."

So much for protecting the integrity of the artist. "I'm sorry you went to all that trouble, Mr. Alvarez, but I don't shun the Amish and I don't want to be on TV."

"Henry—"

"Have a good day."

Henry hung up before the guy could get out another word, and dialed the New York number he knew by heart. If Matt Alvarez tried to call back, he'd get a busy signal. Two birds with one stone.

"Petersen—hey, is that you, Henry? Did the guy from TNC call?"

"I just hung up with him." Then he corrected himself. "On him."

"And?"

"And nothing. I don't much appreciate you giving out my phone number to TV producers, Dave. Or anyone else, for that matter. I'd like your assurance that it won't happen again."

"Come on, Henry, lighten up. There isn't a person in the US of A who wouldn't jump at the chance to be on TNC. They're the number one rated network on—"

"Wednesday nights—yes, so I understand. But I think in

Whinburg Township at least, you'll find a lot of people not only not jumping, but actively running away, me included."

"Henry." Dave's voice sounded so patient that Henry braced himself. "You're not seeing the bigger picture here. Now, the response to your pottery has been great, and orders are coming in even better than we expected. Which is good for you, and us. But what we'd really like is a greater reach of awareness."

Henry sighed. Marketing people should speak a language that was easier to understand. Like Tagalog. Or Pennsylvania Dutch. "What does that mean?"

"It means relative value. It means that if ten million viewers discover you on an episode of *Shunning Amish* on Wednesday night, your relative value goes stratospheric. It means that countrywide, people will be demanding your pieces. It means you'll be one of the most famous ex-Amish people in the country."

"There are famous ex-Amish?" Who knew? But, he supposed, once a man left the church, he wasn't obliged to practice *Uffgeva* or be *demut* anymore, was he? Though it seemed a strange way to court fame—for *not* belonging to something.

Dave rattled off a couple of names that Henry had never heard, and went on, "The thing is, this will be your chance to tell the world why you left the church—and yet, how it still informs your art. Classic conflict, Henry. People will eat it up."

The urge to throw the phone out the barn doors was overwhelming, but it was on a long spiral cord and would only bounce back. Henry controlled himself and schooled his voice to calm rationality. It seemed to him to be the only way to counteract such rampant craziness. "Dave, for one thing, I didn't leave the church, because I never joined it. And for another thing, the Amish faith doesn't inform my art. If it did, I'd be making plain white coffee mugs and sauerkraut crocks like the one I made my cousin's wife not long ago. The Amish don't go for embellishment or anything that could be called *fancy*—and even you can't deny that there is plenty of fancy going on in my pieces."

"Missing the point again, Henry. Okay, so you don't want it to be an exposé. Fine. I get that. But what we need here is some expo*sure*, and let me tell you, it doesn't come any better than this—and at no cost to Frith, to boot."

"But why? You said the orders were coming in better than you expected."

"For now. Christmas is a-coming, the economy is up, and people are buying. But what about in January? If they do the filming this month, the episode will air early next year—right when the Christmas sales have fallen off and we need something to goose things along until the spring catalog comes out."

"Isn't that your job? Isn't that what Marketing is for?"

"Yes," Dave moaned dramatically. From the tone of his voice, Henry could imagine him pulling at his hair in despair. "Which I am trying to do as we speak. This is a terrific opportunity, Henry. Once in a lifetime, even. TNC won't come knocking again. We can't afford to turn them down."

Henry was silent. *We? Really?*

"Tell you what," Dave said, when it became obvious someone needed to fill in the gap. "Why don't you sleep on it, and I'll call you tomorrow."

"There's nothing to sleep on."

"Yeah, there is. A renewal of your contract, for a start. It was for the fall/winter season only, remember, with an option to renew in the new year."

"Dave…" Did he really have to be so heavy-handed? Henry was perfectly aware of the amount of time the contract covered.

"I hate to bring it up, I really do, but you have to plan for success. *Expect* success. I know that's not what the Amish do, or what you've been used to doing in Denver, but this is here and now and I want you to think about it. Talk it over with your fiancée. You never know. Maybe she watches TNC."

Henry gave up. "Fine. I'll talk to you tomorrow. But my answer won't be any different."

"Maybe not, but at least you'll have given it a fair shot." The smile was back in Dave's voice, and for the first time, Henry wondered what kind of pressure was being brought to bear on the man from the people above him.

Maybe when they spoke tomorrow, he'd ask him.

✾

"TNC?" From around the dining table, four pairs of interested coffee-brown eyes pinned Henry to his chair. "They want you to be on *Shunning Amish*?"

Venezia grabbed Ginny's forearm in excitement. "That's my favorite show! Or one of them—right after *Dancing with Celebrities* and *Own That Gown*. I can't believe someone I know is going to be on TNC!"

Immediately after Henry had hung up on Dave, Ginny had called to let him know her parents and sister had arrived from Philadelphia. As he left the kiln to do its job, it was almost a relief to get away from the studio and what was becoming an unwelcome connection with the demanding world outside of quiet Willow Creek.

How had he never noticed what it was like before? Had it been this bad in Denver?

"I don't think Henry has said yes to the press yet, Venezia," Rafe Mainwaring told his daughter. "This isn't the face of a guy who's a hundred percent happy about the idea."

From the first handshake, Henry had decided that he was going to be lucky in his future father-in-law. Rafe's balding head was fringed with grizzled gray hair, and he wore a tweed jacket whose obvious comfort complemented well-worn jeans. He was heavy enough to give his wife's cooking a good testimony, but moved like a man who could waltz her around the room if he had the chance—which, Henry imagined, he would, at the wedding.

When Henry looked at Donnée, Rafe's wife, he could see where Ginny got her cheekbones and her wide-lipped smile. Ginny was the more voluptuous of the two sisters, though; Venezia favored her mother's angular figure. They hadn't even been in the house an hour and he wondered if there was a man on the planet who could keep up with Venezia. She was scary smart, which he supposed was a requirement for managing a sales force in the pharmaceutical industry. She had a frivolous side, though, it seemed, if she watched celebrity dancing shows—and if the sparkly dragonflies in her ears were any indication, she and Ginny had something in common outside of their gene pool. When they were teenagers, had they fought over who was going to wear what earrings?

"Henry's not the television type." With the authority of long practice, Ginny cut the fresh gingerbread cake, dabbed a spoonful of real whipped cream on each serving, and topped it with tiny, jewel-like pieces of homemade candied ginger. Then she handed them around to her family, the biggest servings going to Henry and her dad. "And I've already seen what even the most careful supervision of the filming will do—nothing. Henry watched them film that Frith video, and still it came out almost completely inaccurate—showing what they wanted instead of what he is. Imagine what a TV episode would do."

"How many ways can they misquote you if it's filmed?" Venezia tasted the gingerbread, lifted her brows, and dug in. "It would be you doing the talking, wouldn't it?"

"Who knows?" Henry said. The gingerbread melted on his tongue and he nearly groaned in satisfaction. "Ginny, I swear every dessert you make is better than the last."

"Never mind changing the subject," she said, but he could tell she was pleased. "If you're going to call Dave Petersen back, you'd better have a decision for him."

"I already told him no."

"Why?" Rafe asked. "No judgment, just curious."

"Because aside from the accuracy issue, the whole premise of the show offends me," Henry said, "and I haven't even seen it yet."

"It's on tonight," Venezia pointed out. "We should watch it."

He probably should, just so he'd be informed when he talked to Dave, but the thought didn't hold any pleasure. "I guess what bothers me most is that I don't hold any hard feelings against anyone in the church, now or then. It was a choice. I made it; it's done. If other people need to take their anger and alienation public, that's fine, but I don't see any reason to."

"I can't say I blame you for wanting to keep your private life private." Donnée glanced at her husband. "This need to chronicle every minute of our lives and air our dirty laundry in front of millions of strangers is a little odd to us."

"I'm in the business of confidentiality," Rafe said with a chuckle. "The only One who hears about the dirty laundry is the Lord. I find it's a lot safer that way."

"I have to agree," Henry found himself saying. "And besides, what if the folks around here somehow got wind of it? The kids carry cell phones, I know they do…and people watch these programs on them now, not just on TVs. It would cause a lot of grief and offense, and I'm not prepared to live with that."

Rafe nodded in understanding, and then said, "So you're still a God-fearing man? Do you and Ginny go to church?"

"I don't think the Mennonites will have us," Ginny said. "Not when my ex still goes. And there isn't a community church closer than Strasburg. We're in plain country down here."

"I think you'd find it helpful," Rafe said. "Does that mean you don't plan a church ceremony? Or are you going to do the deed at home in Philly?"

"I was hoping *you* could marry us, Daddy, right here in the garden." Ginny smiled at him with such love that Henry couldn't help comparing their two families. Hers, who still remained close even though the daughters were scattered all over the country. And his, who made a return to the church a condition of complete fellowship and love. Oh, they'd never say so, but he felt it sure enough. Even with Sarah Yoder he felt that wall of separation that never quite came down—that unspoken requirement for complete friendship that was as palpable as it was invisible.

"I'd be honored and delighted," Rafe said. "Have you talked this over with your intended?"

"Of course," Ginny said.

Henry came back to himself with a bump. "Anything you want is fine with me, you know that."

"What if, deep down, she wanted you to do this silly show?" Venezia asked him quietly.

"What?" three voices chorused. Henry couldn't have said it better himself.

"Venezia, girl, give your head a shake," Ginny said. "Haven't you been listening?"

"Henry has just got done telling you all the reasons why he can't do it," her mother added, frowning. "It's obvious she doesn't want him to do it. What are you thinking?"

"I'm thinking of his career," Venezia told them all, but her gaze held her sister's from across the table.

"My career doesn't need this," Henry put in, since no one else seemed inclined to.

"But maybe you do. Maybe you need this kind of recognition to erase what happened in Denver."

"How do you know what happened in Denver?"

"I told her, never expecting she'd bring it up at my own table, right in front of you." Ginny glared at her. "So much for confidentiality."

"I'm not a pastor—or a pastor's wife."

"This isn't recognition, Venezia," he explained gently, before things got out of hand. "Recognition is winning an award, or getting a good review in the Arts section of the *Post*. This is notoriety."

"It all depends on how you present yourself. You could make it a condition of the shoot that you review the final film, and if there's anything you want them to change or take out, they have to do it."

"I don't think you make those kinds of conditions with TNC," Ginny observed. "That kinda negates the point."

"It's worth a try," Venezia insisted. "I'm speaking as the sales manager here. Not only does your pottery get its moment in the spotlight, the Rose Arbor Inn does, too. This could be a windfall for the two of you as you start your lives together."

Donnée's eyes widened. "Girl, you really want your sister's man to go against his principles so she can get some free nationwide advertising? Do you think these two are going to go for that?"

Ginny gave her sister a look over a pair of imaginary glasses, and her earrings—sea-green parrots to match her blouse—swung. "Of course not."

But Venezia wasn't giving up. Henry saw the woman who took on big business as part of her workday retrench and come at the pitch another way. "I'm just looking at every angle so Henry can make the best decision. There's no law says he has to listen. But someone has to bring it up."

"You all have given me a lot to think about—Venezia, too." Henry rose from the table and pushed back his chair. "I need to get back to the studio—this firing will be done. But I'll be back for supper, and we can watch the show together. Then I'll see what I think."

Venezia subsided into her chair and dug into her gingerbread, but it seemed that Ginny had had enough. She pushed her plate away.

"Fair enough," Rafe said. "Want some company?"

"Daddy, you'll be getting a tour of the township tomorrow," Ginny protested.

Henry pulled her to her feet and kissed her. "It's okay. It's been a while since I had a man older than fourteen around the place to talk to. I'll bring him back safely, I promise."

She smiled into his eyes. "All right, then. You can check each other out and kick each other's tires all you want. Just be here by six or my soufflé will be ruined—and Henry, for goodness' sake, put some cream on those hands. You make me hurt just looking at you."

"Count on it."

As they went outside, Henry could already hear female voices clashing against one another, and even Rafe's footsteps picked up their pace. "You sure you're ready to take on the women in this family?" his future father-in-law muttered.

Henry had to laugh. "As long as it's only one at a time."

CHAPTER 10

"Your kitchen smells wonderful."

Ella Peachey put her worn leather handbag on a kitchen chair and breathed in the scent of the elderberry syrup that Sarah had been working on for the past hour or two. Smiling, Sarah dipped a clean spoon in the saucepan and offered it to her.

"Taste and see whether it's sweet enough."

Obediently, like a small child taking cough syrup, Ella took the spoonful and rolled it around in her mouth with an expression Sarah could only describe as thoughtful.

"I would say it's just right," she said at last. "What's in it—and how will it help?"

"This is so easy that I'll give you the recipe so you can make it at home." Sarah took the saucepan to the sink and began to fill the series of pint jars she had just sterilized. "You pick a couple of pounds of elderberries—it's the season for them, so they're everywhere—and cook them in water until their skins burst. Run that mixture through cheesecloth to get the skins and seeds out."

She screwed a lid on one of the jars and handed it to Ella. The thick syrup inside had a deep purple, jewel-like tone that delighted her. Unfortunately, even though she'd been as careful as she could, her spatulas and the two towels she'd used now bore permanent purple stains that weren't so delightful. Ah, well. Now they'd be for exclusive use at elderberry time— or when she was making blueberry pie in summer.

"Then what?" Ella asked, stashing the jar carefully in her handbag.

"Put the liquid back on the burner and reduce it by half, and then add the same amount of honey. Or if anyone doesn't like honey, you can use raw sugar. I like the honey, though... it seems more syrupy, doesn't it? You can use it just like that, but"—she indicated the jar in the purse—"I added a little licorice root and a bit of sage for their soothing effect."

Ella nodded, clearly committing the recipe to memory. "I'm glad you gave me some to taste. Sometimes, while these cures are good for you, they taste awful. I had a bit of Linda's tincture you were giving her." She made a face, and Sarah laughed. "I was glad it wasn't me."

"You'll like this one," Sarah told her. "And the beauty of it is, you can use it just as you would any fruit syrup—even on your pancakes or over ice cream."

"Really?" Ella's gaze took on the focus of intense interest. "And will it keep colds away? The boys don't get them so much, but Arlon is a martyr to them in the winter, especially if it's a wet one like last year."

Sarah nodded. "Oh yes. I don't think you'll have any trouble getting your menfolk to take their cold syrup. It will just be a matter of how many different ways you can use it."

Ella's smile changed her whole face—in fact, Sarah couldn't ever remember seeing such brightness in her face in all the time she'd known her. Maybe it was simply because here was something she could give her husband that would not only help him, but please his taste buds, too.

A few worn bills changed hands, and then Sarah was seeing her new patient off down the lane, the lamps on either side of the buggy lit. At five o'clock in the afternoon, the sun was already down, leaving only the afterglow in the sky to see by. The chickens had gone into their shed by themselves, so Sarah had just enough light to count beaks and make sure everyone was in their place before she refilled the waterers with the garden hose for morning.

When she closed up and walked across the orchard, she pulled her black wool jacket more tightly around her. There would be frost again tomorrow, just as there had been the last several mornings. The frost had its own beauty, but it signified the end of their Indian summer in no uncertain terms.

And the end of her garden's season. She would have to get more serious about clearing it out—thank goodness Simon was home, because it was hard work. More than one person could do on her own, especially if an unexpected buggy came rolling down the lane bearing someone else needing a cure. Since Caleb had his responsibilities on Jon Hostetler's work crew now, Simon would be picking up his little brother's daytime chores until he found work again.

Hard work would be good for him. It would keep him from thinking up mischief like chasing girls who were already spoken for.

As she emerged from under the pear at the corner of the orchard, she caught sight of two dark figures coming down the hill path between her place and Henry's, one tall and thin, one stocky and solid.

Henry.

And a stranger.

Sarah didn't know whether to be glad or sorry that Henry was coming to see her. In her deepest heart of hearts, she had to admit that it would be easier if he didn't. That way, she wouldn't need to hear about his wedding plans, or about his bride-to-be...though when Priscilla shared the odd detail about her boss in passing conversation, Sarah couldn't stop herself from pricking up her ears.

It was like a fine kind of torture—wanting to know and yet dreading to hear.

Or maybe she was just crazy and needed to turn her mind to something more profitable. Like cleaning up the kitchen. Or compost.

"Sarah!" Henry had seen her now, though how he could in the falling twilight was a mystery. He must have very good eyesight.

"Hallo, Henry," she said as the two men joined her on the lawn. It was *gut* that her voice sounded so calm—she just hoped no one saw the rapid pulse giving itself away under her bib apron. "How are you?"

"I'll get to that," he said in a tone as easy as hers. "Sarah, this is my future father-in-law, Rafe Mainwaring. Rafe, my neighbor Sarah Yoder. Her boy Caleb has been a lot of help to me since I moved here in April."

"Happy to meet you, Mrs. Yoder." The man extended a hand, and Sarah's was clasped in a broad, warm grip. His eyes were kind and brimming with interest in a face the color of strong coffee. So this was Ginny's father. He had a wonderful handshake.

"Please," she said, "we do not use honorifics. Call me Sarah."

"I'd be happy to." He released her hand and gazed past her at the orchard, the lawn, the chicken shed, and in the distance, at her garden. "You have a real nice place here. It smells good."

That made her smile. "Only because I don't keep cows. I grow herbs, vegetables, and flowers…though nearly everything is over for the season. Please, come inside. It's chilly out here."

In the lamplit kitchen, she pulled out chairs for them and slid into the oven the chicken pie that she and the boys would be having for supper when Caleb got home. "Can I offer you something to eat? A whoopie pie? A cookie?"

"No, thanks. We'll be having our own dinner shortly, and we just stuffed ourselves on gingerbread cake—though the air in here smells good enough to eat," Henry said. "Have you been baking?"

"Making elderberry syrup for a patient with a persistent cough."

"Ah. Well, this is more of a business call."

She had already seen it. "Henry, what has happened to your hands?" Already, she was filling another saucepan at the sink. "Sit, and I'll brew up a quick soaking bath for you. That must hurt."

He spread them on the table and gazed at the cracked, bleeding joints. "I don't know what happened. I mean, I knew the water here was hard, and clay dries out the skin, so I've been using this stuff I got at the drugstore."

"A moisturizer?"

"I guess. Smelled like a flower garden. Then I ordered some gloves to give my hands some protection, and it's gotten worse. Now it's getting so bad people are remarking on it like you just did."

"What kind of gloves?" Sarah liked Rafe's voice. It was deep and resonant, the way she imagined an Old Testament prophet's might have sounded. She put the saucepan on the stove and turned on the flame.

Henry looked a little confused. "Why would that matter? Not gardening gloves, certainly. I ordered a box of those thin latex ones that surgeons use. I need to be close to the clay—though I have to say, even that barrier is almost too much. It might be necessary, but it sure is distracting."

"Then I recommend you find something else," Rafe said. "Looks to me like you're allergic to latex."

Sarah stared at Henry's poor hands and wondered how long it might have taken her to come to that diagnosis if she'd been left to her own devices. She wore latex gloves herself sometimes, when she was working with nettles, for instance. Since they had no effect on her, it would never have occurred to her that someone could be allergic to them.

"How did you know?" she finally said to Rafe, feeling very humble indeed. "Are these always the symptoms?"

Rafe nodded. "One of my congregation owns a restaurant—best cheese steaks you'll ever eat, if you're ever on Broad Street—and when the new food prep laws came in a few years ago, they had to wear gloves. Turned out he and some of his kitchen staff were allergic to latex, and their hands looked similar to this. Not quite as bad, though. They hadn't let it go on so long before they said something." He cleared his throat meaningfully.

"I'm saying something now," Henry said. "Can you help me, Sarah?"

"If you stop wearing the gloves, it should clear up."

"But my hands were cracked before the gloves. That's why I got them. To help with that. I have to do something different—my hands are my livelihood."

She ran over what she knew and came up empty. "Let me get my book. Once this water warms up, I'll make a quick calendula bath for them—it's an antibacterial so at least it will clean out the wounds. They're looking pretty angry." Hurrying into the compiling room, she called, "How have you managed to work like that?"

"It hasn't been easy."

The two men's voices fell into a low conversation as Henry pointed out things in her kitchen that weren't likely in that of his future mother-in-law. Like the propane fridge and stove, and the pole lantern, the jars of elderberry syrup, and the rows of pickled beets on the counter that she'd put up this morning and hadn't got put away downstairs in the pantry yet.

From her shelves, she chose a jar of calendula tincture and spooned a tablespoon into a bowl. Then she got out the book of herbal medicine that Ruth had recommended and had come in the mail.

Chafed skin, chapped hands, chilblains. Hm. The cure was the same for all three: the sticky sap from the tree the country people called balm of Gilead. In spite of her hurry, Sarah smiled as the verse came to mind—*Is there no balm in Gilead; is there no physician there?*

She carried the bowl of fragrant liquid into the kitchen and carefully poured lukewarm water into it to dilute it. When it was ready, she set it in front of Henry. "Soak your hands in this for fifteen minutes while we talk."

He glanced at the clock on the top of the stove. "We need to be home by six."

"You will. It's only over the hill."

"I mean, Ginny's home."

Her stomach dipped as she realized how much had changed while she was determined not to look. "Well, maybe ten minutes will still do some good. I'll put some more in a quart jar and you can take it with you when you leave. Soak them again in the morning before you start work. I don't want those wounds to get infected, Henry, or you'll be in even more difficulty."

"I know, and I appreciate that." He submerged his hands obediently.

"Is this the cure, then?" Rafe said, watching the proceedings with interest.

Sarah shook her head. "According to my book, the best thing is balm of Gilead, which is made from the sap of poplar buds."

Rafe looked as though she'd just given him a present. "You mean there really is balm in Gilead?"

She smiled at him. "It seems there is somewhere—I just wish I had some."

"You don't?" Henry asked.

"No," Sarah admitted. "Poplars bud in very early spring, and we're only in October now. But Ruth will know where to get some. Oh, I wish you'd come sooner. I was there for my lesson only yesterday and I could have asked her."

"Ruth is what the Amish call a *Dokterfraa*," Henry explained. "Sarah is learning herbal medicine from her, but Ruth lives in Whinburg, which you would have driven through on your way here."

"Whinburg's not so far," Rafe said. "Just a few minutes."

"Not with a horse and buggy," Sarah told him. "It's an all-day journey for us, there and back."

"Ah. Well, maybe we could take you over tomorrow in the car," Rafe said. "Ginny's promised me a tour of the township, and I can't think of anything more interesting than meeting another Amish woman in your line of work—a *Dokterfraa*."

Sarah smiled at his pronunciation, but gave him credit for trying to say it. "Would eight o'clock be all right, then?" she asked. "Ruth usually opens her door for the day at nine, but she won't mind if we come a little early. Like us, they're up at four."

Rafe glanced at Henry. "Is Ginny planning on serving breakfast?"

"I'm sure she is. But we'll be back by nine."

"Donnée will appreciate the sleep-in, then...she hardly ever gets a chance to do that. She works as hard as I do."

"What do you do for your living?" Sarah asked.

"I'm a pastor at the Episcopal Gospel Church of Douglas-town. That's a neighborhood in Philadelphia."

Sarah nodded, and hoped her thoughts weren't open for anyone to read on her face. She bottled up the quart of the calendula wash for Henry in a Mason jar and sent them on their way so they wouldn't be late for Ginny's dinner. When they were gone, she sank into what had become her reading and sewing chair in the front room.

Caleb would be home any minute, and Simon had promised to be back for supper, so she might only have a few minutes alone to think.

She'd resolutely managed not to think about Henry for all these weeks, and now here he'd come into her kitchen, needing help and undoing all the good work she'd accomplished. And with a worldly pastor as a future father-in-law! There was some kind of ironic justice in that, wasn't there—to run so far from God, only to marry into the family of a man who made God his business.

But at the same time, there was a big difference. Henry could enjoy his father-in-law and even worship in that church with the long name. It wouldn't be the same as giving his life to God in service. It wouldn't mean *Uffgeva*, that giving up of one's own will and doing the will of the Lord, as

Jesus had done—of saying, "Not my will, Lord, but Thine be done."

And what about her? she thought in despair. Was this the Lord's will for her—that her greatest temptation should be brought into her own kitchen for treatment so that she had to see him time and again before he was married? Even though Scripture said that God would not tempt her more than she could bear, Sarah wondered how she was going to manage it.

Because this would rip the scab off the wound that Henry had dealt her on that summer evening in June, when she had met him on the hill and he had told her he was going to marry Ginny.

Oh, she'd known then. Her own treacherous heart had been revealed to her in all its pain and glory, and it had taken her months to recover from it.

She had made the mistake of allowing herself to care, and she'd been paying the price ever since.

It had come on slowly at first—so slowly she'd hardly been aware of it. She and Henry had been friends, neighbors— as much as an Amish woman could be with a man who had walked away from the church and chosen to be *Englisch*. Somehow their lives had become entwined with those of several others over the summer, and they had become a team, time and circumstance binding them together with invisible cords. They felt good, those cords, soft and sweet and ever so dangerous because the sweetness hid the tiny thorns. Even Sarah couldn't deny that having a male friend to whom she could say anything was a treasure she didn't get to hold very often. Not since Michael's death. So she had held it close— taken it out to examine its beauty—hoarded every feeling and look and shared moment of laughter or discovery.

And then—the hill.

She had realized to her mortification that his relationship with Ginny had progressed much further than she'd had any idea of because he hadn't told her—further even than his own relatives knew. But God had told her.

God had revealed her once and for all as a complete and utter fool.

It simply wasn't fair that when Henry needed help with his cracked hands, he turned to her instead of doing the sensible thing and making an appointment at the Mennonite cash-only medical clinic, or even going to the county hospital outside Whinburg. This was clearly God's doing. He had brought Henry back to her to test her strength, and now it was up to her to be kind and professional and get his hands fixed up in the shortest time possible, and deliver him unscathed back to Ginny.

Sarah curled up in the chair, pulled the afghan off the back of it, and buried her face in its comforting softness. And by the time Caleb and Simon came in a few minutes later, every last trace of her tears had been scrubbed away.

Chapter 11

The blessing a person always found at the bottom of a well of tears was the end of herself. There she found the place of prayer.

As she knelt by the side of her bed the next morning, Sarah felt a kind of weary relief that she could hand the day over to God.

Lord, You know my struggles, and how little sleep I've had. I know that I could tell Henry just to go to the clinic. But Your strength is sufficient for me, so I must trust You. I pray that Henry will find healing in Your hands for his—and for his spirit, too. Lord, if it's Your will, I pray that You would draw him back to Yourself in love.

She'd risen at four to make breakfast for Caleb and say prayers with him and Simon, and had his lunch bucket ready when he left at five. He got a ride with two of the other men on the crew, so he was always on the work site by six, which meant she had the use of the buggy if she needed it. When the car rolled into the driveway at eight, she and Simon had already had another cup of coffee together and cleaned up the kitchen, and she even had time to strip the dried flowers from a whole sack of lavender stems she'd collected earlier in September and had been drying upstairs.

"I smell lavender this morning instead of fruit," Rafe said as he held the car door for her, indicating she should sit in the front.

There was no way she was going to sit beside Henry in the backseat, so she smiled as she folded herself in on the passenger side. "That's because I was bagging it for sachets," she told him as he backed the car around and headed up the lane. "I have them hanging in bunches upstairs in the boys' rooms because it's cleaner there than in the barn."

"Boys' rooms are cleaner than a barn?" Rafe's pretend amazement made Sarah laugh.

"Mine are. They learned early that he who brings in dirt has to clean it out again, so they keep things tidy up there. And the lavender makes them sleep like logs...there's a method to my madness, you see."

If only she'd thought to hang a few bunches in her own room last night.

"How are your hands this morning, Henry?" she asked over her shoulder. "I see you have them wrapped in gauze."

"That was my daughter," Rafe said. "Turn here?"

"Yes, take the county highway for twelve miles, and turn right at the stop sign in Whinburg," Henry said. "Ginny didn't want me dripping blood on the furniture, so she soaked some gauze pads in your daisy water and wrapped them. Same again this morning. I don't know if it's healed them, but the skin around the cracked part isn't so red."

"Then it's done its job," she assured him, pushing away the

mental picture of Ginny ministering to him. While it would be Sarah's place to do that if she were going to take him on as a patient, she couldn't very well begrudge Ginny the privilege of loving service to the man she was going to marry.

The fact that it irked her was annoying, even so.

"We were watching a show on television," Rafe said, driving with comfortable confidence. Henry stirred restlessly in the backseat. "It's called *Shunning Amish*. Have you folks heard of it?"

Sarah gazed at him, a little at sea. "A television program? About the Amish?"

"More about those who have left the church," Henry said.

"Oh my," Sarah said. Then, when she couldn't control her curiosity and amazement any longer, she said, "Why on earth would you waste time with such a thing?"

"Now see what you've done," Henry grumbled to Rafe.

"The folks who make the program want Henry to be on it," Rafe told her.

Every sensible word left her head as she goggled first at him, then at Henry, who looked as though he had a headache. "I know what you're thinking, Sarah," he said.

"You do? Because I don't know what to think. Are there really such crazy things out there? Why on earth would anyone want to watch a program about people who have left the church? Why not make a program about people who have left the...the Episcopal Gospel Church of Douglastown?"

Rafe laughed while Henry simply shrugged. "It's a mystery," Henry said. "I'm with you—I don't see the attraction. But apparently there is one."

"On the good side, millions of people will see Henry's pottery," Rafe put in.

"And the Rose Arbor Inn," Henry added. "Don't forget that."

"And on the bad side?" she asked. "You talk about why you left everything you knew to take your own way in the world?"

"Way to sugarcoat things, Sarah." Henry shifted again and appeared to be trying to adjust the seat belt without using his sore hands to push against the upholstery of the car. "I write to my sisters the way I always have, and taking my own way doesn't mean turning my back on God. Not that any Amish person would believe that."

Oh dear, she'd made him angry blurting out exactly what she thought. When would she learn to school her tongue to a soft answer? "I'm sorry, Henry. I sinned in saying those words and judging you. Please forgive me." She swallowed. "But it's so strange. I don't understand this *Englisch* television at all."

"You might have liked the episode last night," Rafe said. "It was about this group of young women who make quilts together. They all have low-income jobs, but they pool their spare change and make quilts out of used clothes they get at thrift shops and cut up. Apparently it's cheaper than fabric yardage."

"Like a quilting frolic?" Sarah asked.

"Yes," Henry said. "One of them even makes pictures of Amish life and stitches them down. I forget what it's called."

"Appliqué?"

"That's it."

"Many of the Mennonite ladies are very good at it. But we don't use appliqué here. It's too fancy."

"I know," Henry said, "but this young lady isn't bound by those rules anymore. I had to give her credit for taking what she knows and making art out of it. And a living, too, I hope."

"A better living now, I suspect," Rafe said. "It's a good bet those quilts are going to sell as fast as those girls can make them, after being on the show." Sarah saw Rafe's gaze lift to the rearview mirror, as though he were looking at Henry instead of the buggy they'd just passed.

"If that's a hint, it's not a very subtle one," Henry told him. "Don't tell me you're going over to Venezia's side."

"Being outnumbered by females, I don't take sides," Rafe told him comfortably. "But I was impressed with one thing— the show didn't sensationalize those girls or try to make them more or less than they are. The focus was on their taking the skills they learned in their Amish homes and translating that into making a living in their new world."

"If you're drawing a parallel here, Rafe, I didn't learn pottery until after I moved to Denver."

Sarah kept her thoughts to herself as Henry turned to look out the window at the familiar countryside. From what she could see, these girls they were talking about were living something close to an Amish life. But they had abandoned the church and its standards—of dress, of humility, of putting God first—and kept the parts they liked or could use. On the one hand, it was *gut* that they could make a living using what their mothers had taught them. On the other, couldn't they have done that without giving up their faith?

Didn't Henry see the real parallel? In some ways, he was living an Amish life. He hadn't put electricity in yet, even after half a year, and was running his home and studio on propane and the generator. He was the first to lend a helping hand when it was needed and the last to take credit for it. He might be on the Internet in a video for that department store, but he led a humble, self-effacing life otherwise.

When someone left the Amish church, people called it "jumping the fence." Why couldn't he see that the only fence he had really jumped was that of his own will? It wouldn't be such a leap to return to the church he had been brought up in, would it?

Nor such a leap to come to her. *Neh, you can't think that way. That's presumptuous and vain and just adds to your sins this morning—because what makes you think he would choose you anyway, even if he did come back?*

Sarah spent the last few miles hauling on the reins of her emotions, thankful beyond words for the stiff black brim of her away bonnet. In its sheltering modesty, no one could get a good look at her face.

When they pulled into the Lehman yard, Isaac stepped out of the barn, wiping his hands on a rag. "Hallo," he called when they got out. "Sarah, is everything all right?"

She bumped the car door shut with her hip. "*Ja*, Isaac, all right. But Henry here is in some pain, and I wanted to see if Ruth has a certain cure on hand for him. So they drove me over." She made the introductions quickly. "Rafe is interested in Ruth's practice," she explained.

"Then let us find her." Isaac led the way into the house, and across a kitchen smelling of warm peanut butter to the *Dokterfraa's* compiling room, which had once been a screened-in porch.

After Sarah had introduced Rafe and explained Henry's problem, Ruth removed the gauze from Henry's hands and looked them over, turning them this way and that. At last she nodded. "I agree that balm of Gilead is the right thing to use here. I have some, but it's in the Gerlings' freezer, two places down the road. They're *Englisch*, but after I treated him for eczema, they offered their freezer if I needed it. I never thought of using such a thing before, but for out-of-season cures like this, it's come in real handy." Her granite gaze took in Henry and Rafe. "Maybe you'd want to visit with Isaac in the barn? We won't be gone long—twenty minutes at most. Luckily all these peanut butter cookies are out of the oven."

The Gerlings had a deep chest freezer and had allotted Ruth one of the wire baskets that sat in the top. She retrieved a zip-top bag labeled POPLAR SAP, and after a few words of conversation with the lady of the house, she and Sarah set off again.

"Is it true what I hear, that Henry is going to marry the woman who runs the Rose Arbor Inn?" Ruth asked as soon as they were on the road and out of earshot of anyone else.

"Yes." Best to keep this brief. "Before Christmas, I understand."

"This is the second time I've seen you here with him."

"Only because of the car."

"That's not his car."

Sarah stopped, and simultaneously, both of them reached up to pick several bunches of rich purple elderberries from the wild tree nodding by the fence. When she'd filled her apron, Ruth was smiling. "I told you in the beginning that you had a calling. You look where you're walking the same way I do. But I can also see through a grindstone when it has a hole in it. Be careful, Sarah."

"There is nothing to be careful of." If only her throat wouldn't close up on the words. "There's nothing," she repeated.

"I'm glad to hear it. Because I can't think of anything more painful."

Was it so easy for others to read her feelings in her face? After all these months, Ruth knew her pretty well, and Henry's name had come up now and again in conversation. Maybe more *again* than *now*. But perhaps there was a way to pull herself out of the hole she'd dug herself into, before this went any further.

"There is a man," Sarah said hoarsely, past the lump in her throat. "In Letitz. We—we are corresponding."

"I'm glad to hear it," Ruth said with some surprise. "Do we know him?"

Better to have his name on people's lips than Henry's. "You remember Silas Lapp? He came with us that day with your cousins Fannie and Zeke."

"Oh yes, I remember. He seemed like a good man—and I wondered then if he was interested in you."

Not for worlds would she tell Ruth that Silas had asked to court her back then and been turned down. She just needed the idea of him now, not the reality. And she hadn't fibbed. He had corresponded with her, and she owed him a letter.

They turned in at the Lehman drive. "No more now," Ruth said. "But I am glad. Maybe we will see something of him this autumn. I hear one of the Esh girls will be the first bride of this year, and we will be into wedding season before we know it."

They talked of weddings and who might be going to which service between the *Gmee* in Whinburg and the one in Willow Creek, and when they reached the house, they found Henry and Rafe waiting for them. Once again, Ruth led her guests back to the compiling room.

"As it says in your book, you'll want to use the sap to make an olive oil–based salve," she told Sarah. "I'd add calendula petals and lavender as an antimicrobial, both particularly good for the skin. And you might think about including a little vitamin E oil, too, as a preservative and to promote healing."

Sarah nodded. "I have all those on hand. I made sure to plant lots of calendula flowers all around the garden, and now I'm glad. I use the petals a lot, and the plants are hardy."

"Latex gloves," Ruth mused as she wrapped the thawing poplar buds so that they formed a packet that looked like a Christmas cracker. "I've never seen such an acute reaction as yours, Henry—not that I've seen a lot of cases. Most of our people don't work in situations where the gloves are necessary, except maybe for the girls cooking in the restaurants." She gazed at Henry as she handed Sarah the packet. "I hope this works for you. If it doesn't, you may need to see an *Englisch* doctor."

"Thanks, I will," he said, handing her a few bills in payment. "But so far Sarah's cures have worked."

"I'm glad to hear it. Let me know in either case, so I can add the information to my journal. And now I must get these cookies finished. We are invited to Amelia and Eli's this evening, and our little Elam sure loves my peanut butter and jam thumbprint cookies."

Sarah smiled as they took their leave. That had been Simon's favorite cookie, too, as a boy—and still was. Rafe wasted no time in getting them over the twelve miles back to Willow Creek—but the men would still be a few minutes late for breakfast.

"I'll mix up the salve today and bring it over," she said

to Henry as he took her place in the passenger seat of the car. "If you're not home, I'll leave it on the kitchen table."

"Thanks, Sarah," was all he said, and absently at that. He was probably looking forward to his breakfast with his intended. Which was just as it should be.

She must concentrate on doing what he had asked of her as an herbalist, nothing more. God must take care of the rest, because one thing was for sure—she didn't have the strength.

❀

Dear Silas,

Thank you for your letter, which Amanda brought over the other day. I hope you'll write down our address so my in-laws won't need to be my delivery service.

I was just over at Isaac Lehman's—you remember his wife Ruth, the Dokterfraa. I'm treating a man with a pretty severe case of dry skin compounded by a latex allergy, and fortunately, she had what I needed to help with a cure. When I was a child I used to wonder why God made so very many kinds of plants and trees and insects and animals. Now I'm glad He did—because it seems I need more and more kinds of cures the longer I practice this humble form of medicine.

I hope you are well, and that you have decided to do something with your fields despite the fact that the cell tower brings in enough to live on and more. God meant for us to be close to the earth so we would be reminded of His creation and our place in it. Tomorrow my place is in my garden, digging up the last of the potatoes and onions and getting them into the cellar.

Give my regards to Zeke and Fannie when you see them. I very much enjoyed their visit in the summer.

Your friend,
Sarah Yoder

Chapter 12

On Friday, while she went about her work cleaning the rooms at the Rose Arbor Inn, Priscilla watched the weather anxiously. Dan and Malinda Kanagy had invited the *Youngie* over to their place for a get-together, and if the weather stayed clear, they'd have the very last volleyball game of the year outside. In some districts, where maybe the weather didn't cooperate so well, local fathers might actually make arrangements with a high school for the *Youngie* to play in their gym, but since Willow Creek didn't have a high school or even a rec center, volleyball became a seasonal thing, like ice skating.

Well, even if it rained or snowed, they'd still have fun playing board games or even team games inside in the big room downstairs where church was held. Pris's favorite was the relay race where teams of eight stood in a line, boy-girl-boy-girl, and each boy had to put a pillowcase on a pillow. His female partner took it off and passed it down the line to the next boy. She always had to laugh at how many boys were really good at pillowcases—and how inventive they could be sometimes when they weren't.

And speaking of pillowcases, she had plenty to do right here at the Inn in that department. While technically the

Mainwarings weren't paying guests, Ginny still wanted Pris and Katie Schrock to do their rooms as neatly as if they were. Tomorrow Ginny was going back with her family to Philadelphia to find a wedding dress, and since there were no guests booked, the Inn would be closed until she got back on Tuesday.

Ginny's father was an early riser, but her mother and sister luxuriated in being able to sleep in on the comfortable beds. So when they got up at last and went down to breakfast, Priscilla would slip in, make the beds and tidy up, and then do the bathrooms after they'd gone to do whatever wedding business they had planned for the day. Ginny had said with a laugh that they were giving Whinburg more business than it had seen in a while—though Pris knew for a fact that the more liberal Mennonite brides got their flowers from the Whinburg florist and their cakes from the bakery there, too.

When she'd finished for the day, Pris stuck her head into the front parlor, where Rafe was reading the local paper. "Good-bye," she said shyly. "Have a safe trip home tomorrow."

He got to his feet, as if she were someone important, and came over to shake hands. "Thank you for all you've done for us, Priscilla. My wife is going to expect this kind of service at home now—and I'm not nearly as good at it as you are."

She laughed at the idea of this man, so kind and dignified, on his knees in front of a toilet, scrubbing. "I will see you at the wedding, then, on the twelfth of December."

"You will, God willing."

Still smiling, she let herself out and went through the rose arbor for which the Inn was named, now a tangle of brown stems and yellowed leaves. There was a buggy in the parking lot. Goodness. Had Joe—

"Hey, Pris." Simon levered himself off the white pickets of the fence, and grinned. "Surprised you."

He certainly had. Her mouth hung open so far that if it had been summer, flies probably would have flown in. "What are you doing here?" she finally managed when he looked as though he was trying not to laugh at her expression.

"I thought you might like a ride home."

"Simon Yoder, I've been working here since April and not once have you offered me a ride home—or even thought of it."

"I thought about it plenty when I was out in Colorado."

"Well, that doesn't mean a thing."

"So? *Ja* or *neh?*"

For a moment, she was tempted. It was a couple of miles, and if she got home early, she'd have a little extra time to get ready for tonight. On the other hand, it would be just her luck if one of the Bylers was driving in the other direction and the news got back to Joe that she was out riding with another boy.

Of course they were all friends, but still. It would look bad.

"*Neh*, I'm fine walking home. The maples in the creek bed are gorgeous right now—it's a treat to go home that way."

To her surprise, he merely nodded, as if it didn't matter to him one way or the other. Which made her a little ashamed of herself. Just how proud was she that she'd automatically assumed he was there because he wanted to give Joe some competition?

"Going to the Kanagys' tonight?" he asked as he climbed into the buggy.

"*Ja*, it sounds like fun. Rosanne says all the *Youngie* from hereabouts are going, and they're expecting some of the Blackbirds from over Strasburg way, too."

Simon grinned. "They'd better expect some competition from us Woodpeckers, then, if they set up the nets. Looks like we might get to play, doesn't it? Not a cloud in the sky."

It did indeed. As Priscilla walked home along the creek, the skies stayed clear, a vibrant blue against which the yellow and scarlet of the maples and poplars stood out in sharp, burning relief.

She had to shake her head at herself. Six months ago, she would have died of happiness if Simon had asked to take her home. But now? Sure, she'd had a tiny moment of indecision, but really, there was only one thing she could have said, and Simon should have known it. She hoped he'd get work soon, and turn his mind to more profitable things. Maybe there'd be a nice girl among the Blackbirds who would catch his eye, and Pris could stop feeling so jumpy in her spirit whenever she saw him.

Joe came and picked her up right after the supper dishes were done—so promptly that Mamm offered to finish drying so Pris could run upstairs and get her coat. Once they were clip-clopping down the road, Joe transferred both reins into his right hand and squeezed her fingers with his left. "On the way home, I wonder if I could talk something over with you."

It was the same distance home as it was going over. Why not talk now? "Sure. What is it?"

"Nothing I want to get started on now, but after...I been thinking about some stuff and wanted your opinion. So don't go letting other fellows drive you home, okay?"

Had someone seen Simon at the Inn and thought she'd got

into his buggy with him? "I didn't go home with Simon this afternoon, if that's what you're hinting at."

Joe slanted her a look. "Simon?"

"*Ja*, he was waiting for me after work and offered me a ride. But I said I'd rather walk, even though I could have used the extra time."

"Why didn't you go with him?" Joe sounded sincerely curious, like maybe he wouldn't mind if she had.

"It wouldn't look right."

"Huh." And that was all he said, but he held her hand all the way to Willow Creek Road, where he had to use both hands on the reins to make the turn.

Rosanne was as glad to see her as if they hadn't been together practically all day at the Amish Market the previous weekend. "Come and help me with the food—I don't know how many people will come, but Malinda says we should prepare for lots. Did you hear a bunch of Blackbirds are coming?" Rosanne looked almost as if she was nervous about it.

"*Ja*, but what's wrong with that? Are they fast?"

"Faster than us Woodpeckers, but not as bad as that bunch that Jake Byler got tangled up with. You know, with the car incident. I mean, some of those boys actually own their own cars and have licenses and everything."

"They'll have to give them up when they join church," Pris pointed out.

"I know, but in the meantime they're just putting a great big temptation in the way of boys like Jake. Oh look, there's Amanda Yoder. My word, she never comes to anything. I wonder what brought her out tonight?"

"Bird-watching?" Priscilla joked as Malinda greeted Amanda and immediately made the other girl comfortable by asking for her help scooping the onion dip out of a big mixing bowl and into smaller bowls that could be spread around the big room downstairs.

After the snacks were laid out and board games set up for those who didn't want to play volleyball, Pris followed Rosanne outside to the lawn, where the game had already started despite the fact that not everyone was there yet. But it would be dark soon, and a little too chilly for all but the hardiest to play very well, so that made sense. Most of the boys had already formed teams—and here came a buggy full of Blackbirds, who spilled out almost before the horse came to a stop.

Amid raucous greetings from those who knew them and introductions for those who didn't, Joe called to Pris, "Come on and join in! We have two spots left on our side but they'll be gone quick."

"Not me." Rosanne shook her head. "You guys spike the ball too hard."

"I will," Pris said. "Come on, it's the last game of the season."

"Can I join?" asked a quiet voice, and Pris turned to see Amanda at her shoulder.

It took a second to get her mouth working through her surprise. One, Amanda hardly ever came to the young people's doings. And two, she was well over twenty-one and, to Pris's knowledge, had never done things in groups with boys, or actually had a date. The courage it must have taken to say those few simple words was staggering.

"Take my spot and welcome," Rosanne said. "I'm happy to cheer from the sidelines until it's time to eat."

"Hurry up before those Blackbirds beat you to it!" Joe said.

It felt good that he wanted her on his team. Pris and Amanda dashed over and filled the fourth and fifth places at the net—right where she liked to be. That meant, though, that Amanda would be up next to serve. And since three Blackbirds—two older boys and a girl about Pris's age—had just filled up the other team, would Amanda be a good server?

Not that it mattered. They played for fun, not to win. But still...

Their team took the first point and then lost the ball on Simon's second serve. The opposing team got three points so easily that Joe said, "We're just warming up. Watch out, now, here comes our star server."

He was so nice. Amanda smiled at him the way she would at a little brother, and tossed the ball off her fingertips to test its firmness.

Then her eyes narrowed as she measured the distance between the ball poised on her left palm and a spot on the other side of the net. *Smack!* The ball sailed exactly an inch over the net—the other team thought it had touched—no one leaped—and it fell right in the middle, between the two rows of players.

Right about where Amanda had been looking.

"Two serving five," she said quietly.

By the time they'd evened up the score, the Blackbird boys were beginning to get wise. And a little more serious about where that ball was going. When one of them got under her low-flyer, she changed it up and dropped it just this side of the line Rosanne's father had staked with string. "Eight serving five."

"Where were *you* all summer?" Simon wondered aloud from the side of the court.

Amanda flubbed the serve and it bounced off the net, but on the other team's serve, Pris spiked the incoming ball and then it was her turn to serve. She only got two points, but by then the other team were too far behind to catch up, and the home side won.

They played two more games before it got too cold, and by the last one, the other team was requesting that Amanda join their side to make it more fair. Flushed and smiling, Amanda went in to supper looking much happier than when she'd arrived.

At the table, Pris and Rosanne found themselves next to Malinda, Amanda, and the taller of the Blackbird boys, whose name turned out to be Jesse Riehl. Joe and Simon sat opposite, and even Jake had come in, though he wasn't sitting with his twin. Not that it was any of her business, but Pris couldn't help noticing that Jesse spent most of the time talking to Amanda—though he was as interested as any of them in Simon's and Joe's stories of their adventures in Colorado. Later, during the games, Amanda wound up on his team for at least half of them. Well, good for her. Maybe Jesse was a year or so younger than she was, and maybe he lived a fair distance away and she might not see him again for weeks, but at least Amanda was having fun.

When Pris's brother Chris came in later, he found her in the kitchen helping Malinda and Rosanne and their Mamm finish up the dishes. "I'm going, Pris, if you want a ride."

If Joe hadn't said something earlier, Pris might well have hopped in the buggy and gone home with her brother. But she was buzzing with anticipation of what Joe's news could be, and nothing was going to get in the way of her hearing it. "Joe's taking me. See you at home."

Of course, they had to run the gauntlet of a whole lot of good-natured teasing from the Kanagys and the others as she climbed into Joe's buggy, which looked as shiny and new as it had the last time she'd been in it. And she was pretty sure she was still the only girl to have sat here, too.

She'd gone home from church last week with her family, so this was really the first time they'd been together in public since he'd come home...which meant it was the first time the *Youngie* had had a chance to rib them and make jokes about open versus closed buggies as they drove away. "Never mind them," Joe said comfortably as he shook the reins over the horse's back and they rolled out of the Kanagys' lane. "They just wish they were us."

Pris expected him to drive slowly so they could talk, but to her surprise, he kept the horse at a normal trot until they came to the dirt farm track that entered Henry Byler's fallow field. This was the field where the infamous band hop had happened last spring and caught the grass on fire—the one she and Joe had helped to put out. It was only by dint of Henry's kindness that they hadn't been in as much trouble as Jake had been over that car incident, and in one way, it had been a blessing. Dat had found her the job at the Rose Arbor Inn in what he'd thought of as punishment, but it hadn't turned out that way. Now she chose to be there—and enjoyed it, too.

"Henry's going to let me and Jake lease this field for soybeans next year," he said. The buggy bumped across the fallow field and then Joe let the reins go slack so the horse could graze while they talked. "We'll let it sit this winter, and then turn it over come February."

When he fell silent, she could contain herself no longer. "What did you want to talk to me about?"

He chuckled as he took her hand, finding it in the dark without even fumbling. "Kept you in suspense, did I?"

"*Ja*, and I've been patient. Come on, now. Tell me."

"It's not that big a thing, Pris. I just wanted your opinion about something."

"About whether you're going back to Colorado?" There. It was out. The thing she wanted to know the most and wanted to happen the least.

"Would you be upset if I did? I made good money out there."

"Money isn't everything. It's not worth being away from your family and friends, is it?"

"*Neh*, not really. Not for good. I don't think I'll be going back. Me and Dat had a long talk the other night."

When he fell silent, Pris wasn't sure if he was collecting his thoughts or simply didn't want to go any further. So she waited.

"I got his opinion, so now I want yours. Do you think I'd make a good herbal doc?"

This was so not what she'd expected him to say that it took her a second to recover. "An herbalist? Like a *Dokterfraa*, like Sarah?"

He chuckled, a whiffle of air through his nose. "Not *Fraa*, exactly, but *ja*, to do like she does."

"Where would you find the time?" was the first thing out of her mouth. "You have to go out and find the plants and then make things out of them, chopping and boiling and whatnot. You have to go to classes with Ruth Lehman. And get books and study. How would you do all that and get the crops in—never mind weeding and fertilizing and harvesting them?"

She heard the soft rustle of his clothes as he shifted. "That's part of what I talked over with Dat. He listened for a good long time. Longer than I expected he would."

"He wasn't too happy, then."

Joe's fingers tightened on Priscilla's, then eased off as though he realized what he was doing. "More surprised that it even entered my head, I guess. I could see him holding back a lot—he's always wanted me and Jake to take over when he and Mamm got too old to farm. It's been kind of hard to see Jake going off the rails this summer while I've been gone, and then to have me come back and want to do something that a woman does…"

Pris made a rude noise. "Herbs aren't something that just women do. Lots of men powwow. And Sarah told me there was an Amish man—in Indiana, maybe?—who was so famous as a healer that *Englisch* folks would come to see him from as far away as California."

Joe thought this over. "So what do you think?"

Without hesitation, she said, "I think it's hard on your dad. I also think you have time to do what it's your place to do, which is to obey your dad, and to pray about it, so you can obey *der Herr*. Look at Sarah—she didn't start her work until just this year, when her boys were grown. You're still only eighteen."

"I know. Dat said much the same thing. But it's still on my mind. Do you think I should talk it over with Sarah?"

He must be serious about this. So she would be equally serious. "*Ja*, I do. She was pretty happy about the way you handled that horse stepping on Simon's foot. She'd be able to tell you what it's like. You might have to plant a big garden like hers and have to look after that, too—or your wife will. Better make sure you find a woman with a green thumb."

"Do you have a green thumb?" His voice held a smile.

"*Neh*, you'll have to wait for my sister Saranne. She has a row of little pots all along the windowsill in her room, full of plants she thinks won't survive the winter. I keep telling her God has been looking after the plants since the beginning of time, but she's convinced she has to help in case He misses these ones."

"Well, maybe I could manage with a girl who just has a normal-colored thumb."

"Maybe you might have to," she said primly. "Come on, we'd best get home or Mamm will be worried."

"All right." He found the reins with unerring ease in the dark, and turned the buggy back toward the road.

They traveled the few hundred yards to the Mast lane in a companionable silence. Pris had never felt this sense of humility and gladness before—being a young man's confidante (second only to his father) on a matter as important as how he would make his living was a completely new experience. It made her feel like a grown-up. As though her opinion mattered to a young man who had done more than most of the boys around Willow Creek—and who still felt responsible enough to come home and do the right thing by the ones he cared about.

"Do you want to come with me to see Sarah?" Joe asked her as he pulled up in the Mast yard.

"I don't want to interfere," she said a little uncertainly. "But it would be interesting."

"You're pretty close to her, and you might think of things to ask that I wouldn't."

"All right, then, if you think I'd be useful."

"Dat has me and Jake bringing in the potatoes this week, but as soon as I can, I'll come over and we can go, maybe in a couple of days."

Though the main light was still on in the yard, shining right in the windscreen of the buggy, he still reached around her shoulders to pull her close. "And you know what? You're more than useful. I like being with you. There must be a better word for it than that."

But when he kissed her, his mouth soft and warm on hers, words fled Priscilla's head altogether.

CHAPTER 13

Henry had come over to the Rose Arbor Inn early Saturday morning and eaten a farewell breakfast with Ginny's family. Ginny cooked a big breakfast for her guests nearly every day between May and September, but when it was family, Henry could see, it wasn't business. It was an act of love for her to feed the people she cared about.

Just like Sarah did with her herbs—not only because she had to make a living, but also because she cared about the people who came to her. It was her way of showing love to the *Gmee* and also extending it to people outside.

People like him.

Were all women like this, or just the two that had come into his life so unexpectedly since he'd moved here? And what was he doing thinking about Sarah when Ginny was offering him one more croissant stuffed with Brie and cranberries?

"I'll have it for supper," he told her, wrapping it in his paper napkin. "After frittata, sausage, fruit salad, and these, I can't even face the thought of lunch."

"My girl sure knows how to cook," Donnée said with satisfaction.

"And everyone in these parts knows it," Henry added. Even the coffee tasted amazing, and he'd seen her make it himself exactly the way everyone else did. But that could have been because he used instant coffee these days, with a pot of hot water on the stove. If he wanted the real thing, either he'd find the time to have the house wired for electricity, or he'd find the money to buy one of those fancy glass drip affairs that would do the job.

When Ginny began to clear the table, he put his hands on her shoulders and turned her toward her suite beyond the kitchen. "I'll do it. You go finish what you need to do."

He was just drying the last of the dishes when she came out, pulling a rollaway suitcase, her wool coat over her arm. Her eyes widened. "Henry, don't tell me you spent all this time washing the dishes by hand?"

The saucepan went into its place on the triple-shelved lazy Susan under the counter. "I did. Wasn't I supposed to?"

She laughed, shaking her head. "You are so Amish sometimes. They invented this thing called a dishwasher, you know. It lives right there." She pointed, her eyes dancing, and he had to laugh at himself, too.

"I never even thought of it. I'm so used to doing up my own—and I've never lived in a place that was fancy enough to have one, not even my apartment in Denver."

"I'll teach you how to use it when I get back. But in the meantime, here's a thank-you for treating my china so well." She kissed him soundly on the mouth, to the point that he didn't hear her father come in the back door after taking the first of their suitcases out.

"PDAs," Rafe said cheerfully. "Come on, you two. If we don't hit the road, the stores will all be closed by the time we get there."

"Daddy, we're talking about an hour's drive, for goodness' sake. Go away and let me say good-bye to my man."

Henry held her close and, not for the first time, thanked his lucky stars that she'd come into his life, bringing laughter and optimism and great food and a family he was really beginning to like. "I don't deserve you," he murmured into the black spirals of her hair, held back this morning by an orange bandanna with little black cats on it in celebration of the month of Hallowe'en. At least, that's what she'd said. But orange looked great on her.

"No, you don't," she agreed pertly. "No man deserves a woman—we just tolerate you all because of the way you improve the scenery."

"Is that going on a T-shirt?" He touched the tip of her nose with his.

"It should, huh? They sell, you know. After Sarah came up with the idea about putting your mugs in the rooms, I thought, why not hang one or two of my T-shirts in the closets? And it only costs the time to design them—I do everything else over the Internet. But that one will have to wait until I get back. I'm gonna find me a wedding dress!" She spun out of his arms with a smacking kiss. "See you Tuesday. Be good."

He put the luggage belonging to both her and Venezia in her car, and waved the two vehicles off from the little parking lot.

Venezia hadn't even tried to convince him one last time about appearing on *Shunning Amish*, for which he had to give her credit. Evidently even the greatest saleswoman in the world could see when a mark wasn't having any, and it was time to back off.

He drove the two miles home, waving at his cousin Paul Byler and his wife, Barbara, on their way somewhere on a Saturday morning in their buggy. Then he turned in his own driveway, thinking about everything he needed to do today. The pottery he'd fired would be ready for glazing with the new mixture he'd prepared. He was anxious to see how it would work on that pumpkin pitcher. Even if it was too late for D.W. Frith to get it in their catalog, they'd still ordered one for their flagship store in time for Thanksgiving next month. But the color had to be perfect. He'd done a couple of test glazes on mugs, but the big test would be—

He stopped the car abruptly, realizing that the side of the yard where he usually parked was blocked by a sleek Jaguar XK and a vintage BMW.

Tourists, at this time of year? He sighed and got out of the car. Time to take down that ARTISAN sign at the end of his lane.

"Henry!" a familiar voice called from just inside the open barn doors, and Dave Petersen stepped outside.

Not for the first time when dealing with Dave, Henry felt a moment of mental vertigo. Had he forgotten an appointment? Was he supposed to be in New York, and when he didn't show up, they'd sent Dave down to Pennsylvania to get him?

"Dave." He shook hands, and as he did, another man stepped out from between the rolling doors leading into his studio.

"Henry, I'd like you to meet Matt Alvarez, from TNC. I believe you and he spoke last week."

"You know perfectly well we did." Politeness demanded a handshake, but his own didn't have the feeling of welcome that Rafe's did, or even Caleb's. "Nice to meet you, Matt."

"You're probably wondering why we're here and poking around in your barn," Matt said with a smile that revealed teeth of a startling whiteness in his tanned face. The kind of whiteness very rarely found in nature.

"I am, in fact," Henry said. "I can give you a proper tour, if you want. But I can't give you what I suspect you came for."

"I'll settle for the tour." The grin flashed again.

Henry had never been exposed to television people in his career—he'd only met the folks who had done the D.W. Frith video with him as its subject earlier in the year. Whatever he thought a producer was supposed to look like, Matt didn't. He had on worn jeans and a plaid button-down shirt that had seen more time on the road than Henry ever had. But unless Frith was doing better than he thought, that Jag didn't belong to Dave.

He showed them over the studio, making a point of showing Dave the pieces that would be shipping to New York in time for their Thanksgiving displays, and his sketches for the big matching set he would be doing for Christmas. And when they'd seen everything with the exception of the cartons of clay in the old horse stalls, he took them outside and walked them through the orchard. He'd be willing to talk apples until the cows came home if it meant avoiding the topic the two men were there for.

He was just reaching through the gnarled, uncared-for branches for a nice-looking stripy Gravenstein that the birds hadn't discovered yet, when a flash of burgundy caught his eye through the branches.

"Hey, Henry," Dave said at the same time, "there's an Amish lady heading down the hill in this direction."

"Better brace yourselves," he muttered, but only Matt, who was standing closest to him, caught it. He moved out from under the tree into the grass and waved, and Sarah waved back.

"Henry," she called, "I wanted to know how your—oh, I'm so sorry. I didn't know you had company." She half turned away, her skirts billowing against her shins with the motion. "I'll come back another time."

"No, it's all right. These folks won't be staying long." Dave and Matt exchanged a glance. "Sarah, this is Dave Petersen from D.W. Frith, and Matt Alvarez from TNC, that TV channel we were talking about the other day. Gentlemen, this is my next-door neighbor, Sarah Yoder."

"You talked about it with an Amish person?" Dave blurted.

"Sure. Sarah's a friend—almost a relative. Her sister-in-law is married to my cousin on the farm across the highway there. We talk about all kinds of things, including why people are so interested in the Amish—or ex-Amish, as the case may be."

"Do you, now?" Matt said, his face alive with interest. "Do the Amish folks ever wonder about that?"

"We don't often have time to wonder what the *Englisch* think of us," Sarah said shyly. "It is enough to be concerned about what God thinks of us."

Matt clearly wasn't about to be deterred into a philosophical discussion. "What's the church's stand on those who go outside and then talk about it publicly?"

"I don't know. We don't take stands on such things. I suppose they're free to talk about it if they like."

"Do you want to talk about it?" Matt said, as smoothly as a knife through soft butter. "On camera?"

She gazed at him, and Henry waited. Then he saw the twinkle in her eyes as her brows rose slightly. "You're as bad as my son Caleb, taking up my words to get what he wants. Except he only tries it once."

"You haven't said no, though."

"No." She smiled at him, the kind of smile a mother wears when she's taken the measure of the opposition. "If I were to appear on your camera, that would be making a graven image, and those are not permitted."

"Is that the reason," Dave said on a note of discovery. "I always thought it was because the camera steals the soul or something."

Sarah gazed at him, puzzled. "That isn't possible, as any child would tell you. God decides what happens to our souls. That's why the safest place for mine is in His hand." She turned to Henry and handed him a glass pint jar, its lid screwed down on a glossy reddish-brown substance. "I made up the balm for you last night. Rub some in morning and evening, and keep bandages on the open wounds so dirt doesn't get in."

"Open wounds?" Dave's eyes widened. "What have you been doing, sword fighting?"

Henry opened his free hand and showed him the Band-Aid strips on his fingers. "Turns out between the hard water and the clay, my skin dried out, and then when I put on latex gloves to protect my hands, I discovered I was allergic to latex."

"Ouch." Matt leaned in to see. "That's gotta hurt."

"Sarah made me a salve for it. She's our local herbal healer."

"In training," Sarah put in. "Ruth is really the *Dokterfraa*. I'm just helping her with some of her patients."

While it was massively tempting to make Sarah the focus of the other men's attention, Henry knew that would be the easy way out—and besides, Sarah didn't deserve it. This was his battle to fight, and he just had to keep his wits about him and stick it out.

"Too bad you're still in the church," Matt said. "That would make a great episode—doctoring the exes with the plants growing in empty urban lots because they can't afford healthcare or whatever."

"What an imagination you have," Sarah said, straight-faced, in a tone that could almost be admiring.

But Matt flushed. "Just thinking out loud. Filing it away for later."

"I'll leave you, Henry." Sarah turned those long-lashed gray eyes back on him. "Please let me know how your skin reacts. I made it pretty strong, so if it hurts more than helps, I should adjust the mixture. I don't want to add to your pain."

"Thanks, Sarah. I will. What do I owe you?"

"I think perhaps . . . twenty dollars?"

After he'd bought gas, his wallet only had a couple of dollars in it. He needed to go to the bank. "I'll bring it over to you after supper. Thanks."

All three men watched her take the path back over the hill, where the last thing they saw was her white prayer *Kapp* floating for a moment against the bright October sky before it disappeared down the far slope.

"Nice lady," Dave said. "She was in the video, wasn't she? Long shot, working in the garden. Probably from the top of that hill."

"Yes," Henry said. "The crew were under strict instructions to show no faces or recognizable features."

"The whole graven image thing," Matt said, clearly having retained what Sarah had said. "But Henry, you make actual physical images of plants and gourds and stuff. How do you get around that?"

"I'm not Amish." Pointing out the obvious always sounded a little blunt. "And they're not images for worship—which is how an Amish person might see a family gathered around the TV, like an altar, with all their attention on it instead of each other or on God. My pieces are kitchen objects, meant for use. Even the Amish would make that distinction—Sarah has one of my early daffodil batter bowls and has no problem using it. I've been giving away the pieces that don't quite come out the way I want them to, and the ladies around here are delighted."

"So do you have this problem with graven images on a personal level?" Matt asked. "In other words, do you object in principle to being filmed—of being the object of that theoretical family's attention?"

"Obviously not, since he did our website video," Dave put in. "I don't see this as being much of a stretch beyond that."

Henry could feel a hard sell gathering in the air. "You don't?" He marshaled his thoughts together so they would get it once and for all. "Well, let me lay it out for you. I am not going to go on TV and say how glad I am that I've left the church and my family and friends. That they were abusive and I had to run away in the dead of night, like that girl who quilts."

"This week's episode," Matt said, clearly pleased that Henry had seen it. "It's trending in the top ten on Twitter. Cool, huh?"

Henry had no idea what Twitter was, and he didn't care. "I have to live here, among people like Sarah and her boys and my cousins over there, where you see those silos. How can I go on TV and say how glad I am that I don't worship the way they do, and make myself some kind of celebrity at their expense?"

"I don't see how you'd do that," Dave said. "He's not asking you to bad-mouth your neighbors and family. In fact, you'd bring a whole other side to the conversation. After all, how many exes can coexist peacefully with their old church?"

Matt shook his head. "Coexistence doesn't make very good TV, I have to tell you. And people are people. But I haven't mentioned the thing that I should have said right up front. You wouldn't be doing this for free, Henry. We also offer an appearance fee of fifty thousand dollars."

Henry gaped at him. "Are you joking?"

"Not at all." Matt leaned in confidentially. "It's a nice chunk of money, and I'll bet it would go a long way around here. You could spruce up the studio, buy some new tools and stuff."

"Put in electricity," Dave suggested.

"Maybe even finance a few research trips. Not that money matters more than art, but it's a consideration."

This guy was good. Henry had no idea that people were paid to appear on the show. What would Ginny say to this— she who had already put up the cash for flowers and catering and a wedding cake? Sure, she'd told him that people owed her favors, but still. Fifty thousand would buy her a pretty wedding dress, unlike the plain one she had worn for her first marriage, and he'd be able to afford to take her on a real honeymoon. They could go to the Bahamas. Or even Europe.

"What are you thinking, Henry?" Matt asked. "Can you see your way to balancing what people would think with the positive changes the show might make in your life?"

Henry turned away, realizing with a sudden sinking feeling that the young man had somehow seen more than he'd meant him to. Visions of himself and Ginny walking hand in hand through some Art Nouveau palace in Vienna dissolved in light of the view from right here. How could he go on this show and talk about something so personal? How could he look in his cousin Paul's eyes ever again? And what if the film crew decided it had to go out to Ohio and film the family farm? What would Anna and Lizzie have to say about *that* in their next letters? Would they mourn him as lost forever and never speak to him again because their bishop would decide this finally warranted *die Meinding*?

Fifty thousand or not, he couldn't do this. Ginny was happy with a quiet wedding and a honeymoon in Colorado, and so should he be. He had to send Dave and Matt on their way while still appearing to be a team player. But how?

To give himself a few minutes to figure it out, he said, "I'm going back to the house to put some of this salve on. You're welcome to walk around the place if you want—just don't climb any fences. Paul used to keep bulls. I don't know if he still does, but he leases my land. You'll want to keep an eye out."

From the alacrity with which they followed him back through the orchard to the house, it was obvious they were a lot more comfortable with human conflict, not the kind that came from running away from livestock.

In the bathroom, Henry peeled the old Band-Aid strips off and dabbed the salve into the cuts. It smelled good— with a hint of lavender and the orange daisy that grew all over Sarah's quilt garden. There were petals in the mixture, as though they'd been preserved in amber. With fresh bandage strips applied, he went out into the kitchen to find his guests had pulled up chairs at the table.

The battle wasn't over, but at least he felt a little more able to cope—as though the scent of the balm had breathed strength into him. "Can I make you some coffee?"

"Not for me," Dave said. "Trying to cut back. So Henry, Matt and I were talking while you were in the bathroom, and

he reminded me of something in your contract that I'd forgotten."

And . . . here we go. "What's that?"

"Well, buried down there on about the fourth page is an
assurance from you that you'll do everything in your power
to promote your pieces. It even spells out magazines and television."

"But not reality show tell-alls."

"I think one is a subset of the other. And if you signed an
agreement for television, I think it's a tacit agreement to do
this show."

"I disagree. D.W. Frith's style strikes me more as NPR or
National Geographic, not *Shunning Amish*."

"You remember what I said about extending our reach,"
Dave said. "That means to other demographics we haven't
touched yet. And TNC reaches a huge demographic that cuts
across all ages and economic levels. Just the people we're trying to access for your pieces, Henry."

"I can't see your average economic level being able to afford a four-hundred-dollar batter bowl."

"Maybe not, but the show is watched by everyone from
urban professionals to construction workers," Matt told him.
"Money completely aside, Dave and I both agree that this is
a one-of-a-kind opportunity to show your work to the world,
and if you're going to abide by the terms of your contract,
you should see your way to doing it. We can work with you
on the focus. Give you script approval. Whatever you need
to come aboard."

Henry gazed at them, feeling in some part of his mind the
tingle of the salve going to work on his hands.

From Sarah's hands to his. What would she make of this
conversation? Would she shut it down with a graceful ref-

erence to Amish customs? Because he was coming to realize with a feeling of cold dread that being Amish would be about the only thing that could save him right now.

But he had to try.

He shook his head. "I'm sorry. I can't. Thanks for your offer. I appreciate it. I really do. But if the contract didn't specify this show, then I'm not obliged to make a spectacle of myself and my neighbors to fulfill its terms."

With a sigh, Dave got to his feet. "You're not leaving me too many options here, Henry. I'm going to have to go back to New York and take it up with the legal beagles. I'm sorry about that."

"You go right ahead. I'm fine with television in a general sense, Dave. A news program. An interview by a real reporter. Just not this. So if you'll excuse me, I'll go back out to the barn and start glazing those pieces for the Thanksgiving display."

There was something in Dave's gaze that made Henry's nape and shoulders prickle—as though the two of them were picturing that display and seeing two completely different things. But that wasn't Henry's business. His business was getting his hands healed up and those pieces finished. It was what he knew how to do, and he'd focus on doing it to the very best of his ability.

He stood in the open barn doors and watched the Jag and the BMW roll cautiously down the gravel lane, like a pair of stylish ladies trying not to hurt their bare feet on the rocks.

It would be all right. No sane lawyer would hold him to such vague contract terms—especially when this had come up after the contract was signed. He had nothing against television in a general sense. But reality TV was a different creature, meant to sensationalize human conflict and emotion and turn people's pain into entertainment.

Fifty-thousand-dollar bribe or not, he just didn't have it in him to do it.

His hands tingled, and he flexed his fingers absentmindedly. Was it supposed to feel like this? Maybe it was a good thing Sarah was expecting him this evening.

After today, her quiet kitchen would feel like a haven of peace.

CHAPTER 14

S arah loved the peacefulness of Saturday evenings. In their district, people didn't visit after supper on a Saturday, so that they could lay aside the busyness of the week and prepare their spirits for the Lord's Day. Once in a while you'd hear of some of the *Youngie* taking a drive or getting together to go for a walk, but not often—and Sarah was glad for it. How sad would it be to have prayer time and Scripture reading—something the whole family did together—with some of its members missing?

Her boys were busy every day and some evenings, too, so Sarah hoarded Saturday nights like a miser, hugging them close to her heart and savoring them before she let the minutes fall through her fingers.

Caleb washed the dishes while Simon dried them and Sarah went into the front room to put away the afghan she was crocheting for Amanda's Christmas present. It was long enough to cover her whole lap and fall over her knees now, which was *gut* since the evenings were getting colder. She tucked it away into her basket, tidied the cushions on the couch, and then raised her head as the sound of a knock came at the kitchen door.

"I've got it, Mamm," Simon called.

But Sarah already knew who it was. She'd been waiting since four o'clock, the earliest time a person could call *evening*, and finally, at nearly six, here he was.

"Simon, Caleb," she heard Henry say. "Good to see you both."

"And you, Henry." Simon sounded a little surprised. Sarah hadn't said anything about Henry coming, in case he changed his mind and waited to complete their business transaction on Monday. If he had come tomorrow, she wouldn't have been able to take his money ... but he wouldn't have come tomorrow. He might be *Englisch* now, but a man would have to be far gone in worldliness not to remember that the Amish did not transact business on the Lord's Day.

"I came to give your mother this," Henry said.

She walked out into the kitchen in time to see him pull a bill from his wallet. "You didn't drive all the way into town just to get that for me, I hope," she said.

"No, I got myself some supper at the Dutch Rest Café while I was at it." He handed her the bill and she led him into her compiling room, where she kept the books. "I forgot to get groceries this week, so I went over to the Country Market in Whinburg. Luckily they were still open, or I'd have been begging you for a dozen eggs."

"You'd better not buy eggs when we have so many," Sarah chided him, making a note in her ledger and tucking the money into her pouch for the bank. "We could supply you with eggs from now on for nothing, simply because you've been so good to Caleb."

"The chickens aren't laying so well now, Mamm," Caleb said from the hall behind Henry as he headed for the stairs. "The days are getting shorter and they're stopping for the winter."

"That's true. But if you need some now, we have an extra dozen. You're welcome to them."

"Thank you, I will," Henry said. "Though I came for another reason besides paying for the salve and begging eggs." He held out his hands and turned them over, palms up. "Is it supposed to tingle like this?"

"I don't know. As I said, I made it fairly strong, but the book doesn't mention any such sensation." She looked up, suddenly stricken. "Oh dear. You don't suppose you're allergic to poplar sap, too?"

"I don't think so. It doesn't feel painful, just tingly."

"Maybe it's the balm doing its good work. May I look?"

As Henry sat at the little table where she'd got into the habit of examining people's cuts and bruises, Simon stopped in the doorway. "Mamm, are we going to read?"

"*Ja*, I'll just have a look at Henry's hands and be right in. Call Caleb back down before he gets his nose in a library book."

With a look at Henry but no comment—for which Sarah was grateful—her elder son went upstairs to do as she asked.

She peeled back one of the bandages and had a look. The cut did not look inflamed, nor did the flesh around it. Henry's hand was warm, but not hot, so that was a good sign, she thought as she pressed the backs of her fingers to it. "I don't think the balm is doing anything other than what it should," she finally said. "The skin and the cut are both well."

"That's a relief. I wasn't worried, really, but I don't want to take chances and risk not being able to work."

"Do you want me to dilute the salve a little? It could just be that you're extra sensitive still, from the gloves."

"No, that's okay. I'll give it overnight and then see how it feels in the morning."

"If it's not looking like it's healing up, you might need to go to the clinic. Church is all the way over at Jon Hostetler's tomorrow, so we'll be leaving earlier than usual and won't be back until midafternoon." What was she babbling for? She said it as though she expected him to know Jon Hostetler, when where church was every other Sunday was probably the last thing to enter his mind.

"I'm sure it'll be fine. Thanks for checking, Sarah."

His hands looked so defenseless, there on the table, when she knew perfectly well the kind of brute labor and skill they were capable of. Now that she looked at him more closely, his face was drawn and his color wasn't all that good.

"Henry, are you all right?"

He busied himself putting the Band-Aid strip back on, though of course it wouldn't stick. She got up to get him another one. "Of course. It's just been a rough day."

"Those men in the orchard? The ones from that television program?"

He nodded. "They offered me fifty thousand dollars to do the show. Can you believe it?"

"Fifty—" She handed him the box of strips and sat rather abruptly opposite. "Are you serious?"

"That's what I said, more or less. They were completely serious. And I have a feeling Dave Petersen will be bringing some legal pressure to bear if I don't do it."

"What kind of legal pressure?" Sarah didn't know much about that kind of thing, but she did know that lawsuits, which the church forbade, could throw a man into poverty and take everything he had. Anybody could bring a lawsuit for any reason at all. But for refusing to be on a television show? That would be crazy.

"I don't know yet. I'm hoping they give it up as a bad job

and go bother some other Frith supplier. But still, it's going to be hard getting to sleep tonight."

"What does your fiancée say?" Surely he would have talked this over with Ginny. Surely he should be there right now, having dinner with her instead of eating by himself at the Dutch Rest. Had they quarreled?

"She's out of town. Went back to Philly with her family to find a wedding dress, and I don't want to spoil her fun with this."

"Oh." What kind of dress would a woman wear who had already been married once, and who was no longer plain? She'd seen a few very fancy confections in shop windows, but she couldn't imagine a woman who loved Henry actually wearing one of them.

But that was none of her business.

"From the discussions we have had about it," Henry went on, "she's leaving the decision up to me. I'm the one who has family and friends who could be affected, after all. The worst she might have to deal with is an unflattering view of the Inn in the fall without its roses."

"How would it affect your family and friends, Henry?" she asked in spite of herself. She shouldn't show any interest in such a worldly thing—it had nothing to do with her. But she couldn't bear to see the heaviness in his shoulders, as if he were carrying a burden and couldn't seem to shrug it off. "What happens on *Englisch* television has nothing to do with us."

"Maybe not. Maybe I'm being arrogant in assuming that anything I do would affect anyone else. But just the thought of there being people out there who would think badly of my family or of you and Paul and Jacob and the other folks around here...I don't want that. I couldn't stand it."

"Does it necessarily have to be negative, this thinking?" If he were forced into doing this, why couldn't he say good things—uplifting things—about his experience? "Surely there could be some good things you could tell people."

"Good things don't make good TV, I'm informed," he said wryly. Then, at a noise from the door, he turned to see Simon and Caleb both standing there. "Hi, boys. Sorry I'm holding your mother up."

"Seems like you need a cure for more than your hands," Caleb said with his usual obliviousness to the finer points of privacy. But he was quite right, in Sarah's mind. "Are you going to do it, Henry?"

Henry shook his head. "Not unless they force me, and I don't think that would make very good television, either. Not too much you can do with a man who refuses to say anything, I wouldn't suppose."

He got to his feet, and something in the way he stood, as though bracing himself to go back to the quiet of his house, compelled words to fly out of Sarah's mouth before she had time to think. "Would you like to stay for prayers with us, Henry?"

His brows rose and surprise chased away all the worry lines that had begun to engrave themselves in his face. He wasn't the only one. Simon's hand made a convulsive movement, as if to stop something, before he controlled himself and merely said, "Mamm," in a tone that clearly asked, *What are you doing?*

"But you can't have fellowship with me," Henry said.

Something was rising in her chest—the same feeling she would get when Caleb was little and had fallen down and hurt himself. The same feeling she got when a bird fell out of its nest and a cat was on its way to investigate. Someone had to do something—and she and her boys were right here at hand.

"We could pray for you." She lifted her chin. "And you could pray for us. The Word of God is open to anyone. Do you still remember your *hoch Deutsch*?"

"I think it might come back to me. But Sarah—"

"No one's going to tell on you," Caleb pointed out, his eyebrows waggling. "It's not like a crime or anything."

"I hope Bishop Daniel wouldn't differ with you on that," Henry told him. "I have to say that I'd like to, but...Simon? What do you say? I don't want to intrude on your family time."

Simon's lips had thinned a little, and his jaw flexed, as if he were chewing the inside of his cheek to keep from speaking. Sarah could practically follow his thoughts through the corn maze of a young man's logic. While it was true that they could not have real fellowship with a man who had left the faith, to refuse to pray for that same man was not godly. And for Simon to refuse a man whom his mother, to whom he owed obedience, had already invited, would be even worse.

She saw the moment when her son realized the best thing to do would be the thing that was right under these particular circumstances, even if it might not be right strictly by the letter of the law.

"You would be welcome to pray," he finally said. "Come into the other room. We're reading from the book of Ruth."

They took turns reading the verses, which were some of Sarah's favorites in the whole Bible.

And Ruth said, Intreat me not to leave thee, or to return from following after thee: for whither thou goest, I will go;

and where thou lodgest, I will lodge: thy people shall be my
people, and thy God my God:
    Where thou diest, will I die, and there will I be buried:
the Lord do so to me, and more also, if ought but death
part thee and me.

Tears came into her eyes as she read softly. This had been
Michael's favorite passage, too...because while her parents
had both passed on some years before they'd met, she had still
left her sisters and their families in Mifflin County after their
wedding to move with him to Whinburg Township.

Caleb took up the reading when she stopped, and then Simon, and before she took her turn again, she allowed a little
silence to fall. And then Henry read two verses, hesitantly, his
mouth working around the shapes of words that had become
strange to him.

When he stopped, Sarah picked up smoothly, and then the
chapter was done. "Caleb, will you say the Lord's Prayer for
us? And then we will pray for Henry."

Caleb did, not racing through the words by rote as some
might, but taking care over them despite their familiarity.
They said this prayer morning and evening, and over meals,
too, but *Thy will be done* was not a promise to be trifled
with. It was a reminder of to whom they owed their lives.
When they had said "Amen," Sarah took a breath and spoke
in *Deitsch*, the language of home and family, not in English,
the language of the world.

"Oh Lord our Father, we come before Thee on Henry's behalf to pray for peace for him. He has made a hard decision,
one that may have him fighting battles in the days to come.
We pray that Thou wouldst give him strength to do the right
thing according to his conscience, and also according to Thy

will. We pray that Thou wouldst come into his heart and find willingness there, that Thou couldst draw him to Thyself in love and give him true peace. We ask it in the name of Jesus."

"Amen," chorused the boys softly, and after a moment, Henry whispered, "Amen."

The boys got up from their knees in front of the sofa and said their good nights. Soon Sarah heard the sound of water running as they got ready for bed.

"Would you like me to light your way up the hill?" she asked, crossing the kitchen to take the lantern from the table.

Wordlessly, he nodded, and turned his head—but not before she saw a suspicious hint of moisture in his eyes. How long had it been since he had prayed? Or had anyone to pray for him? Did he and Ginny not pray together?

But of course she could not ask such a thing, and break the silence that seemed wrapped around him. She almost got the feeling that if she said any more, this delicate filament of connection that God might have spun among them tonight would be torn.

She could not risk it.

So instead, she opened the kitchen door and preceded him out into the windy night, across the lawn, and up the path on her side of the hill, lighting the way before him.

CHAPTER 15

As Priscilla made her way into the Hostetler meeting shed with her buddy bunch on Sunday morning, she saw that Jesse Riehl had not gone home yesterday, but in fact he and the brother and sister he'd come with had stayed over a second night. Since Amanda was older than she was, she'd already gone in, but Pris was dying to know what she thought of it. Was she the reason Jesse had wangled an invitation to stay with one of the local families?

He'd certainly thought ahead, because he was wearing Sunday clothes, and unless he'd borrowed some, he would have had to pack them in advance.

"That's interesting," she whispered to Rosanne, sitting next to her.

"I know. I heard that Jesse has a reputation for being a little wild. I hope Amanda is careful and doesn't give him too much encouragement."

Pris couldn't imagine anyone more careful than Amanda Yoder, but Mamm was already looking over her shoulder, so she subsided into a more respectful silence.

The sermon was on the Shepherd, and when the last hymn had been sung, Bishop Daniel got to his feet. "As you know, there will be a baptism two weeks from today at the Jacob

Yoders'. There are several who have been taking classes, and we look forward in grateful humility to welcoming our brothers and sisters into the church."

Would Benny Peachey really go through with it when baptism classes began again? Priscilla hadn't seen much of him lately, which was probably a good thing, now that Joe was home. By then Benny would know exactly what the step of baptism entailed—and that joining church was a serious business that involved giving his life completely to God. It meant marrying a girl who had been baptized, too, and being willing for the lot to fall on him and possibly make him a minister or a preacher or even a bishop. The thought of harum-scarum Benny Peachey preaching as solemnly as Young Orlan Stoltzfuss had done this morning was enough to make a person burst out into incredulous giggles, but the power of God had made stranger things happen.

After a light lunch of *Bohnesupp* and more homemade bread with peanut butter spread than was probably good for her waistline, Priscilla and Rosanne met Joe, Jesse, and Amanda outside on the lawn.

"A harder frost this morning," Joe said, looking out at what remained of Betsy Hostetler's garden. "That means we'll be digging up *die Grummbeere* and sweet potatoes this week for Mamm."

"Do you always think about work on the Lord's Day?" Jesse nudged him, teasing.

"Do you *ever* think about work?" Joe shot back, apparently not too bothered. "Better that than girls."

"Hey!" Pris said, pretending indignation.

"Except you." Joe smiled down at her, and while of course he couldn't take her hand in front of the whole *Gmee*, in that smile Pris felt as though he had.

"So, Pris," Jesse said, "Joe and I were thinking of taking you girls for a drive. That sound all right?"

"A drive where?" Amanda said softly.

"That would spoil the surprise," Jesse told her.

Pris resisted the urge to roll her eyes. "Probably over to Millers'," she said. "That's where supper and singing are tonight, but they're way over on the other side of the district from here. At least it's close to home."

Jesse nodded. "Sam and Mamie are heading back Strasburg way with some of the others this afternoon, but I thought I'd stick around and go back after singing."

"How can you do that?" Pris wanted to know. "It's a long way—you'd be getting home just in time for milking, probably."

"We don't have a dairy, but never mind. It'll be okay."

Priscilla couldn't imagine it, but how this boy got himself around the county was none of her business. Besides, if Amanda was okay with it, then it must be fine. "All right. I'll just let Mamm know that I won't be going with them."

Pris felt a little bad when Rosanne declined to come… though not exactly surprised, given what she'd said about Jesse earlier. Pris couldn't see anything wrong with five in the buggy—they'd fit perfectly well and it wasn't like Rosanne would be forward enough to wedge herself between Jesse and Amanda, even as a joke. Amanda was so sweet and self-effacing that Pris couldn't imagine playing jokes on her.

No, she thought as Rosanne crossed the lawn and rejoined their buddy bunch, she would have to make an extra effort not to leave her best friend out. While it was natural to want to do things with Joe, her friendships with the girls in her buddy bunch meant a lot to her—and would for the rest of her life. Mamm still got a circle letter once a month from the women who had been in hers, even though some were as far away as Indiana. Pris might be only seventeen, but she already knew that her friendships with her female friends would stand for her whole life. They wouldn't bloom without care and attention, though, just like plants.

Joe hadn't brought the courting buggy this morning because of the cold. Instead, he had the family's old one, which still shone with good care and had recently had new wheels put on. She and Joe sat in the front, while Jesse and Amanda climbed into the back. It was a good eight miles from Hostetlers' back through Willow Creek and then west and south again toward Millers'... except that right in the middle of town, Jesse leaned forward and said, "There, Joe. Behind the gas station."

"Are we stopping to pick something up?" Pris wondered aloud. "On a Sunday?"

Willow Creek was deserted on Sundays, except for the *Englisch* ladies' quilt shop, the gas station, the Dutch Rest Café, and the Hex Barn, which never seemed to close no matter what time you went by. Even if Dat hadn't forbidden her to get a job there, the chances were pretty good that when she refused to work on a Sunday, they'd have fired her anyhow.

Joe guided the horse past the gas pumps and around the corner of the building. There was nothing there except an old white car and some trash cans—not even a rail to tie the horse.

"Here we are," Jesse said with a smile. "Hop out, Priscilla."

"Here we are where?" Pris got out. "I thought we were going to Millers'."

"*Neh*, actually we're going to Gap for a hamburger and some fries."

"Oh, ha ha. If we leave now, we might get there in time for breakfast."

"If we leave now, we'll be there by three." He pulled a set of jingling keys from his pocket and walked over to the old car. "Hop in."

It took a lot to deprive Priscilla of the power of speech. Gaping, she looked from Jesse, sliding in behind the wheel, to Amanda, who was actually walking over to the passenger door.

"Are you joking?"

"We don't have to go, Pris, if you don't want to," Joe said.

"He has a car," she said blankly. "How does he have a car, much less know how to drive it? Has he been hanging around with Jake?"

Jesse just laughed and started the engine, which coughed, blew out a cloud of black smoke, and got itself going, even though it sounded like an old tractor. "Are you coming or not? The cheeseburgers at the Burger Shack are great— fries—and they give you a big milkshake with any kind of fruit you want in it."

"We can't let Amanda go in that car with him," she said urgently to Joe in an undertone. "She only met him two days ago."

"Then I guess we'll have to go, too. You get in while I find a place to leave Atlas where he has some grass."

So five minutes later, Pris found herself doing something she never would have imagined—racing down the county road at fifty miles an hour in what she was informed was a 1965 Ford Falcon, unearthed from someone's barn and driven by a boy who most certainly was not about to join church if he'd gone out and gotten his driver's license and spent all his money in such a crazy way.

Amanda had already joined church. What was she doing here? What were any of them doing here?

"Do your parents know you have this?" she asked a little breathlessly from the backseat. There were bench seats in front and back, but they in no way resembled the seats in a buggy. She made sure her seat belt was good and fastened.

"Maybe. I'm not living at home."

"Where do you live, then?"

"With my aunt and uncle. They're Mennonite, so driving is no big deal to them. My uncle even helped me study for the test, and helped me practice."

"So, what...you drove here and then your friends picked you up so you could look Amish when you came to church?"

"I am Amish," Jesse said with what looked like a show of patience instead of the real thing. "I'm dressed Amish, just like you, and I listened to the preaching and sang the '*Lob Lied*,' just like you. And I'm riding in a car, just like you."

"*Neh*, not like me. You're driving it and you own it. The *Ordnung* doesn't forbid riding in a car, but it certainly does the other two."

"Pris, are you going to argue all the way to Gap?" Joe asked. "You got in of your own free will, so no sense hounding Jesse about it."

I got in because of Amanda, and so did you. But she couldn't very well say that, because one, Amanda and Jesse were both older than she and Joe, and two, Amanda probably didn't need either of them looking out for her. For all Pris knew, she'd wanted to be alone with her new friend and Pris and Joe had come along and messed it all up.

"I'm sorry, Jesse," she finally said. "It's not my place to criticize. I'm just surprised, that's all."

"I wish my brother Jake had had the sense to study up and get his license before he got behind the wheel of that girl's car," Joe went on, as if they'd been talking about that all along. "As it is, he's lucky the police didn't charge him."

"They didn't?" Amanda asked. "I thought he went to jail."

"They took him down to the station and kept the car in their back lot until the girl's parents came to get it. But they let him off with a warning."

"What did your father have to say about that?" Pris couldn't resist asking.

"Plenty." Joe grinned. "Enough that Jesse here is safe from me ever wanting to take his place behind the wheel."

"You're assuming I'd ever let you behind the wheel."

"Hey, I can drive a tractor—as long as it's got lots of *horse* power."

Jesse and Amanda laughed, and while Priscilla smiled, too, her mind was busy on another subject. Jesse Riehl was probably the last person she would ever have imagined Amanda Yoder taking up with. Had something happened that had propelled her behaving so out of character? Or had she just decided that she needed to come out of her shell, and picked the unlikeliest boy she could find to help with the project?

She didn't get a chance to say anything privately to Amanda until they got to the Burger Shack in Gap, a town that was busier and bigger than Willow Creek by about ten times. Pris was already hungry, and ordered a cheeseburger, fries, and a raspberry milkshake, which was so wildly out of season that she had to do it just because she could.

"We'll go get a table while you boys wait for the order,"

Amanda suggested. But the place was crowded, so they had to go outside, where it was cold, in order to all sit together, collecting stares from the *Englisch* folks as they did so.

"They must not see many Amish kids here," Pris ventured, pulling her jacket more closely around her and making sure her purse was safely in her lap and her arm through the strap.

"Not on a Sunday, probably," Amanda agreed. "I'm a bit surprised about it myself."

"Then why did you come?" Pris couldn't help it—the words just jumped out.

"Because he asked me," Amanda said simply. "And because I wanted to do something completely different. Something that wasn't me."

"Why?" The Yoders were a wonderful family. What was wrong with being Amanda Yoder? She ought to try being Priscilla Mast sometime, and working two jobs, plus looking after her remaining chores at home.

Amanda gazed at her across the plastic all-weather table as the breeze picked up her *Kapp* strings and blew them back over her shoulders. "It's easy for you. You're pretty and lively and boys want to date you."

"But you're all those things."

"Not young. Not pretty. Most girls in my buddy bunch are planning their weddings this fall—like Sylvia Esh. The first bride of the year—and she used to be my sidekick. That's why I don't go to singings so much anymore. I'm one of the oldest ones there. It's hard to play volleyball when you'd rather be planning a home with someone."

"Someone like Jesse Riehl?" Try as she might, Pris couldn't keep the incredulity out of her tone.

"*Neh.* But he's the first one to ever see past my bad skin and the fact that I can't talk to people very easily, to someone who might have a brain in her head and want to do something other than stay at home and sew for her brothers' *Kinner*."

Pris had never heard so many words come out of Amanda's mouth in all the time she'd known her—and that was her whole life.

Maybe she had a point.

"What would you do?"

But Amanda's attention had shifted to the door, where the boys were coming out burdened with boxes and bags of gloriously greasy, non-homemade food. And in the commotion of eating and joking around and having a food fight with the last of the French fries, the subject didn't come up again. Which was fine. There were things you couldn't talk about in front of boys. Priscilla was still recovering from the fact that Amanda had opened up that much to her, a girl so much younger than she. And, Pris had to admit, it was very strange that Amanda looked up to her in some ways. That she thought she, Pris, was pretty and lively and didn't think of herself that way. Humility was one thing, but did Amanda really not see her own good qualities?

Was wild Jesse Riehl really the one who did?

And how could that be, because goodness, it would never work between the two of them.

"So, Joe," Amanda said on the way back up the steep hill out of Gap that buggies didn't seem to be allowed on, "tell us some more about Colorado. What was it like being in a place where the nearest Amish folks were a hundred miles away?"

"It took some getting used to." Joe pulled at his seat belt, as though being restrained by anything but his own good sense irritated him. "And the ranch hands, well, they don't pay a lot of attention to Sunday. Me and Simon got used to going for long walks—you know, to at least get out where we could hear God and look at the mountains He made—but when Simon got hurt, we couldn't even do that. It was hard."

"But nobody judged you." Amanda craned her head to look at him over the seat. "They didn't make comments about it?"

Joe shook his head. "Everybody knew we were Amish so they cut us some slack. Some of the guys, they played pranks and stuff to get us to react, but most of them were live and let live. Cowboys are like that. You spend a lot of time out there on the back of a horse and I guess you get used to leaving other people alone."

"Do you think an Amish girl would do all right?"

Joe's eyebrows shot up. "Handling horses? On a seven-day trail ride? I don't think so—unless she's got muscles built up from swinging hay bales at home."

"I was thinking in the kitchen, cooking. Or being a *Maud*."

"You thinking of going out West, Amanda?" Jesse said with a quick glance at her before he swung his gaze back to the road flashing by. "Are we the first to hear?"

"Of course not." She dropped her gaze and fiddled with her purse on her lap. "I was just asking."

If you asked Joe an honest question, he gave you an honest answer, so he didn't tease her. Instead, he said thoughtfully, "I think an Amish girl would do all right if she didn't mix with the cowboys and hands. Some of 'em are pretty rough, and some are there because they can't get work anywhere else. Because the work is seasonal, the family takes what they can get. She'd be pretty lonely, though. Other than Teresa and the lady of the house, there were only the two housekeeping girls. And they were as rough as the hands."

"Guess I'd better look closer to home for work, then," Amanda said lightly. "If Priscilla ever leaves the Rose Arbor Inn, maybe she'd put in a good word for me." She smiled at Pris over her shoulder.

"Katie Schrock is getting married this fall, you know," Pris said suddenly. "She might work for a few months afterward, but when the babies start coming, she'll give her notice. I can tell Ginny you're interested, if you want."

Amanda's laugh held self-mockery. "I only just thought of it this second. But maybe you're right. Maybe I'd like being a *Maud*."

"You do more than clean bathrooms and make beds," Pris told her earnestly. "If the guests come and Ginny isn't there, I give them the tour and make sure they're comfortable. She always has food and sodas in the TV room, so I show them that. And they always want to know about where the quilting places are, so I get out the map and give them directions."

"So you're like an assistant?" Jesse teased. "You should ask this lady to pay you more."

"*Neh.*" Pris raised her chin. "I just do what any of us would do when company comes over. Make them feel comfortable and welcome, and offer them something to eat. That's all."

"Seems to me that's what they come to the Inn for anyhow," Joe said with a smile, and all her pique dissolved in the warmth of it.

They arrived at the field behind the gas station a few minutes later, and there was Atlas, patiently standing where Joe had left him, with all the grass within reach cropped down to stubble.

"We'll see you at singing, then," Jesse said as he swung the car to the side of the road.

"Actually, Jesse, I'm not going to go," Amanda said. "Can you take me home? You don't have to bring the car all the way in—I can walk from the road."

"I'm not ashamed of my car."

"I didn't say you should be. But Dat and Mamm wouldn't like it."

"We can take you, Amanda," Joe said. "It's no trouble."

"No, she's with me, so I'll take her home." Jesse's tone was firm enough to settle the question, which made Pris glad. If he cared enough to see her safely home, then maybe there was more going on here than even Amanda suspected.

Pris and Joe got out, and while Joe untied Atlas and offered him some water from the jug in the back, Priscilla waved from the door of the buggy as Jesse looked both ways and swung the car in a U-turn.

While Amanda would only have ten minutes alone with Jesse in the car as they zoomed home, she would have half an hour with Joe in the buggy as they...didn't. It was a happy thought. In fact, she thought as they set off through town, taking their time and talking about whatever came into their heads, it worked out just about perfectly.

Not until the last hill before County Road 26 did Atlas snort and a hitch enter his smooth gait. On the other side of the hill, a plume of dirty gray rose into the air, hanging like dust.

"Easy, boy," Joe said. "Whatever that is, he don't like it. Easy."

Priscilla practically stood in her seat as they crested the hill. Down in the hollow, the fields on the north side narrowed into a cattle culvert where the dairy cattle would cross under the road to their barn on the south side. Some of the cows were already on their way in. A clump of them huddled in the culvert as if they didn't know what to do.

And hanging drunkenly off the road above the culvert, nearly perpendicular and facing backward, was a car.

A white one.

A 1965 Ford Falcon.

CHAPTER 16

S arah felt the drumming in the ground beneath her feet as she let the chickens out into the yard, and lifted her head like a pointer sniffing the air.

Hoofbeats. Coming fast.

No one drove a buggy that fast unless the boys were racing—and they wouldn't dare do that so close to people's farms. Someone was riding a horse at a dead gallop—something so rare that it was like hearing the phone ringing in the shanty in the middle of the night. Nothing that out of place could be good news.

Closer now. Coming up the driveway.

Her heartbeat spiking, Sarah picked up her skirts and dashed across the lawn in time to see Priscilla Mast plunge out from under the trees and bring up the horse in a stamping, skittering halt in the yard. She was astride it, her green skirts and white slip blown back over her legs, using nothing more than a leading halter to give the animal guidance.

"Priscilla! *Was duschde hier?*"

The girl slid off the horse, half sobbing, half trying to breathe. "Sarah, you must come. Jesse Riehl and Amanda Yoder have been in a car accident!"

A bucket of ice water thrown over her couldn't have made

the blood in her veins chill more than this sudden stab of horror and fear. "How badly are they hurt?"

"I don't know. The car went off the road and I couldn't see them, but Joe sent me to get you. He's the one who knows how to ride a horse but he said I wasn't strong enough to pull them out, and besides, Atlas used to be a racehorse and girls were lighter and—"

"Priscilla!" Sarah took her by the shoulders and gave her a shake. "Take a breath. *Gut? Ja?* Now tell me where they are. Did the car leave?"

"*Neh*, I told you, it's over the edge. Joe's trying to get them out."

"Is it on top of the buggy?" Sarah's voice cracked. If that were true, chances of their survival were practically nil.

"No, Joe and I were way behind them. They've gone down Lev Esh's cattle culvert—the last hill before the county road."

"Then—" She stopped. There was no making any sense out of this. The important thing was that two young people were probably injured, and they needed help. "All right. You get back on that horse and fetch Henry Byler. Ask him to call an ambulance, and then ask if he can drive me there. I'll gather my things so I can help them before the ambulance arrives—and if it doesn't come soon, we can try to take them to the county hospital in Henry's car."

Sarah boosted her back up onto Atlas, who stamped and backstepped, but once she had his makeshift reins in hand, seemed to remember his old life well enough. "Go across lots. It's faster."

The girl leaned over the horse's withers and kicked him into motion, and they thundered over the lawn and through the orchard, heading for the hill.

Sarah ran into the house, snatching up her basket on the

way into the compiling room. Blankets. Bandages. Scissors. B and W salve. There was no time to make a healing soak for the bandages, but she had a good tincture she could give the *Youngie* for shock and pain.

She had taken a first aid class at the hospital in the summer, but her skill at setting bones left a lot to be desired. So she would do what she could, and let the EMTs do their job when they got there.

The crunch of gravel in the lane told her Henry was already here. She grabbed a heavier jacket than the one she'd gone out with, and dashed outside. He was already pushing open the passenger door.

"Where is Priscilla?" she said breathlessly, reaching for the seat belt.

"She's gone to get Amanda's father."

"She won't find him—he and Corinne are still at Hostetlers' with Caleb."

"Then we'll call them. Here." He handed her his cell phone.

She pecked at the screen with one finger as he accelerated down the road, concentrating so she wouldn't make a mistake. It was a good thing church had been at Hostetlers'—the only reason she knew the number in their barn was because Jon employed Caleb and she'd memorized it.

"Hallo? Jon Hostetler? *Ja*, this is Sarah Yoder. Is my father-in-law still there?"

"Sure he is, Sarah. One minute and I'll get him. Is everything all right?"

"*Neh*. There's been an accident. I need to speak to him urgently."

Jacob came on the line much faster than she might have imagined. "Sarah, are you all right?"

"*Ja*, I'm fine. It's Amanda. I don't know how bad. Henry is taking me there right now, but I need you and Memm to come home."

The breath whooshed out of Jacob on a groan Sarah could hear even above the sound of the car. "Where did it happen?"

"Lev Esh's cattle culvert. The buggy was hit by a car."

Jacob breathed out a prayer. "We will leave immediately. Lev and Sallie are still here, so they will come, too. You will do—what you can?"

"Henry called the ambulance, so it should be here soon. We're nearly there—I must go."

"God be with you, Sarah—and Amanda—both our daughters."

Sarah swallowed, fighting back tears as she disconnected. Henry crested the hill and they saw the car below, dropped drunkenly over the edge of the slope, facing uphill. He coasted down and pulled over to the shoulder on the opposite site. "Where's the buggy? Surely they couldn't have left."

Joe popped into view from under the car's rear wheels as he climbed out of the culvert. "There is no buggy. Amanda and Jesse were in his car. This car."

Sarah could not wrap her mind around this—so she focused on the important part. "Where are they?" She struggled to keep her tone from spiraling up into panic. "Are they still inside?"

Joe shook his head. "Over here, on the other side. I got them out and checked them as best I could, but—"

She and Henry scrambled around the car to find Amanda and Jesse on the ground on the other side of it, well out of the way in case it decided to change its center of gravity and roll all the way into the muddy cattle path at the bottom.

"Amanda?" Sarah dropped to her knees next to her young

sister-in-law and lifted her chin to check her eyes. "*Ischt du okay?* Are you in pain?"

"Sarah?" Amanda's voice was small, her skin white. Her *Kapp* was gone and her thick *bob* was coming out of its pins. "I'm so sorry."

"You have nothing to be sorry about, *Liewi*." Amanda's eyes responded to the light, contracting just as they should. And she recognized her. No concussion, then, probably. Thank the *gut Gott*. "Are you injured? Tell me where it hurts."

"I hit my forehead. And my ankle hurts."

An ugly bruise was already forming on her temple, and she'd have a black eye by tonight. Fortunately, there was something Sarah could do about that. "Let me put some salve on it, dear one. I have bandages right here." She glanced at Joe, who had already taken a blanket and tucked it around the other boy. "And Jesse? What is his condition?"

"I'm fine," the boy said. "You look after Amanda." But he didn't sound fine. He sounded dazed, and his breathing was shallow.

"Broken rib, maybe?" Joe hazarded. "Bruises from hitting the steering wheel. Lucky they were wearing seat belts. Some of these old cars don't even come with them."

"It's the law," Jesse mumbled. "Stupid cow. It got out of the culvert. I tried to miss it, but hit the post on the guard rail and spun and—" He seemed to lose the thread of the sentence and broke off.

Sarah couldn't even allow her mind's eye to consider what could have happened if Jesse hadn't obeyed the law. And at some later time she would find out what Amanda had been doing in this car...but that time was not now.

"The ambulance should be here by now, shouldn't it?" she said anxiously to Henry, fixing a gauze pad smeared with

B and W salve to Amanda's forehead with tape. Then she took out a small bottle of tincture of valerian, cava-cava, and milky oats that she kept just for trauma. "Amanda, open your mouth. A little of this will calm your system."

Obediently, she opened her mouth and Sarah squirted half a dropperful onto her tongue. "Joe, the same for Jesse, please, until I get over there to have a look at him."

Joe administered the dose to Jesse as calmly as though he'd done it a hundred times before. "You have a real knack," she said with approval as he handed the bottle back to her.

"Maybe we could talk about that sometime," he said. "Do you think Amanda might be able to walk up to the road? I don't think Jesse can."

"If you think he has a broken rib, I won't risk moving him."

"I'm all right," came a slurred demurral from Joe's other side.

"If her ankle hurts, I don't want her walking on it, either. It's already swelling and we've got no ice. Listen—is that the siren?"

Joe scrambled up the slope to meet the ambulance while Sarah had a look at Jesse. This wasn't good. His gaze didn't track properly when she passed a finger before his eyes, and if his rib really was broken, he could puncture a lung if they weren't careful. Without moving him, she tucked the blanket between his shoulders and the ground.

The siren chirped as the ambulance stopped above them, and Sarah heard Joe giving the EMTs what information he could. And then the two men were coming down the slope, a backboard between them and a big red case over the shoulder of one.

"It's all right, ma'am, we've got them now," one of them

said to Sarah. "The boy up there said you were treating them?"

Rapidly, she told them what she'd done—such as it was—and the one who seemed to be in charge nodded. He knelt by Amanda. "What's your name, miss?"

"Amanda Yoder," she said softly.

"Do you know what day it is?"

"Sunday. I shouldn't have been riding in a car, should I?"

"I hope it didn't get banged up as much as you did. It's a collector's item," the man said with a smile. "I need you to move your arms and legs for me, Amanda. Great. Now, wiggle your toes. Good. How many fingers am I holding up?"

"Three," Amanda said.

"Good girl. You're doing okay, but I don't like the look of these contusions—or that ankle. We're going to take you in and get you fixed up, all right?"

"But Jesse—"

"We'll look at Jesse now. You stay right there and I'll be back in a second."

It didn't take much more than a look before the backboard came out and Jesse was lifted on to it. "My car—" he mumbled restlessly as the men hefted him up and began to negotiate their way up the slope. Henry walked beside him.

"Don't worry about the car. Once the police are done with it, I'll have it towed to my place." The sheriff's cruiser had already pulled in a safe distance behind the ambulance.

"Doesn't look like it took a lot of damage," one of the EMTs said as they put Jesse on a gurney. "Those old ones were built to last."

"You should make him an offer," the other one joked as the sheriff's deputy joined them.

"Don't tempt me. Come on, let's get the little lady aboard and get going."

Sarah could tell that Amanda didn't want to go in the ambulance, but there was no gainsaying the EMTs and their backboard—or the tape that held her to it. "You must go to the hospital, *Liewi*," Sarah urged. "They'll make sure you're completely fine."

"I am completely fine. I want to go home."

"When the doctor tells us that, I'll take you home," Henry said. "What would your mother say?"

"She would say I was to go," Amanda said reluctantly. "Are they coming? The hospital is so far away. They can't get there before dark."

"I can have them there in half an hour," Henry said. "Don't you worry about a thing except letting these nice folks take care of you."

The EMTs loaded Amanda into the back, where she lay next to Jesse, fussing with her skirts and the blanket, trying to return it to Sarah. Henry pulled Sarah away. "The sheriff will need a statement. We can do that for them."

It didn't take long. Rapidly, they told the deputy what Jesse had said about the cow—about Pris's mad ride across country to fetch Sarah—about their arrival and what they had found. The sheriff had a look around and, after he measured the skid marks and found the fence broken down at the bottom of the culvert, agreed that Jesse had swerved to avoid hitting a cow that had probably hightailed it back down into the culvert and gone with its companions to the barn.

"Hard to say what would have been the better move," he said, writing in his notebook. "Swerve right, you go into the culvert. Swerve left, you run the risk of hitting someone coming in the other direction." He closed his book and shoved it in a pocket. "Guess we'd better get that car out of there before it goes to join the cows."

"I told Jesse I'd call a tow truck and have it taken to my place."

The deputy nodded. "It's not a crime scene. You're welcome to it. Nice little car. Turns out there's more damage than he thinks and the kid wants to sell it, he can call me." And to Sarah's astonishment, he pulled out a card and gave it to Henry. "It's a 'sixty-five. Those things are in major demand."

Shaking her head, Sarah watched the sheriff pull out, leaving only the two of them and the disabled car. While Henry called a tow truck, Sarah heaved a sigh that didn't seem to loosen the tightness in her chest one bit. Maybe she should take a dropperful of her own tincture.

Amanda riding in a car with Jesse Riehl. If she hadn't seen it with her own eyes, she would never have believed it. She'd seen them talking together after church, but it was a far cry from that to joyriding on a Sunday afternoon when everyone else was visiting friends and family. Were they dating? Did Jacob and Corinne know?

Well, if they didn't, they certainly would soon.

Henry hung up. "They'll be along in about an hour."

Sarah shook her head. "We can't wait. The sooner we get Jacob and Corinne to the hospital and they know Amanda is all right, the better. Joe, will you stay and make sure they take the car to Henry's?"

Joe nodded. "Then I'll find Pris. Atlas still needs to pull the buggy home."

"Okay." Henry took her arm and they crossed the road together. "We can probably be there and back before the tow truck gets here anyhow. Where do you suppose we should start looking?"

"If they left fifteen minutes ago, they should be just about to the intersection where Willow Creek Road crosses the highway."

He got in, and she made good and sure her seat belt was fastened.

"That's pretty specific," he said as he swung onto the road. "Are you psychic?"

"Of course not." As an attempt to lighten her spirits, it was pretty feeble, but she appreciated his trying. "I know how fast a buggy goes, and I know how long it takes to get there. We should arrive at the intersection just about when they do."

And she was right. They passed through the intersection and hadn't gone much more than a few hundred feet when Sarah saw Magic, her in-laws' buggy horse, coming along at such a spanking clip that it took Jacob a few seconds to get him slowed down when they saw Henry waving out the driver's window.

Once Jacob turned into the nearest driveway, Corinne leaped down onto the asphalt and Henry called, "It's all right. She's alert and banged up, but she'll be okay. They just took her to the hospital to patch her up. If you folks come with me, Sarah can take your buggy home."

Which was such a perfect solution that Sarah wondered why she hadn't thought of it herself. She couldn't help Amanda any further, and it was her mother and father's place to be by her bedside.

"Thank you," she said on a long breath of gratitude, and before she got out of his car, she threw her arms around Henry's neck and hugged him. "You've been such a good friend to us."

One arm came around her waist and he buried his face in her shoulder, breathing in as if he were inhaling her very scent.

Sarah blushed scarlet and pushed out of the embrace into which she'd so thoughtlessly thrown herself. "*Denki*, I must go," she blurted. She snatched up her basket and practically fell out the door.

It was lucky that Corinne was looking up at her husband as they crossed the road together. With a brief, hard hug for her mother-in-law, Sarah said, "Go. Henry will get you there almost as soon as the ambulance."

Corinne was blind to anything but getting to Whinburg General as fast as possible. By the time Sarah seated herself in their buggy and took up Magic's reins, they had already disappeared over the hill.

Magic looked around several minutes later to see why no one was asking him to walk on. But Sarah couldn't drive. For she had just realized something. From the moment the sheriff had left, she and Henry had been speaking exclusively in *Deitsch*. The language of the family. The language a couple spoke to each other. And when she had lost control and compounded her error by hugging him, he had responded...he had...

The tears flooded her eyes, blinding her—their salt and heat stinging as her own body rebuked her for looking where she should not.

For reaching out to hold a man who belonged to another woman.

CHAPTER 17

Corinne Yoder wouldn't hear of Henry's going home to his solitary kitchen that evening, after he'd brought her and Jacob and Amanda back to the farm. "With all you've done for us today, Henry Byler, you must let us give you dinner. It is the least we can do to thank you for your kindness."

"My kindness, as you call it, was the least I could do for my neighbors." He hustled to hold the kitchen door open as Jacob hovered next to Amanda, his strong, sinewy hands ready in case she should lose her balance. She navigated the steps and her new crutches with much more skill than Henry would have anticipated.

"Does it hurt, *Dochder*?" Corinne asked anxiously. "Do you need one of the pills the doctor gave you?"

"*Neh*, Mamm. It only hurts when I put weight on it. The real question is, how are you going to manage to keep house for six weeks without me?"

"We'll think about that later. For now, let's get you into your bed and I'll bring you some supper on a tray."

A few minutes later, with Amanda apparently comfortably settled, Corinne hurried back in and pulled a bib apron from the back of the kitchen door. "Has anyone found Jesse Riehl's parents?" she asked. "He looked so alone in the emergency room—not that he was in any shape to appreciate company after the drugs took hold. But someone ought to let his family know. Amanda says he is staying with a Mennonite aunt and uncle."

"The sheriff would have called, I think," Henry said. "If he's living at their address, then the license plate would have been registered there and it would have been straightforward to get a phone number."

Jacob shook his head. "Imagine an Amish boy driving a car."

"Imagine an Amish girl riding in it," his wife said tartly. "But that's a conversation for another time. All I can say is I'm glad you were there to help, Henry. They would have been lying on the side of the road yet if it hadn't been for you." She put a pot of coffee on and laid out bread, jam, honey, and sliced cheese, in case anyone was hungry before dinner.

"Sarah sent Priscilla to get me. You should have seen that girl, astride a buggy horse and riding like the wind. It was straight out of Paul Revere." Suddenly he found himself starving, and helped himself to bread and jam. Raspberry. Heaven.

"Priscilla is a good girl," Corinne said. "And Joe Byler is a fine young man. They are young yet, but I hope something comes of it someday." She got a parcel wrapped in white butcher's paper from the refrigerator. "I wonder where Sarah is. I thought she would be here waiting for us." She began to cut up onions and mushrooms. "And what of you and Ginny Hochstetler? How are your plans coming along?"

Henry felt the stiffness in his spine begin to relax as he watched the comfortable movements of a woman at home in her own kitchen. "Ginny's in Philadelphia as we speak, searching for a wedding dress with her mother and sister. She'll be back on Tuesday."

"Caleb has told us you're undecided about whether to sell the old place," Jacob said. "It seems it will take a little figuring out."

Henry nodded. "It's the studio that's the problem. I need the barn, but I can't sell to an Amish family without it. And since the house isn't wired for electricity, an English family wouldn't buy it without a lot of renovation first—and that would affect the asking price. Not that I could get a lot for it anyway... it needs a lot of work."

"You could move away altogether," Corinne suggested. "Sell both places and find one that has what you need." She moved the sautéed vegetables to a bowl and began to fry pork chops.

"We talked about that, but neither of us wants to leave here. Willow Creek has been Ginny's home for going on fifteen years, and the Inn has built a nice reputation even as far as New York. It would be a shame to give that up and start over fresh where we didn't have friends and family."

"Your friends would be sad to see you go." Jacob agreed, pouring them both a second cup of coffee. "It's *gut* that Caleb has his job with Jon Hostetler now, but we are grateful for the work you gave him when you first came."

Henry smiled. "I do miss him popping in and out, but I'm glad he has more steady work. I'm sure Sarah appreciates the help with expenses."

As though her name had conjured her up, there was a commotion on the porch outside, and Sarah, Caleb, and Simon all poured in, panting as though they'd run across lots.

"Ah, *gut*, I'm so glad you're back," Sarah said. "I went home to leave a note for the boys that I was here when they got back from the singing—but it turned out they hadn't gone."

"Word spread pretty fast from Hostetlers' place after you called," Jacob agreed. "Did you boys come home with Paul and Barbara?"

"*Ja*, and weren't they upset that Joe and Pris were in the car before the accident," Caleb said, sitting down opposite Henry and smearing a piece of bread with jam and peanut butter. "I think Priscilla will be grounded again. For a girl who doesn't do hardly anything, she sure gets grounded a lot."

"I think Amanda would disagree that she doesn't do anything," Sarah said, brushing his hair out of his eyes with a tenderness that made Henry focus on his coffee cup. She hadn't looked in his direction once since she'd come in.

Was this how it was going to be? Him doing stupid things like overresponding to a simple hug of thanks, and both of them ignoring it because an apology would be too awkward? And what was wrong with him that he kept on doing that? Couldn't he see that she was a warmhearted woman, and a hug meant nothing more than—than a pat on the back?

Well, if she could treat it like nothing, then so could he. And the truth was that Ginny deserved better than to have him get all flustered and awkward over a simple gesture of friendship. And besides, after they were married, he couldn't imagine he'd be seeing much of the Yoders anyway. With the money from D.W. Frith, he and Ginny might do a little traveling during the off season, even if it was only to the states bordering Pennsylvania.

Sarah made the gravy and roasted potatoes, and when the meal was served, Henry bowed his head for the silent grace.

And for the first time in many years, he prayed—not the Lord's Prayer, which he might have said years ago, but one born more of feeling than words.

Lord, you probably don't recognize me, it's been so long, but I need some help. I don't know what it is about this woman, but one of us is in the wrong place and it's definitely the wrong time. Maybe You've sent her to test me, or sent me to test her, I don't know—but please give me the strength to put her out of my life. To feel nothing, and treat her with nothing but the friendship she feels for me. This is kind of a selfish prayer, Lord, and I don't have anything to offer in return. But it is a needy one. Help me, in Jesus' name.

As prayers went, it wasn't much, but he felt a little better as he raised his head.

At which point he realized that the entire family had been sitting silently, waiting for him to do so.

Chagrined, he felt sweat break out on his forehead. Would someone say something? Make a comment? Then, belatedly, he realized that no one in an Amish family would dream of commenting on the length of another's prayer—even when that other was *Englisch*.

Instead, Jacob merely smiled and picked up his knife and fork, which was the signal for everyone else to reach for bowls of vegetables and pickles, and for the pork chops in rich gravy to be handed around. Sarah made up a plate for Amanda and took it up, but came back down the stairs almost immediately.

"She's asleep," she said, covering the plate with foil and slipping it into the still-warm oven. "Rest is the best thing for her now—probably better even than food."

With everyone else there, it was surprisingly easy to avoid talking with Sarah. He traded news with Caleb. He discussed the weather and how it might affect the last of the apple harvest with Jacob. He even chatted about Colorado with Simon. He'd been through the area where the ranch apparently was, so they traded notes and impressions for a big chunk of the dinner hour—almost until dessert, in fact.

If Sarah noticed that he spoke to everyone at the table but her, she gave no sign of it. In fact, she seemed quite happy to let others do the talking and do none herself. Maybe she was still recovering from the shock of seeing Amanda hurt. He knew they were close, and he could imagine that she probably wanted to hover over Amanda's bedside, just to make sure that she kept on breathing.

Or maybe she was just doing as he was doing, and keeping her distance. Reducing the possibility that this strange connection might accidentally re-form between them again.

By eight o'clock, when he saw that Jacob and Corinne were ready for bed, it being Monday the next day and an early start, he wasted no time in thanking them and taking his leave. He barely had time to get out to the car, congratulating himself on managing his escape pretty well, when he heard the rapid sound of footsteps on the stairs.

"Henry?"

He opened the door and the interior light came on. "Right here, Sarah. Can I give you and the boys a lift?"

"*Neh*—I mean, no. Thank you." The combined lights from the yard pole and the inside of the car made her *Kapp* seem as though it were made of moonlight. "I wanted to check your hands. How do they feel?"

"They're fine." He had to get out of here, away from that concerned gaze.

"That's a man's standard answer when he doesn't want the woman to trouble herself about him." Her tone held a smile. "What he doesn't realize is that if he doesn't let her help, the trouble might wind up being worse than when he started. Come over to the house and let me look."

"I'm not going to your house, Sarah." The words were out before he thought about how they would sound. "I mean—"

"If you're worried about what happened in the car, then I am sorry. I was forward. I should not have allowed my emotions to carry me away."

"Nothing happened." *Liar. You fell into that hug as if you'd been waiting for it for a year.*

"Well, then, you won't mind coming home so I can look at your hands and bandage them up again."

He did mind. Ginny would mind even more. But the boys were trooping out the back door and Caleb had caught sight of them now. "Is Henry giving us a ride home?" the boy asked, loping over.

Maybe that would be the best thing. The more the merrier. Get it over with in the boys' company, and then leave. "I've offered, but your mother says no."

"Come on, Mamm," Caleb begged. "It's pitch dark and cold."

"All right, then, if Henry doesn't mind. Let me get my basket from the kitchen."

The drive was short and noisy, and when Sarah led him into her dispensary and fired up the pole lamp, there was no question that the door to the room would be left open. Oh, Henry knew the rules as well as anyone—they'd just never mattered as much as they did right now.

"Wash your hands well with soap," she said, "and I'll take the bandage strips off."

He took a kerosene lantern into the bathroom and scrubbed. When he sat down at her little white wooden table, he spread his hands, palms up, and waited. Her own were gentle and efficient, her fingers smooth and warm, as she removed the Band-Aid strips and bent to look.

"Improving," she said. "The redness is gone, and look, this shallow one is beginning to close up. Do they still tingle?"

"They must not. I haven't thought about it all day."

"Then maybe it was just the salve doing its good work. Now that the skin has become used to it, it has stopped arguing."

He smiled. "I don't think an MD would phrase it quite that way."

"He might if he had boys."

"Your boys never argued with you."

She smiled, clearly thinking of the boys as they had been ten years ago or more. "Not after the first few tries anyway. Arguing is a form of disobedience, and a mother wants to train that out of her children early."

"I remember," he said ruefully. Her gentle touch was making goose bumps rise on his arms, running all the way up and ending between his shoulder blades. It was a good thing that he wore not only a long-sleeved flannel shirt, but a jacket as well. "I'm not sure my mother ever succeeded. Or if she did, it cropped back up when I was nineteen, and by then it was too late to change."

"Is that when you left home?"

"Yes. She never stopped trying, though, even after I'd moved to Denver. A letter came every week, faithful as the sunrise."

"We mothers don't stop loving our sons just because they're disobedient." She got up and found the jar of salve in the cabinet. "Neither does God," she said to the cabinet door as she closed it.

"Sarah..." he warned.

"I'm not saying anything more than the truth."

"Your truth."

"*Ja*, mine... and maybe that of a man who is thankful for his food at the dinner table." She took her seat and scooped up a fingerful of the reddish-brown salve.

"I can do that. I've had a little practice."

She dabbed it on the cuts where his fingers met his palms and, when she'd finished, pushed the glass jar toward him. "All right. You finish and I'll get the bandages."

Caleb stuck his head in the doorway. "I'm going to bed, Mamm."

"Good night, son of mine." Her hands were sticky, so she leaned over to kiss him on the ear as she passed him. "We're up early tomorrow, so I won't be long. Where is Simon?"

"Out in the barn, I think, saying good night to Dulcie. 'Night, Henry."

"'Night, Caleb. I'd shake your hand but I'd get goop all over you."

"It's good goop, if it makes you better." And with that, he loped upstairs.

With Sarah's help, Henry bandaged up the remaining cuts, and when it didn't seem as though Simon was in any hurry to leave the horse and come in, he stood to go.

"Can I offer you some coffee?" she asked.

"Sarah, you know I can't stay."

She looked away, the lamplight casting one side of her face in shadow, and illuminating the other in gold light, like a picture out of a medieval manuscript. "You're so different tonight. Has my forward behavior spoiled our friendship? Or is it because you're promised to Ginny?"

"Both. I mean, neither."

When she looked up at him, the words fell out of his head and all he could see was the pain in those gray eyes—eyes that should hold laughter, or compassion, or love. Not pain that he had caused. "Sarah, don't look like that."

"How can I not? Henry, I must say it—you're marrying the wrong woman."

"Am I?" he got out, though his chest had constricted and he wasn't sure how he was going to take his next breath. "And who is the right one?"

"The woman God has chosen for you," she whispered. "A plain woman. A faithful woman, to make a home for you and your children."

"I'm with a faithful woman." No, that could be taken two ways. "The one in Philadelphia."

He said it like an incantation, the way a priest would wave a cross to ward off evil. But Sarah wasn't evil. She was just a temptation too great to be borne. He half expected her to say, *Not the right faith*, but she didn't. Instead, tears filled her eyes and she blushed.

"Why are you doing this to me?" he whispered, his voice cracking.

"Why are you doing it to me?" It was almost a groan. "This was a mistake. My pride again." The tears had overflowed now, and one dropped down her cheek with the suddenness of despair. "You have to go," she said, so low he could barely hear her. "I can't treat you anymore. And I must find a way to not see you, either, even if it means moving to the other side of the district."

"Don't do that, Sarah. Don't even think it. This is my fault.

I'm the one who's betraying a good woman in my heart. At least you're free."

"Not for long."

And before he could ask her what on earth that meant, the kitchen door banged open and Simon came in. Sarah turned and began cleaning up the papers from the Band-Aid strips as though her life depended on it. And when Henry wished her good night from the doorway, she didn't look up.

CHAPTER 18

On Monday morning, Priscilla finished the breakfast dishes in record time and said to her mother, "Mamm, I'm going to go over to Yoders' to see how Amanda is doing. Do you want me to take anything?"

"*Ja*, I do, but it might be best to drop in at Sarah's and see if Amanda is well enough for a visit first. I made a big pot of chicken and dumpling soup, so if she's well enough to eat it, I could take it by on my way to the fabric store at ten o'clock. Miriam Yoder is having her annual sale this week, and if I don't go on the first day, all the best colors will be gone."

"Poor Miriam. She'll sure be busy without Amanda to help."

"Miriam likes to be busy. And her girls are old enough to count change—they'll be happy for the chance to help their mother."

Katie turned from where she was putting the dry plates in the cupboard. "Mamm, I wonder if I could help her. I'm good at math, and I'm almost fifteen. It's time I found some work to do."

Mamm gazed at her as if she hadn't quite expected her to grow up so fast. She still looked at Priscilla that way sometimes. "Are you sure? Because with Pris working, you're a wonderful help to me, and I'm not sure I can manage without you."

"Not every day, maybe," Katie said, the light in her face dimming just a little. "Or ever. But I could offer to help this week, while Amanda *ischt krank*."

Mamm reached over and gave her a hug. "My girl has a bright mind and a big heart. Why don't you come with me and we'll ask Miriam. If she says yes, you can stay for the day and see how you like it."

"And the next day?" Katie asked hesitantly.

"That will be up to Miriam, but we can talk about it at supper."

Katie nodded, and ran to change out of her house dress to one that might be suitable for greeting the public. Though the *Englisch* long weekend wasn't for another week, a number of Miriam's *Englisch* customers knew about her sale and saved this Monday for quilt-group trips. Pris hoped it would work out for Katie—she was calm and responsible, and far better at arithmetic than anyone in the family. Counting change and cutting yardage would be the perfect job for her, even if it was only for a week or even a month, until Amanda was back on her feet.

Pris pinned on a freshly washed and starched *Kapp* and took her jacket off the peg near the door. The glorious crisp sunshine they'd been having seemed to have taken a holiday today, and Pris's hand hovered, undecided, over the umbrella.

Better take it. Her nice crisp *Kapp* would be a sorry sight if it got soaked.

It didn't take long to walk the half mile down the road, cross, and make her way down Sarah Yoder's lane. She would just pop in, say hello, and ask if Amanda was seeing visitors, so as not to take up too much time on laundry day. But when she knocked at the back door, no one answered. She stepped into the kitchen, saw nothing but clean counters and empty chairs, and peeked into the compiling room.

"Hello? Sarah? Is anyone home?" In the silence, the clock on the windowsill over the sink ticked, telling her nothing but that it was ten minutes to eight.

Well, the laundry was hung out to dry on the line, despite the threat of rain. Maybe Sarah had taken a healing mixture over to Amanda, and Pris would find them all in the kitchen over there, talking over cups of coffee.

Priscilla crossed the yard, heading for the creek bottom and the shortcut up the hill that would take her to Jacob and Corinne's, when someone called her name. She turned to see Simon emerge from the barn with a curved piece of wood in one hand and a nasty-looking knife in the other.

"Pris—I thought that was you. Are you looking for Mamm?"

"*Ja*, I wanted to know how Amanda is, and whether she's well enough to have some of my mother's chicken and dumpling soup."

"It would be worth running off the road to have some of that." He grinned. "My favorite."

"I think Amanda would probably say the price was a little high. Has anyone heard how Jesse is?"

"Not yet, but Mamm was going to call the hospital from the phone shanty when she got back. She's still worried that this aunt and uncle of his might not know." As he spoke, he put his whittling down on a fence post and ambled over until he was leaning on one of the maples overlooking the creek. "I hear things might have gone a lot worse if you hadn't ridden for help."

She shrugged and pushed both hands into the pockets of

her jacket, the braided loop of the umbrella handle over one wrist. "I thought Joe should go since you and he spent the whole summer riding horses, but he was right in the end. He was able to get them out of the car in case it rolled away and hit bottom and made things worse, where I sure couldn't have."

"Mamm says it was quite a sight." He paused for the briefest second. "But then, you're a sight for sore eyes anyway."

For a second, she thought he was teasing her, and then the warmth in his long-lashed gaze made the light come on in her brain. He'd just given her a compliment.

But it wasn't the compliment that made her blush. It was that gaze, lying on her skin like honey and cinnamon.

But this was ridiculous. She'd practically thrown herself at him in the spring. Why had he decided to wake up now instead of then? How different things would have been if he'd behaved like this instead of the big brother type who always had something more interesting to do than be with her.

"Pris, while I was gone, I had the chance to do a lot of thinking."

"Did you? So did I. What did you think about?"

"You, mostly, especially when I was laid up and didn't even have my work with the horses to keep me from seeing the truth."

Heat prickled into her cheeks. "What did Joe have to say about that?"

He grinned. "You think I'm fool enough to talk about it with him? He'd have thrown me in the stock pond in two seconds."

"Joe's not like that. He'll talk about anything with anybody."

"The subject of Priscilla Mast isn't for everybody. It's special. I guess that goes for both of us."

"Simon, are you trying to flirt with me?"

He laughed, but it could be because she was flushed with embarrassment despite the coldness of the day. "Maybe. Maybe I'm thinking what a fool I was not to notice you before he did. Maybe I'm wondering if you still like me the way you used to—and whether you'd go on a date with me sometime."

"Maybe you ought to talk that over with my special friend first. He might be able to suggest a handy stock pond." There was something thrilling about this—about being wanted by two boys. And the fact that one of them was Simon, whom she'd been dreaming about for a year at least...well, even though she knew perfectly well it was prideful and wrong, she couldn't help the tiny trickle of female triumph that somehow, some way, she'd finally managed to make him notice her.

Even if she no longer planned to do anything about it.

Simon laughed. "Maybe he would. But if you told him that you wanted to date other people, then the stock ponds and I would be safe."

"I couldn't do that, Simon."

He levered himself slowly off the tree, which brought him to within touching distance. "Don't you care for me?"

"I—I—*ja*." Of course she did. As a brother. Or maybe not. Brothers were safe. And there was nothing remotely safe about Simon Yoder. "But not in that way."

"Are you sure?" He reached out, and instead of taking her arm, he tugged gently on the little folding umbrella. Because its loop was over her wrist, her hand came out of her pocket and he tugged some more. If she didn't take a step, she'd lose her balance.

The wind kicked up behind her and blew her skirts flat against the backs of her legs. It also pushed her the last inch, as if it were conspiring to make her stand this close to him.

"*Ja*," she said.

"*Ja, so?*" His voice fell halfway between a bass note and a whisper. The wind got under her collar and tickled the back of her neck, and she shivered. "*Bischt du kalt*, Pris?"

One last tug, and she was in his arms.

He dipped his head and kissed her, the heat of his body warming her hands, the umbrella dangling forgotten from her wrist. His lips were cold. Cold and firm and a bit wet. Not at all like Joe's.

Somewhere, thunder rolled, a long grinding sound that didn't bode well for her staying dry until she got to Yoders'. She wrenched herself away. "Simon—Joe—he—"

At the sound of Joe's name, his best friend set her away from himself. She searched his face, looking for—what? An apology? An acknowledgment that they'd done something unworthy? A gaze that would match the tone of his voice a few seconds ago?

But no. He was looking up, past her hair, over her head.

She turned just in time to see Joe bring his buggy to a halt, the grinding of the gravel under the wheels a sound like thunder in her ears.

Priscilla may as well have stepped into a freezer. Even her blood had chilled to a crawl at the look on Joe's face—at the naked pain and betrayal in his eyes.

Caught.

She had walked into a trap she had set for herself out of pride and greed—why be satisfied with one boy courting you when you could have two with a wave of your hand?—and now she had to pay the price.

"I came to talk to Sarah," he said to Simon, the reins held loosely in his hands. "She in?"

Priscilla couldn't speak. How could he say a single word in such a calm tone when his eyes blazed like that? Wordlessly, she shook her head.

"She went over to Daed and Mammi's to see Amanda," Simon said. "Joe—"

Joe flapped the reins and guided the buggy past them in a wide turn. When the horse was facing back down the lane, he didn't even pull up, just nodded. "*Denki*. See you."

And without another word, the buggy rattled off up the lane. Priscilla felt as though Joe had taken her heart with him, all her blood vessels and sinews that connected it to her body stretching between them to the breaking point.

If it broke, she would be broken forever.

"Now look what you've done!" she snapped, whirling to face Simon.

"Me!" Simon's brows rose in comic dismay. "There were two of us in that kiss, if you remember."

"How can you talk about it like that when you know he saw us!"

He lifted one shoulder in a shrug. "He saw us. It's done. At least we all know where we stand."

"We do not! Didn't you see his face? I've hurt him something awful, and now I have to go make it up to him. Somehow. If I can."

How did you make up for a hurt that deep? She knew Joe cared for her—it was impossible not to know, with the way he always put her first. Whether it was opening a door or passing her a bowl of food at the table, he made sure she knew that, for him, she came before anyone else.

How could she have cheapened that kind of caring by kissing Simon? How could she have thrown away Joe's faithful heart by listening to her own selfish pride?

"Don't get all worked up, Pris," Simon said, his hand sliding into the crook of her elbow. "He'll be okay. I mean, 'I came to see Sarah'? Not, 'Take your hands off my woman'? I know you two were special friends, but maybe it doesn't run as deep as you thought."

"Don't say *were*! And what do you know about it? You've never had a special friend because you think too highly of yourself to share yourself with anybody."

He was still smiling, that aggravating amused smile that he used for nearly everything. "I think highly of myself?" He snorted. "Hardly."

How could she have been in love with this boy? He didn't know the first thing about what it was like to care for someone. "You do—and that's why you can't see how hurt he was. Joe Byler would be the first one to expect that I'd choose someone else. He'd be the first one to encourage me to go ... because he doesn't think he's worthy. He's the humblest, most self-effacing guy I'll ever meet. Don't you see? In his mind, I just proved him right."

"Nothing wrong with being humble."

"Maybe you ought to try it." She yanked her elbow away and heard the whisper of the rain falling through the last of the red leaves of the maple above. "I'm going after him."

"No, you're not. Come into the house with me and have some coffee. I think you're probably a free woman now."

She whirled to stare at him. "How can you be so insensitive? He's your best friend!"

"How can you get so worked up?" he shot back, and she saw she'd finally gotten under his skin. "I've known Joe my whole life, and you've got him all wrong. He doesn't think about stuff the way you do. And he certainly doesn't get all emotional like this. I'll have a talk with him, say we were just goofing around, and it'll be fine."

Boys, honestly.

But they weren't boys anymore, were they? This wasn't the schoolyard, and they weren't six years old, learning to take their turn with the ball. This was real—real emotion, real feelings, real people who hurt and were hurt in their turn.

"It's not your place," she told him stiffly. "I'm the one who's in the wrong, so I'm the one to talk to him."

"He's probably there by now. You'll never catch him."

"Watch me."

Fleet as a rabbit, she ran past Sarah's quilt garden and down the slope to the creek bottom. She took the log bridge in three long strides and dashed up the hill on the other side. It was a quarter mile between places. Joe would probably be just turning in at the mailbox, so if she cut through the hay meadow here and climbed the fence, she'd meet him coming halfway down the lane—right about—

"Joe!" Panting, disheveled, and wet because opening the umbrella would have slowed her down, she slapped both hands on the passenger door to get him to stop the buggy.

"Whoa!" she heard him say to the horse, and the reins scraped against their channels in the windscreen as he pulled the animal up. The door slid open.

"Pris, you're soaking. Get in."

She couldn't get her breath, couldn't speak, couldn't do anything but heave against the constriction of the waistband of her dress. But she had to. She had to apologize, had to make him see that it was all a mistake.

She hadn't known before, but she knew now, and she had to tell him.

Finally she could get a good lungful of air. She sounded like the engine on the corn augur when it started up on a November morning, all puffing and coughing and hesitating.

"Joe—what you saw—Simon—"

"It's okay, Pris." He gazed at his hands, holding the reins so the horse wouldn't pull forward and bring them out from behind the spruces into the yard where anyone looking out the windows could see them.

"It's not okay! I never should have let him. I know that now."

"But you did."

"*Ja*, for one second. Then I pushed him away."

"But that one second was enough to tell me that you still have feelings for him."

"It was enough to tell *me* that I *don't*. That's what kisses do. They tell you."

"And some tell you more than you want them to. I'm serious, Pris. It's okay. I've never really thought this whole time we've been special friends that you and me, we'd be together forever."

"But what if—" She couldn't go on. *What if we are? What if you break up with me and you're the one God wants for me and I've messed up His entire plan for my life? What then?*

"There are lots of guys in Willow Creek, and you're a pretty girl from a good family. I never fooled myself, believe me."

"But Joe, I want to be with you."

"Didn't look like it."

"That was a *mistake*."

"Maybe. But maybe it wasn't. Maybe it was a sign that I should be thinking about other things than courting. Like figuring out what I want to do with my life."

Without me?

"That's why I came to see Sarah. I stopped in at your place to see if you wanted to come with me, like we talked about, and your Mamm said you were already over here. So I rushed the horse a little. Guess I shouldn't have."

Priscilla didn't think it was possible to feel any worse, but now she knew differently. She shrank down into her jacket and her throat closed up and before she could breathe or control it or anything, a great big sob came up out of nowhere and she started to cry.

"Aw, Pris. Don't do that."

But she couldn't help it. He was so humble, so accepting of his belief that he didn't deserve anything better than this, that it broke her heart. Some horrible hussy was going to catch him on the rebound and she'd have to watch as the kindest boy in the whole settlement got treated like dirt... all because of her.

"Here. Use my hanky."

Which made her sob all the harder, which finally made him huff out a breath and wrap the reins around their hook. He slid over and put his arms around her, patting her on the back while she shuddered and gulped.

She would rather he had climbed out and walked down the lane alone to do what he'd come to do. Because his comforting hug only showed her once and for all exactly what that kiss with Simon was going to cost her.

CHAPTER 19

A manda, there's someone here to see you."
Sarah turned at the sound of Corinne's voice. In the doorway of the front room, Joe Byler stood behind her, a smile on his lips and an unhappy expression in his eyes that made Sarah think he might be remembering the accident— or at least some other disaster.

"Joe." Lying on the sofa, Amanda smiled back in a quiet greeting while Sarah tucked a cozy Nine Patch quilt around her.

"How are you feeling?" He folded himself into a chair at the foot of the sofa, opposite Sarah's.

"Like I was in an accident." She laid a hand on her chest, slightly to one side. "And strangely, the worst of it is here, where the seat belt was."

"The alternative would've been worse," Joe pointed out.

"We're not going to think about the alternative," Sarah said firmly. "I've just been treating her with a salve of plantain and calendula for the trauma and contusions."

"What about the ankle?" Joe asked. "I don't see a cast, but it's bound up."

Amanda nodded. "A bad sprain with some torn tissue, they said. It hurts like anything, but Sarah says there's a cream you can get at the pharmacy called Traumeel that's good for it. Mamm said she would go into Whinburg tomorrow and get some."

"Let me go," Joe said. "Has anyone heard anything of Jesse? Maybe I could stop at the hospital and visit him while I'm there."

How kind he was, to give up a whole day's work for others. If Sarah recalled correctly, Priscilla was off tomorrow. Maybe they would go together and keep each other company on the long drive. "I called the hospital and asked after him, and they said he had suffered a mild concussion, but he'd made it through whatever period they have to wait. He may even be released by tomorrow."

"Has anyone spoken with his aunt and uncle?" Amanda shifted restlessly, and Sarah reached behind her to wedge a pillow more firmly behind her back.

"No. Joe, do you know?"

He shook his head. "I don't know that it matters now. If they let me take him, I can just drive him home."

"His car is at Henry's, isn't it?"

"I seem to remember him saying he'd have it towed there, but I could be wrong," Amanda told them. "I'm a little fuzzy on some of it."

"You're not wrong," Joe said. "I wonder if it will run. No sense going all the way out east of Strasburg if I can just take him to Henry's and he can drive home."

"Call over and ask him," Sarah said. "He's probably out in the barn anyway."

"Naw, I'll just drive over there. It's on the way home. Say, Sarah, I wonder if I might talk something over with you?"

"Of course." She tried to hide her surprise. Joe and Simon might be best friends, and Joe might even have done Simon a wonderful turn by treating his injured foot out in Colorado, but the young man was not in the habit of coming to her for advice. But yet there was really only one subject that they had in common, besides a mutual affection for Priscilla Mast. A subject that she'd wondered about more than once. "If you're going to Henry's, maybe you wouldn't mind dropping me at my mailbox. We could talk on the way."

He nodded. "Whenever you're ready. Maybe you could write out the name of that cream so I don't get it mixed up. Glad you're in good hands, Amanda. I'll see you tomorrow."

They could call a driver and go to Whinburg and back in an hour. But maybe it was better this way. Joe was just that kind of boy—putting himself in the place of a servant for Amanda and finding a way to help that rapscallion Jesse, even though he was under no obligation to do either.

After he went outside, she kissed Amanda and said good-bye to Corinne, promising to come back that evening to have another look at Amanda's chest. Joe had already turned his buggy around and was waiting, his gaze fixed on something out past the spruce hedge.

She climbed in, and the tilt of the buggy under her weight brought him back to earth. "What was it you wanted to talk with me about?"

He flapped the reins and the horse set off. "I was wondering about how a person gets started doctoring. What he would have to know first. Whether you thought I might be the right kind of man for it."

She'd been right. Ever since Simon's injury, some part of her had been waiting for this conversation. Joy bubbled up inside as she considered what he'd asked. "The question is not whether I think you're able, but whether God does," she said gently. "Have you prayed about it?"

He nodded. "But a dove hasn't come out of the sky with an olive branch in its beak or anything."

"That's because olives don't grow here."

He chuckled. "Or with a dock leaf, either. But it's been on my mind a lot, so I thought I would talk it over with you. Priscilla was supposed to come with me, but..." His voice trailed away.

"Did she have to work? It's Monday."

"Naw. Ginny's out of town so the Inn is closed. No, she—" Now his throat closed up and he swallowed.

Sarah took careful note of a body that couldn't speak of the pain that was obvious in his eyes. "Joe," she said, hoping she wasn't treading on sacred ground, "has something gone wrong between you and Priscilla?"

His face crumpled and the reins went slack in his hands. His animal slowed and tossed its head, uncertain what he wanted, and Joe visibly forced himself to focus on the road. "She ain't—we ain't—" But the words still wouldn't come out.

He stopped the buggy at the end of her lane and hung his head, as though his whole body were curling around some pain.

"Will you come in? We can talk in my compiling room and I could show you a few things."

He shook his head. "Simon's home."

"Well, sure he's home. He hasn't found work yet, but if he doesn't soon, I'm going to find some for him. Why would—"

And then an overheard conversation from days ago added itself to the equation, and the answer became clear. "Oh, Joe. Did Simon do something? Is that what's wrong between you and Pris?"

He drew a long, shuddering breath. "Don't aim to burden you with my troubles. I'll come another day, Sarah, if that's all right."

"He'll still be here," she pointed out. "He's interfering between the two of you, isn't he?"

A shrug. "Not interfering. Maybe giving Priscilla what she really wants. I came to see you before I came over to Yoders', and" —a breath, then, in a rush— "saw him kissing her."

"Oh, my word." Sarah's hand drifted to her mouth, as though some part of her wanted to stop this conversation— to stop adding to Joe's pain. "But she doesn't care for him, Joe. Not the way she cares for you. I know it."

"They were kissing. She said it only lasted for a second and she pushed him away, and maybe that's so, but still. A kiss is a kiss."

"So you talked with her?" This was unusual. Sarah couldn't think of too many teenage misunderstandings that were hashed out in a reasonable conversation. In her experience and that of her sisters, it meant silence and tears and long walks in fields...until the one came along that meant so much to you that even a misunderstanding wasn't enough to keep you apart.

"*Ja.* Just in the drive there, before I went in to see Amanda. She came after me and met me halfway down."

"I think you should cling to that. Maybe she's willing to meet you halfway in other, more important ways."

"I don't want her to do that. If she wants your boy and he wants her, I'm not going to stand in the road."

"The trouble is, much as I love my boy, he has his faults. And one of them is pride. I'm not talking behind his back— he knows it as well as I do. He thinks that all he has to do to win Priscilla's heart is crook his finger and smile at her."

"She was sweet on him for a long time before she decided to stop trying. That's when I saw my chance. Guess I jumped too soon."

"Priscilla has grown a lot since the spring. Over the summer, while she was writing to you, even I could see it." Oh, if only hearts could have a healing salve applied to them to ease the ache! But maybe there was something words could do. "Joe," Sarah said earnestly, "if she says she would rather be with you than Simon, I think you should believe her. Sure, you're both young. But God doesn't take age into account when He purposes two people for each other. It's your hearts that matter."

He nodded, his eyes on the reins between his fingers. "What if Simon keeps chasing her?"

"Remember what I said about pride? The one thing it can't stand up to is the truth. And if Pris truly cares about you and goes out of her way to show it, then Simon will admit he's barking up the wrong tree. I know my boy. I've seen it before, in other ways."

Overcoming pride was one of the hardest lessons the human heart had to learn. But Joe had the opposite battle, it seemed.

"The Lord knows best," she said. "Don't you think that if He can bring the sea together with the land, and earth together with the roots of plants that need it, He can bring together two hearts that are right for one another?"

"*Ja*," Joe said reluctantly.

"I don't think Simon has a chance, personally," she said with a gentle smile. "He is my son and I love him dearly, but even I can see that he and Priscilla wouldn't be the pair that you and she are."

"How do you know?"

"Because she's the laughing water and you're the creek bank that holds her and keeps her safe."

He gave her a sidelong glance. "Have you been reading library books?"

"Only herbals." She smiled at her own flight of fancy. But it was the truth. "If Henry can see glaze colors in nature, then I'm allowed to see people in nature, too." And why had she brought him into this? She corrected her course quickly. "You just think about it. And as for the other, I can tell you this—I was no more ready to be a *Dokterfraa* when Ruth approached me than you are. Less ready, probably, since at least you came up with the idea yourself, and did something about it. I ran away from it for days until God convinced me it was the path He wanted me on. You're going to Whinburg for Amanda's cream and to see Jesse tomorrow, but next week, why don't you come with me to Ruth's? If you survive one lesson with her, you'll know whether you want to do this and whether it's a calling...or just a good idea."

Again, he nodded, but his back had straightened, and he gazed out the windscreen at the horse instead of at his feet. Maybe he was just being brave, or maybe his heart really was responding to encouragement, like a plant unfurling under the sun.

"I'll get out here," she said. "You do some thinking tomorrow on your way. And some praying, too."

❧

Dear Sarah,

I am so delighted to have your letter that as soon as I finish this, I'm going to drive into town to post it at the post office instead of waiting for Monday's mail.

You will be glad to hear that the cell tower is well, and by this month I can actually see where I might get my mortgage paid in this lifetime. So I am very grateful for the Lord's provision in this matter.

I hope your boys are well. I am glad to hear via Zeke and Fannie that Simon is safely home. He will want to take up a career and get himself settled. Does he have a talent for mechanical devices? Maybe he might do as Eli Fischer does in Whinburg, and convert tools to hydraulic power. Or work for an outfit that does. That seems to be satisfying work that would be of service to the church community.

I have been invited to my cousin's daughter's wedding in Oakfield, just a few miles north of you, on November 10. I wonder if Joshua and Miriam might have room for a visitor afterward for a day or two. I hope you will write and let me know if that sounds like a good idea to you.

I think of you often. I have even checked a few books on herbs out of the library so that I can identify the plants growing in my fields here. I look forward to talking with you about them, and especially about this little one that I pressed and enclose herewith. I can't tell what it is and hope that maybe you can.

I will close for now. I am invited over to a neighbor's for dinner, but with six daughters ranging in age from eight to twenty-eight, at least I won't be required to talk much.

Your friend,
Silas

Chapter 20

The new pieces, delicate greenware ready to be glazed, sat on the shelf that Henry had built especially for this purpose. It had a thin layer of foam on which the pieces sat, and in front was a barrier of foam on a narrow board, just in case the shelving unit got bumped and something wobbled enough to fall against it.

Henry was taking no chances with these pieces.

The Thanksgiving display would lead straight into the Christmas season—which Dave Petersen had told him was their highest selling period of the year. "Even better than Mother's Day for high-end housewares," he said in one of their calls. "I predict you'll sell out, and then you can command even higher prices. It's all about what the market will bear, Henry. Just remember that when you start feeling Amish and modest."

Feeling Amish was not going to be a problem, he kept telling himself. Once he and Ginny were married, he would never have to feel Amish again.

He flexed his hands, newly bandaged this morning, and now speckled with dried bits of glaze. He had been experimenting with the burnt siennas and golds for the pumpkin pitcher and, from the test mugs he'd fired, thought he might have the perfect combination. The sky and water glaze he had developed earlier in the summer had been expanded to include several more variations in the color spectrum. This pumpkin pitcher would be the proof in the pudding, and he could hardly wait to see how it turned out.

Henry was deeply thankful for the pressure of perfection, and for the workload of pieces to prepare. It kept him from thinking of the gentle touch of Sarah's hands, and the huskiness of her voice as she exposed her deepest feelings to him—feelings he had to shut down and close away and flee from, like Joseph from Potiphar's wife. Even the memory of her emotion had to go; otherwise, he'd have a quiet breakdown right here in his silent studio.

He was promised to Ginny, and that was that. He needed Ginny. She was his path to peace, his relief from the silent prayers that he knew his family all around him were sending up to God, urging the Lord to bring the prodigal back. He could feel it in the air, like the pressure before a thunderstorm. Once he and Ginny were married, those prayers would dissipate and be blown away on the winter wind, and he would be able to breathe again.

Live again. Love again.

Ginny was due back tonight, though they'd found her dress yesterday and she could have come home. "My lips are sealed," she'd told him when she'd called to say she was going to stay and do some power visiting. "You're not going to see it until December twelfth, but I'll just say this—it's tea length and classy, and I even found a little hat with a veil that sets it off perfectly."

Henry had no idea what tea length was, but one thing was completely obvious. "You'll be the prettiest bride in Lancaster County."

She had laughed. "Since most of my competition is Amish? What's that about?"

"None of them hold a candle to you, Amish or not."

She had hung up laughing, and even now, he smiled as he remembered the sound of it.

When the phone rang, his first thought was that it was Ginny, so he was still smiling as he answered.

"Henry, it's Dave Petersen. How are you?"

Not Ginny. Business. He roped his thoughts into order. "I'm well, thanks. Just getting ready to start the glaze. I'm excited about these pieces, Dave—I haven't felt this way about my work in years. Ever since that breakthrough with the sky and water glaze, I've been on this creative roll that—"

"That's great, Henry. I'm glad to hear it. But what I'm really calling about is much more down to earth. Like, our promotion plan for your pieces. Can we talk about that?"

Heat prickled in his cheeks. Good thing he didn't have one of those cell phones that showed the speaker's face. He'd forgotten Dave probably didn't have time for rhapsodizing about the creative process. "Sure," he managed past his chagrin.

"So I've been chatting with our corporate counsel over the last couple of days."

For a moment Henry couldn't figure out what that had to do with him, and then he remembered. *Shunning Amish.* Good grief—had Dave really been serious about taking it to the lawyers? "Yes?"

"Have you thought any more about taking up TNC's offer?"

"No," he said truthfully. Once the dust had settled from the departure of Dave and Matt Alvarez, he hadn't wasted a single neuron more on it. Everything had been focused on his life—his hands healing up, Sarah, Ginny, the pieces—

"Well, lawyers being what they are, it took a little while to get plain English out of them, but the upshot is, Henry, that you pretty much have to do the show, per your contract."

Henry closed his eyes as a bolt of cold adrenaline shot through his body from head to foot. It took a second before he was able to speak. "How's that, Dave?"

"I checked the contract language, and it says 'every reasonable effort shall be made to promote.' Every reasonable effort, Henry. TNC is willing to come to you. You don't have to travel. You get final approval over the rough cut. They're willing to work with you in any way that gets this episode made. I think that's pretty reasonable, don't you?"

"Maybe," Henry allowed. "But I'm not working on a logistical level. I'm working on a moral level—the level of what will happen to my friends and family when this comes out. This is supposed to be reality TV, and you said yourself that good news doesn't sell. No matter what I say on camera, they're going to twist it so that some kind of exposé is the end product. I just can't do it and live with my conscience."

"Now, see, there's where you're wrong. You're projecting your own fears on the segment that have no basis in reality. How do you know what the final product will be before it's even made? This is all negative thinking and imagination, with no basis in fact."

"The previous episodes are fact. They're reality. I wonder how the families of those girls who did the quilting feel?"

"Now you're just speculating," Dave said impatiently. "Look. Here's the deal. The legal eagles say that if you're not willing to fulfill the terms of the contract, then Frith isn't obligated to fulfill the order for your pieces. And that means the Christmas spread."

Cold prickled anew over Henry's skin, as though hundreds of bits of hail were striking him all at once. "But I've just finished the prototypes and bought the ingredients for the glazes for those pieces. And you probably already have inquiries about some of them."

"We'll hold up our side for the Thanksgiving pieces, since the catalogs have gone out and we have to fulfill those orders. But the big splash we were planning for Christmas? That's up in the air unless you're willing to do this."

Silence fell as Henry looked at the Thanksgiving and Christmas pieces—weeks of work sitting on the shelves, ready for glazing. At the cartons of clay beyond, in the remodeled stalls, that meant a change in his financial circumstances—that would mean everything to him and Ginny in the months ahead.

Financial security and commercial recognition—the two things he had been working for since he was nineteen—balanced against the feelings of Paul and Barbara Byler, of Sarah and Caleb, of the Yoders, even of Joe and Priscilla. His gaze fell on Jesse Riehl's car, sitting in front of the old hayloft doors, where the tow truck driver had left it on Sunday. What would the camera crew make of that, if it was still here when they came? Would poor Jesse be the next scandal they pursued? Would Whinburg Township be fertile ground for them to plow if he opened the gate and let them in?

But all this work...he dragged his gaze back inside. All this *work*. Where would he sell it if not at Frith?

"Henry? You there?"

"How much time do I have to make a decision?" Henry

asked, his mouth dry, his insides heaving. "I have to talk this over with my fiancée, and she's not back until tonight."

"Let's see. Today's Tuesday. How about Friday? TNC is ready to go to contract. You greenlight this on Friday, the contracts will be on your doorstep by Monday, holiday or not. Matt told me so himself."

"Fine. Friday."

"Great! I know you'll do the right thing for your career, Henry, and I look—"

But Henry never heard the rest of the sentence. He hung up the phone and leaned his forehead on the old wood of the barn door, as though it were the shoulder of a friend.

The comforting silence of the barn settled around him. His Dat's special place had been the barn, where the family was always welcome, of course, but where he ruled supreme. Henry's sisters and brother would run through the milking parlor, or play hide and seek in the hayloft, but in the end, when Dat said it was time to stop playing and help him, they obeyed without question. And when they were all in the house doing schoolwork or reading, Henry knew that Dat would be out there, happily mending or raking or hosing down, as at home in the solitude of his work as he was in the front room with his family for the nightly Bible verses.

With a sigh, Henry pushed himself off the solidity of the door. It was no surprise he was thinking about his father. What would Dat have said about *Shunning Amish*? Probably the same thing Henry did—that it was ninety percent lies and ten percent imagination. But weren't lies and imagination responsible for much of the damage people could do to one another?

Outside, a sound intruded on his wish that, for the first time in decades, he could talk something over with his father—even if all he told him was that Henry would have to pray about it and do as God prompted him. After a moment, he recognized the sound as hooves and metal wheels on gravel, which meant an Amish vehicle.

That was a relief. So far, most of the *Englisch* vehicles that had come up his lane had meant bad news.

He stepped outside and Joe Byler drew up his horse at the rail. "Hey, Henry."

"Hi, Joe." He looked more closely. "Have you been to Whinburg and back already? Is that Jesse Riehl in the buggy with you?"

"*Ja* to both. But if you were hoping he might get his car out of your yard, you might have to wait a little."

"Yeah? I checked it out and it starts. He's going to have to pull the metal fender out of the front tire and pound it back into shape, then replace the tire, but once he does that, if he sticks to the back roads, he should be okay to drive to his aunt and uncle's, at least. If he can't do all that today, no problem. I don't expect him to if you've just sprung him from the hospital."

Joe wasn't tying up his horse. Rather, he stood by the passenger door and gazed at Henry over the horse's harness. "Mind if we go down to the house? Jesse here is about done in."

As if to illustrate the words, Jesse slumped suddenly against the window, as if he couldn't hold himself upright another second.

"Maybe they shouldn't have sprung him," Henry said in sudden alarm. "I can get him back to the hospital in half an hour."

"No," came from inside the buggy.

Clearly this wasn't going to be resolved standing here in

the yard, and the wind was kicking up as though the clouds moving back in meant business. "All right. Take him down to the house and I'll meet you there. And tie your animal up under the cedar tree. I don't have accommodations for him in the barn anymore, but he and the buggy should stay about half dry if it rains."

It looked like his plans for glazing would have to wait until tomorrow. Between this and Ginny's return this evening, the hours of solitude he needed to concentrate just weren't going to happen.

When he got down to the house, Joe had Jesse on the sofa with his feet up and his head on a patchwork pillow, and was filling a glass at the kitchen faucet. "He's kind of woozy," was the succinct diagnosis. "Even if that car worked, I wouldn't trust him to drive."

"Good call."

Jesse rolled his head toward Joe and accepted the glass. "Good meds, man," he said. "I never had industrial-strength ibuprofen before." His gaze rose to Henry as he drank. "I know you."

Henry nodded. "I was there when the ambulance came for you. I brought Amanda's parents to see her, and then dropped in to see you. I'm surprised you remembered."

"Thank you," the boy said. "For doing that."

"It was no trouble. I live practically next door to Amanda." He pointed over his shoulder in the direction of the Yoder farm. "But the question is, what are we going to do with you?"

"About that," Joe put in, folding himself into the stiffly upholstered chair that Henry remembered his uncle avoiding because it was so uncomfortable. One of these days he'd get rid of it. Maybe he should turn Ginny loose in here and see what she could do with the place. Maybe he should call her and ask her to speed up her return.

Henry marshaled his thoughts back to the immediate problem and waited for Joe to go on.

"After I picked up Amanda's cream, I went straight to the hospital and found the sheriff in Jesse's room."

"Joe," groaned the other boy.

But Joe kept going, the way he probably kept his hand to the plow no matter what the mules wanted to do. "Looks like the address on his driver's license ain't quite right, since no Mennonite couple by the name of Riehl live there anymore."

"Why would that bring the sheriff out?" Henry asked.

"Oh, he was just curious, I guess, since he wanted to let them know their nephew was all right and couldn't find anyone to tell. Turns out Jesse's actual current address is probably your yard right here."

It took Henry a second to understand what Joe meant. Then he turned to look at Jesse, who now had one arm over his face. "Are you homeless? Have you been *living* in that car?"

Mumble.

"Jesse, quit hiding and talk to me like a responsible man who would ask a nice girl like Amanda to go riding with him. Does she know you lied about your situation?"

"No."

"Does she know any of this?"

"No. And she doesn't need to. I'm not going to show my face in this district again." He struggled to sit up. "I'll just go."

Henry sighed and pushed him back down with one hand, which was as easy as petting a kitten. "Simmer down. Nobody's making you go, and even if your car was drivable, we wouldn't let you anyway. With your luck, you'd run off the road before you'd gone a mile and the outcome might be worse this time."

"If you don't want him here, he could come home with me," Joe suggested. "As long as the car stays here, Mamm and Dat will be glad to look after him."

The thought of telling an injured boy he didn't want him there made Henry a little ill. Here was a problem he could solve with what he had on hand. Yes, it was inconvenient, but it would be a whole lot more inconvenient to poor Jesse if he turned him out. "Looks to me like he needs to sleep for about a week, and he'd get nothing but peace and quiet here. I've got a spare room and Sarah is just over the hill. I'd feel better if he was handy to my car, in case I have to get him back to the hospital, or over to her. Jesse, are you okay with that?"

But there was no answer. The poor kid was already sacked out, his face pale and drawn and his long, gangly limbs loose on the old cushions.

"There's our answer," Joe said. "Wonder how long he's been living in that old thing."

"Do we know where his family actually is?"

Joe shook his head. "But I can find out. There are Riehls here, too, and they all seem to be related."

"You do that. Meanwhile, I'll see Sarah about something to put on Jesse's black eye."

"And he'll probably have bruises from the seat belt, like Amanda."

Henry realized with a jolt of alarm that he had just committed to do the very thing he'd sworn not to do—see Sarah again. Well, for the sake of this beat-up kid on his couch, he'd do what was necessary. Keep things businesslike. And get out of there as fast as he could.

"Thanks, Joe. Among all of us, we'll see he's looked after—
and maybe talk some sense into him as well."

The corners of Joe's mouth tipped up. "Going home to his
parents can't be as bad as living in a car. I wonder how he's
been feeding himself."

"Odd jobs and kindness?"

"Maybe I'll ask Mamm to make extra for dinner and bring
you fellows over a couple of plates."

"That would be kind of you, Joe, but don't trouble your
mother. I'm sure I can hunt up something around here."

"It ain't no trouble. You're family," he said simply.

It was all Henry could do to keep the smile steady on his
face. How on earth could he go on television and tell the
world what had compelled him to leave the church when the
reality was that, because of the people living here in Willow
Creek, he had never been happier?

Chapter 21

With the days so short now, Caleb was getting home from the construction site earlier, which meant Sarah started dinner around four o'clock. She liked to have everything ready when he came through the door, hungry as a hunter. Simon had spent yesterday and today turning over the last remains of her quilt garden, and tomorrow he'd sow the silage radishes that would provide a natural fertilizer when they in turn got turned under in February.

Now that winter was coming on, construction jobs would be few and far between, even for someone already on a crew like Caleb. She was going to have a gentle but firm talk with Simon on the subject of idleness. Even if all he did was walk over to milk his grandfather's cows morning and evening, she'd be satisfied, but he had to keep his hands busy somehow, or the devil would.

She checked the sausage and potato casserole in the oven. *Gut*, it was coming along nicely. With some creamed corn, pickles, and chunky applesauce and bread, her boys would have a good meal to fuel their strong young bodies.

She was just wondering what she'd done with her sweater before she went outside to see if she could spot one of them, when a knock sounded on the back door. "Come in," she called. Ah, there it was, over the arm of the sofa. Her guest was probably Corinne, coming to tell her Joe had brought the Traumeel cream for Amanda. Maybe there was news of Jesse, too. "Memm, is that—"

She stopped in the kitchen doorway at the sight of Henry, standing with his hands in the pockets of his jacket, his head tipped back. Was he...breathing?

"Henry?"

His eyes opened and he smiled a friendly smile. "Whatever you've got going in that oven smells great."

"It's sausage and potato casserole. Would you like to stay and have some?" The invitation was automatic. Hospitable. Utterly foolish. That was the trouble with being surprised. Things came out of your mouth before you had the chance to reason them away.

"No, but thanks all the same. You'll never believe who I've got on my front room sofa."

She ran through the short list of possibilities. "Jesse Riehl?"

"Good guess."

"What is he doing there? Is he all right? Why hasn't he gone home by now?"

"Well, that's just the trouble. Seems the address he gave isn't current, no one related to him lives there, and he's been living out of his car for who knows how long. So for the moment, he's going to stay with me. I came to see if you had a salve that might help a black eye and some bruising. He's had ibuprofen, but he seems kind of out of it so I don't know if it's doing any good. Looks like the hospital was more concerned about the possible concussion than they were about the rest of him. Joe Byler says that Amanda took a beating from the seat belt, and I imagine Jesse did, too."

Goodness. Whatever next? A hundred questions crowded the tip of her tongue, but she bit them back and focused on the important thing. A young man needed help, and she had help to give. "I do, *ja*. I'll give you a jar of the same thing I left for Amanda. But just so you know, you could have used the balm of Gilead on him."

"I'll remember that the next time an accident victim lands on my couch."

"Come into the compiling room while I fill a jar for you. How did you find out there was no one living at the address he gave? And if they aren't there, where are they?"

"The sheriff went over there, I guess, or tried to call, and found out. And who knows what happened to the aunt and uncle—if they even existed." Henry leaned on the door frame and watched her get down a clean half-pint jar and the larger tub of the salve. "Joe's going to try to track someone down through the family in this district."

"Ah." There were Riehls over by the Peachey place, whose family was so large and spread out it wouldn't surprise her if they knew Jesse's connections. "He'll likely find what he needs to know before the sheriff will."

"He's Amish. Everybody knows you start with the family." Henry smiled, and Sarah concentrated on what her hands were doing before her heart clutched and gave her away. "On a different subject, do you have a second to talk?"

Oh dear. About cures, yes. About anything remotely personal? If he said a single word about how she had thrown herself at him and how he had reminded her quite rightly that he belonged to someone else, she would run from the room in shame.

Maybe she would anyway.

"The boys will be home soon," she finally managed, do-

ing her best to sound as though she had a thousand things
to do.

"This won't take long," he said. "It might even be a yes or
no answer." He stepped all the way into the room and stood
in front of her little white-painted bookcase filled with a
growing library of herbals, along with a cookbook or two that
Corinne had donated that focused on cooking with herbs and
included a surprising amount of information about tempera-
tures and how they affected various plants as they cooked.

Finally, it seemed, among all those words on the shelves,
he found the ones for the question he wanted to ask. "You
remember I told you about this TV program that D.W. Frith
wants me to be on?"

"*Ja.* The shunning one."

"Right. *Shunning Amish*, it's called. Tell me honestly,
Sarah…how do you think folks around here will feel if I do
the program?"

"The Amish folks, you mean?"

"Yes. You, the boys, the Yoders, Paul and Barbara. The
folks I know."

Now she wished she had some of those words herself.
"Why, I hardly know. I suppose you would have to ask the
others."

"And what about you?"

"I think you already know how I would feel. I don't think
it's profitable to dwell on the past. Even less to tell the
world about it, so that they have a view of us that's distorted
through an unhappy young man's eyes, like looking through
those old glass windows in Jacob's hay barn."

"But what if I said good things?" The low tone in his voice
almost sounded desperate. What was going on behind these
questions? Why did her answers matter?

"If you had only good things to say, Henry, they would wonder why you left the church at all," she replied quietly.

He let out a long breath. "I guess if I wanted someone to make me feel good about this, I shouldn't have come here." His mouth canted up on one side, as if he were laughing at himself.

"But why do you care what I or any of your neighbors think? It's none of our business what you do." She screwed the lid on the jar she'd managed to fill without spilling. This would help on Jesse's outside. But what was going on in his inside? He'd had ibuprofen, and yet he was "out of it." That didn't sound right.

Henry began to speak, and she snapped her attention back to him. "Because the store has threatened to cancel the order for the Christmas pieces if I don't do it," he said. "There's something in the contract that says I have to do reasonable promotion. And apparently, spilling my guts about my past is what they consider reasonable."

Ah. She released a long breath. Now she was beginning to understand the tension behind these questions. "So your livelihood depends on doing this? That seems dangerous." She wasn't sure how he would take it, but it had to be said. "You might do better not dealing with these people at all, if they're going to force you to do things as silly as this program. Things that go against what you think is right."

"That's one option, all right," he admitted. "Not the greatest one. It puts me back at Plan A, which is selling pieces at the Amish Market in summer, and doing goodness knows what in the winter. Making mugs for restaurants, I guess."

"Is that so bad?" It sounded perfectly reasonable to her. "Do you want so many people to know about and admire your pieces, even when it could cause harm to others?"

Which maybe wasn't the smartest thing to say to a man who was obviously already torn on the matter. "I'm sorry, Henry, I shouldn't have said that."

"Why not say exactly what you think? That's what I came here for, and you've never failed to deliver before."

She bowed her head, uncomfortably aware that he was right—her tongue did run away with her. Here she was, doing it again—poking her nose in where it didn't belong and giving advice before she prayed for the words in season. When was she going to learn?

"Sarah, don't look like that. I only meant that I value your opinion. You never whitewash it, you never play games. I may not like it, but I appreciate it. Does that make sense?"

He was not angry with her for not showing him humility. Her heart expanded a little in relief. She would still have to approach *der Herr* later and ask for His forgiveness and guidance, though. "What does Ginny say about all this?"

"I'm going to talk to her about it later tonight, after she's home. Because whatever I do, it's going to affect both of us."

Struck speechless after this reminder, she wiped off the small jar of salve and handed it to him.

"What do I owe you?"

She must not show how she felt. So she said the first thing that came into her head. "I could use one or two of those mugs you were talking about."

"Done. Thanks, Sarah. For the salve, and for the talking-to."

But she could no longer ignore the prompting of the still, small voice—the tiny anxiety that fluttered behind her breastbone. "Henry, something is bothering me about what Jesse said. About the ibuprofen. It doesn't sound right."

One eyebrow rose in surprise. "He did say he'd never had it before."

"I wonder..." She thought quickly, then plucked a book from the shelf and paged through it until she found what she wanted. "I know it's an imposition...but would you mind if I came to see him? Does he have a rash?"

"I didn't think to look. All I saw was bruises. But he doesn't feel good, I'll tell you that."

"I have the ingredients for a tea here that might help. I wonder if he might be allergic to ibuprofen. If he is, this might balance out his system and help him absorb it better."

"It's no imposition. But your boys are due home any second, aren't they?"

Did he not want her to come? Was this his way of giving her a graceful way out? But she couldn't ignore the urge inside any more than she could a pang of hunger. "I'll turn off the oven and leave them a note. The casserole won't suffer, and I don't feel right leaving this until later."

Swiftly, she gathered what she needed and filled her basket. Then she turned off the oven and put a lid on the corn so it wouldn't dry out, scribbled a note, and followed Henry out. There was just enough light to see them over the hill.

"I'll start a fire," Henry said as he let her precede him into the house. "I should have thought of it before, but it was kind of an upside-down day."

"And I'll need to boil some water for these twigs."

While he busied himself with wood and kindling in the old-fashioned woodstove that marked the dividing line between kitchen and front room and heated the entire house, as Sarah remembered from coming here for church, she got the water going on the kitchen stove and then turned to her new patient.

"Hallo, Jesse, *wie geht's?*"

But the eyes he turned to her were half closed and he was far paler than a young man ought to be. Restlessly, he scratched at his arms through his torn shirt. "Who are you?" he asked.

"I'm Sarah." She reached into the basket for the salve she had prepared. "I'm going to give you some medicine."

"Don't need it."

"Yes, you do. You seem to be allergic to whatever they gave you at the hospital, so I'm going to give you something to counteract it. But before I do that, I'm going to attend to your bruises and that rash you've got going."

"Don't want any more."

Henry closed the door on the fire just beginning to leap in the stove, and joined them. "Sarah is a *Dokterfraa* and you'll do as she says."

She could have handled Jesse, even if it had meant wedging his jaws open with the spoon and pouring the tea down his throat. She was not the mother of two teenage boys for nothing. But not for the first time, she was grateful that Henry's first instinct was to back her up—to demand obedience on her behalf when hers was the place of authority.

His gaze sliding between her and Henry, Jesse nodded. She unbuttoned his shirt and frowned in distress at the bruises spreading in a pattern similar to those on Amanda's chest. "Joe said you might have a broken rib, Jesse. Is that what the doctor said?" His ribs didn't seem to be wrapped. He just looked as though a cow had used him for a welcome mat.

"No broken ribs," the boy managed. "But it sure feels like it."

When she had compiled the tea, she propped up his head

and let him drink it slowly. He swallowed and made a face. "What is this?"

"This is called Mormon tea, with some coneflower and agrimony to settle your stomach. Come now. I want you to drink half of this mug now, and the other half in an hour. And some more in the morning."

Unwillingly, he swallowed. "Yuck. Did you give this to Amanda?"

"No, but if she had needed it, I would have." Her tone was soothing. "It will make you feel better. I'm using this salve I'm going to put on you on Amanda's bruises, though, so you'll have someone to keep you company in your misery."

Along with the bruising, there was the allergy rash on his arms. As gently as she could, she massaged the salve into his chest, shoulder, and ribs, and dabbed it on the rash. When she was finished, she glanced at Henry. "Can we move him to a bed, do you think?"

"We can try." Jesse tried to sit up, and between the two of them, they got him into Sadie's old room at the rear of the house and into bed. Henry pulled off his jeans, and took the sorry garments out to the kitchen when Sarah sat next to Jesse to dab more salve on the rash on the boy's legs.

"I'll wash those and mend the shirt," she said to Henry when she came out of the bedroom, and joined him on the sofa. The woodstove was going now, and the room warming up. "He can't go around in these pants—look, they're stained with blood." She rolled up the jeans and tucked them into the basket. "I hate to ask this, but can you check on him at least once during the night, and give him another half mug of the tea? It doesn't matter if it's cold."

"Sure," he said, nodding. "Ten to one I won't be able to

sleep much anyway, what with thinking over this TV thing and listening for him to fall out of bed."

With a smile, she said, "Hopefully he won't do that. Like Amanda, he needs rest. I wonder if tomorrow we might take him over to Corinne's. She's already worried about him, and it might make her feel better to nurse both of them."

"Joe offered, too. At this rate, the kid will be adopted by somebody."

"I hope so. The poor boy, cut off from his family and hurt. At least when Simon got hurt, he knew he could turn to us, whether we were a thousand miles away or not. I wonder who Jesse turns to."

"If he didn't know before, I'm sure he knows now," Henry said in a gentle tone that told her the sooner she got out of his front room, the better.

Quick steps sounded on the front porch, and then came a rapid knock. Both of them jumped at the unexpected sound, and before Henry could open the door himself, Ginny whirled in, bringing a gust of cold air with her.

"Henry!" She bounced across the room and threw herself into his arms, giving him a smacking kiss on the mouth that Sarah could hear on the other side of the room.

"Well, hey, you," he said, glancing over her hair at Sarah. "Why didn't you call me? I'd have come over."

"Haven't been home yet." She kissed him again. "I couldn't wait to see my man and tell him all about my adventures. Except for the dress. Mum's the word about that."

"Ginny—"

"But I found a great pair of shoes and saw about a hundred relatives, all of whom want to come this time because they couldn't come last time."

"Gin—"

"And Mom and Daddy wanted me to tell you that you're not to worry about paying for everything, because since they kinda got left out last time, they want to chip in."

Sarah couldn't stay silent another second, listening to a conversation that was none of her business. And if she had to see another kiss, she'd probably start to cry, and that would be disastrous.

"It all sounds wonderful," she said, surging off the sofa and crossing the room, hands outstretched. "I don't want to intrude anymore, and you'll have lots of news to tell each other, so I'll be on my way."

Ginny's eyes rounded as she turned in Henry's embrace. His arms fell away as she shook Sarah's hand automatically. "Sarah? I'm sorry—I didn't see you. I—where did you come from?"

"I've just been treating Jesse Riehl."

"I'm sorry—who?"

Henry cleared his throat. "Jesse, the boy who ran his car into a guard rail over a cattle culvert on Sunday. Remember, I told you about him?"

"Vaguely." Her brows wrinkled. "But what does that have to do with—wait. He's here?"

Sarah nodded. "In Sadie's old room, down the hall. I just treated him with a salve for some pretty awful bruising, and had just asked Henry if he would give him another dose of this"—she held up the mug—"sometime in the night."

"Is there a reason this boy isn't in the hospital?" Ginny asked.

"He was just released today. Joe brought him back here in the buggy because his car is here. The kid is homeless, Ginny. Sarah and I were just talking over what to do with him when you came in."

"Sarah and you, huh?"

Her tone began to change, with just the slightest edge a woman got when her man paired his name with that of another, even in the most ordinary way. Sarah picked up her basket. The sooner she got out of here and they got back to kissing and exchanging news of wedding preparations, the better.

"I'd best get back to my own boys," she said, "or there won't be any sausage casserole left for me. It was nice to see you, Ginny. I'm glad your trip went well and you're safely home."

"Me, too," Ginny said, but by then Sarah was safely out the door.

CHAPTER 22

The Rose Arbor Inn on Wednesday was the quietest Priscilla had ever heard it. Not only were there no guests from the weekend to clean up after, but there was also no singing. No humming. And none of the usual chatter that would follow her "Good morning, Priscilla—isn't it a beautiful day?"

Come to think of it, Ginny hadn't even added that last part, which was really strange, because even when it was the dead of winter and snowing like mad, Ginny found something to appreciate about every new day.

Well, that was fine. Today Pris didn't feel much like looking for the good in a gray, rainy day like this, except that it would make the ground softer for people turning over their gardens.

She'd finished polishing Ginny's antique furniture in the public sitting room and was dusting the contents of the china breakfront when Ginny leaned in the doorway behind her. "Pris, when you're finished with the dusting, you may as well go on home. The rooms are all ready in case we get a booking, and I hate to keep you when you probably have a ton of stuff to do."

That was true. "I do. Evie Troyer says that I should make

a whole bunch of pot holders for the Amish Market's final weekend of the season. Lots of *Englisch* folks come from the cities to look at the fall colors and buy preserves and things. She says I could maybe make all my Christmas money in one weekend if I have enough stock."

"Then how about we just call this week a bust and you spend your time doing your sewing?"

"Are you sure?" Ginny's eyes looked tired, as though she hadn't slept much. "Are you feeling well?"

Half a smile quirked up one corner of Ginny's mouth. "Yes, I'm fine. Shopping takes a lot more out of me than it used to—especially a marathon like this past weekend. We tried on dresses at six stores over three days, can you believe it?"

"Did you find one?"

"Yes—the very first one I tried on turned out to be The One." She turned away and took a couple of steps across the hall to the guests' dining room. "I just hope I get a chance to wear it."

Pris must have misheard. She followed Ginny into the kitchen. "Sorry—I didn't catch what you said."

Ginny put on her oven mitts and opened the oven door. "Never mind. Man trouble. Want a pecan tart?"

A couple dozen were already cooling on the worktable. "I'd love one. After your sticky buns, these are my favorite."

"Exclusive to the Rose Arbor Inn." Ginny set the new batch to cool, piled a few cooled ones on a plate, and poured them each a glass of milk. When she sat opposite, she took a bite and then sighed. "You ever have man trouble, Pris?"

Priscilla gulped her milk and swallowed. "All the time. Which up until this summer I never would have thought I'd ever say. But most of it is my fault."

"Tell me."

So she did. About Simon, and how she'd liked him so much but he never saw her as more than a friend—until his friend did. About Joe, and how nice he was, and how badly she'd messed up in letting Simon kiss her. And even about Benny Peachey, who still had the nerve to make jokes about courting her, even though Joe was home and he'd seen them together.

Ginny licked the pad of her thumb and pressed it into the pastry crumbs to pick them up. "Sounds like you might be giving poor Benny a chance, then, huh?"

"No," Pris said bluntly, setting her empty glass aside. "He's too wild—even though most of it is just his silly jokes and horsing around. Joe is the one for me, and I spoiled it."

"There isn't another girl involved, though, is there? You don't have any competition?"

Pris shook her head, making her *Kapp* strings dance on her shoulders. She'd flipped the knot over her head to keep them out of the way while she cleaned. "Not yet. But Joe is so humble. He doesn't think he's worthy of me—when it's me that isn't worthy of him—and so to him, it's perfectly normal that I would choose someone else. Expected, even."

"Isn't that taking *Demut* a little too far?"

Pris sighed. "I don't know if it's *Demut* or if it's just the way he is."

"No self-esteem, you mean." When Pris nodded, Ginny said, "Have you talked with him about it?"

"Yes. And he just says that if I want Simon, I should date him. Which misses the point of me apologizing and wanting him, not Simon. It was just a silly little kiss. An experiment, almost," she said half despairingly. "The only boy I've ever kissed and meant it was Joe."

"Well, that's the thing," Ginny said thoughtfully. "With people, you can't experiment. You can't stay half on one side and half on the other. You have to go all in. Because if you don't, you haven't given the relationship a chance."

"Is that what you're doing?" Priscilla ventured. "With *Englisch* Henry Byler?"

"Is that what you folks call him?" Ginny's smile didn't hold the brightness it usually did.

"There are two other Henry Bylers in the district, but both of them are older."

"What happens if he decides to join church? What will you call him then?"

Now it was Pris's turn to smile. "I don't know. I suppose Amish Henry Byler wouldn't be very helpful, would it?" Ginny's face seemed to go still. Almost bleak. "Ginny? It was supposed to be a joke. Did I say something wrong?"

"No, honey." Ginny reached across the table to squeeze her hand. "I was just thinking, that's all. Look, here's my advice. You go find that boy of yours, sit him down, and give it to him straight. Tell him you're all in, if he is, and all this stuff about being worthy or not is all backward. God's love makes us all worthy, and our love for each other is all we've got in the end." Her lips trembled, and Priscilla held her breath. "But you gotta be all in. You tell him that."

Ginny pushed away from the table and walked into her private sitting room. The door closed quietly behind her.

After a minute, Pris finally thought to close her mouth, which was hanging open in astonishment. Then she got up, put the next batch of tarts in the oven, and set the timer for twelve minutes.

They both might be having man trouble, but that was no reason not to bake the tarts. Sometimes you needed more than philosophy to make something good out of a rainy day.

She tracked Joe down in, of all places, *Englisch* Henry's house, where he was sitting on the side of Jesse's bed trying to get him to drink some bitterly aromatic tea. Jesse looked relieved when Joe's surprise made him take the mug away. "What are you doing here?"

"Your mother said you were here. Hallo, Jesse."

Jesse croaked something that sounded like hallo.

"He's giving me trouble," Joe said. "Sarah says he's supposed to drink a cup in the daytime and a cup at night until the rash clears up."

"It's clearing up," Jesse managed to say, pushing himself up to a sitting position with a groan. "Between the salve and the tea and who knows what else she sent over, I'm either going to be dead from the accident or dead from the cure."

"You're not going to die," Joe said patiently.

"He sure isn't." Pris mustered up some cheer. "Crankiness is a sign that you're on the mend. If you were just lying there moaning, I'd be worried. Now, drink your tea before Joe holds your jaws open and I pour it in."

He must have seen something businesslike in her face, because he took the mug and gulped it down fast, so he wouldn't have to taste it.

"That's better."

"You take time off work to come over and see this guy?" Joe asked, taking the mug and getting off the bed.

"No, Ginny gave me the rest of the week off so I could make pot holders for the Amish Market. And I came to find you."

"Good," Jesse mumbled. "Take him away, please."

"How is he doing, really?" Pris asked once they were out

on the porch. It was still raining. Ginny had come out of her
sitting room when the timer had buzzed and taken the tarts
out, and had given her a ride home so she wouldn't have to
walk the two miles in the wet. But Mamm wouldn't hitch up
the buggy just to take her down the road to the Byler place,
so she had put on her gums and been thankful for whoever
had invented umbrellas.

Joe sat on the railing, and after a minute, Pris perched
there, too. The old-fashioned eave was deep enough that it
kept them both dry, and the whisper of the rain masked their
voices if there had been anyone around to hear them.

"He's better," Joe said. "The rash is going away and the
bruises are doing what they do—turning color. The salve
seems to be moving the process along faster, though. I wonder how it does that."

But Pris had not slogged all the way across three farms to
talk about rashes and salve. "I came to find you for a reason,"
she said.

"Everything okay?" His brown eyes lit with concern, and
his gaze ran over her as though he was checking whether she
needed some salve, too.

"*Ja*…everything but you and me."

Joe being Joe, he only looked at his hands, tapping restlessly as though they were looking for something to do.

Maybe it wasn't her place to be so forward. Maybe she
should just step back and wait for God's will to be revealed
to her. Or maybe this *was* God's will, and she should listen to
the urge in her chest that was telling her she needed to make
this right.

"I was wrong to let Simon kiss me," she said. "I know you
say you've forgiven me, but it's still not right between us."

"I got nothing against you, Pris," he said after a moment.

He knotted his fingers together, as if to still them. "I got nothing holding you back, either."

"That's just it." *Oh Lord, please give me the words.* "I don't want to go forward or back. I want to be with you. By your side." When he didn't reply, a cold chill settled in her stomach. "Unless...you don't want to be my special friend at all. That Simon's kissing me was just a good reason to break up."

"No."

"No, what? Talk to me, Joe," she begged. And then the words came to her, like a flock of butterflies landing all at once. "Because you know what? Not being ourselves together is no good for me. I want to be able to tell you things. I want to know that when we say our prayers at night, we're praying for each other. And most of all, I want to save my kisses for you...because to be quite honest, Simon isn't very good at it. And as for Benny Peachey, I'd sooner kiss a horse."

This made a smile flicker on his lips. "You're not supposed to kiss and tell, I hear."

"I'm not supposed to be this forward, either. I'm supposed to pay the price of my own foolishness and let you walk away."

"Seems like a heavy price for one kiss."

She hardly dared to hope that he might be hearing her—or at least, the words that seemed to be pouring out of her without let or hindrance. "I came all the way here to say that I'm all in, Joe. I know we're young and maybe God will take our lives in a different direction tomorrow or next month or next year, but for now, I choose you. And I hope that you'll choose me, too."

She slid off the rail. There was nothing else she could say, and maybe it was best to leave him to think it over before her mouth got going again and she spoiled it all.

"You going to go before I do what you asked?"

"What's that?"

"Talk to you."

"Oh. Well. *Neh*, not if you don't want me to." She seated herself again on the rail, facing him and swinging one foot in its ugly gumboot.

"I ain't very good with words," he said, his gaze dropping once more to his hands. "Not like you, in real life and in your letters. But I got feelings. And Pris, I can't tell you what it felt like to see you kissing him, whether you liked it or you didn't."

Miserably, she nodded, accepting responsibility once again for the wrong she'd done him.

"But me and Jesse, we were talking just before you came in. I was sort of trying to keep him distracted so I could get the Mormon tea down his throat. So I broke your confidence and told him a few things."

"All in the name of medicine," she said. "*Ischt okay.*"

"He doesn't know why Amanda came with him on Sunday. He doesn't even know if she likes him. But I think he likes her, and he doesn't have the first idea how to make all this up to her."

"Telling her the truth would be a good start."

"*Ja*, that's what I said. No girl wants to date a man who's got no family and even owns a car, never mind lives in it. And best I know, she doesn't know he's homeless yet."

"No family? But there are dozens of Riehls around here."

"I shouldn't be telling tales out of school, but his dad kicked him out when he took the driving test. The car came after, when he was working. He only gave the last address he knew of his aunt and uncle because you had to have that for the license."

"You mean he hasn't even seen them? Or knows where they live?"

He shrugged. "He's mixed up."

"I'll say."

"So I'm talking to him, and the more he tells me, the more I think that maybe one little kiss that you're sorry for isn't such a bad thing. I know how Simon is. How pride is. I ain't saying I've got none of that, because I probably have too much, but compared to the row Jesse's got to hoe, maybe I ought not to discount the blessings I have just because my feelings got hurt."

Relief trickled into her heart, then became a flood as he finally looked up into her face.

"Besides which, I don't want Benny Peachey *or* his horse swooping in when I'm not looking and taking you away."

She laughed, and it ended on a hitch of her breath. "I'm really sorry, Joe. For putting you through that. For causing you even a second of hurt feelings."

"That's all in the past now." And at last, he reached over and took her hand, pulling her closer to him. "From now on, it's you and me until the *gut Gott* tells us different."

And right there on *Englisch* Henry's front porch, he pulled her in close and kissed her... and it was like running up the steps and bursting in the kitchen door after a long, long time away.

Chapter 23

By Friday, Jesse was too restless to stay in bed, and Henry was too worried over his own concerns to keep him there. So he made breakfast for the two of them, and made sure he was out in the barn when Sarah came for her morning visit.

When Jesse limped through the open doors, Henry looked up from his glaze recipe book. "Everything all right?"

"Yeah, I guess. She didn't bring me any more of that tea, so I must be getting better. The rash is almost gone."

"Don't be tempted to take any more ibuprofen, though, even if you're in some pain. I don't think it's worth it."

Jesse huffed a laugh. "Sure isn't. I'm just going to have a look at my car, okay?"

"It's your car," Henry pointed out. "I don't have much in the way of tools, or much more in the way of knowledge about what goes on under the hood, but the toolbox is in the tack room if you need it. There's a hammer to pound out that fender, if nothing else."

"Thanks, Henry. For everything," Jesse said a little awkwardly. "I'll try and be out of here as fast as possible."

"Why? You don't take up a lot of room."

"I know, but it's an imposition. Your lady...Sarah..."

Henry looked up in alarm. "What?"

"Sarah. She and you—you're a thing, right?"

Where did an Amish boy get these expressions? "My *fiancée's* name is Ginny Hochstetler. Sarah is just my neighbor who happens to be a *Dokterfraa* and kind enough to look after you."

"Oh. Sorry. I thought—"

"Never mind." Time to change the subject. "Jesse, before you go outside...here's a weird question. Have you ever heard of a TV show called *Shunning Amish*?"

It took the boy a second or two to get the train of his thoughts onto this new and unexpected track. "Sure. I watched it a couple of times at this place."

A homeless shelter? A bar? Henry decided he probably didn't want to know. "What did you think of it?"

"I think that some of those people weren't even Amish. Some of them might have been, I guess. There were these girls that were quilting—I'm pretty sure they were. Why? Are you getting a TV so you can watch it?"

Henry snorted. "Not likely. No, they want me to be *on* it."

If he hadn't been leaning on the tack room door, the boy would probably have fallen right over. "On the show? Are you kidding me?"

"Sadly, no. I'm supposed to let them know today whether I'm going to do it or not, and I just can't seem to walk over there and pick up the phone."

"Why not? I'd be on it. Do they pay?"

"Sure they do. Fifty grand."

Jesse gaped at him and his knees actually buckled before he remembered himself and straightened up. "Fifty thousand dollars? Are you serious?"

"It might as well be fifty pieces of silver. I'm having a hard time balancing what Ginny and I could do with that money with the intrusion it would be into everyone's lives here. The hard feelings. To say nothing of how my family in Ohio would feel if word ever got back to them."

"They're in Ohio," Jesse pointed out a little more bluntly than he had to. "And the fifty grand is here."

"Yes, but is it worth it to alienate all my neighbors and lose their trust? Because after that money's spent, I still have to live here."

"I wouldn't. I'd go as far away as I could get. Maybe even Australia."

Henry looked at him for a moment. "Jesse, no matter how bad it was for you at home, no matter why you left, family is important. You can't outrun who you are."

"I can outrun who they want me to be."

"And where would that leave you as far as Amanda is concerned? She's joined church—if you want her, you have to want everything she stands for."

"I could say the same to you."

Maybe he should have tied the kid down to the bed. "I don't know what you mean."

"I haven't seen this lady you're supposed to be engaged to, but I have seen you with Sarah Yoder. And I don't think you have any business preaching to me about girls in church."

"Okay, that's enough." Henry abandoned the recipes. "If you want to hang around here, that's fine by me. But you won't say that again or you'll be on your way even if you have to walk. Understand?"

Jesse's brief moment of bravado faded. "*Ja*. Sorry. None of my business."

"You're right. It isn't. And now, since you've brought up

her name, I'm going to go see my fiancée and talk this over with her."

His temper didn't get riled up very often, but when it did, it took him a little time to get it calmed down again. He couldn't see Ginny when he was angry about something else, so he'd just walk along the creek instead of driving over there. The weather had improved marginally, so he might not even get rained on.

He found Ginny in her office off the sitting room, going over the accounts. "Sorry—am I interrupting?"

She rolled her chair away from the computer and rubbed her eyes, as though she'd been at it for some time already. "You're here awfully early. It's not even ten o'clock. And no, you're not interrupting. Any excuse not to look at the bills and my bank statement is a good one." Over her shoulder, he could see the columns of numbers on the spreadsheet, many of which were red. "Come and I'll make another pot of coffee."

He followed her into the kitchen, where she waved him into a seat at the worktable. "I thought I might see you yesterday," he said.

"Likewise." She ground fresh beans, and the rough fragrance of coffee filled the kitchen. "I had a lot of things to catch up on after being gone four days. Even without guests, the place has to be run."

"Is it running all right?"

She shrugged, leaning one hip on the counter, her arms folded. "It's running. *All right* is up for debate. I've got a big balloon payment coming up in April and with fewer guests this past summer, the place hasn't brought in as much. I was hoping I wouldn't have to go all out with the Christmas promotions, but I might. An innkeepers' association has been bugging me about joining, so I may do that just to get the extra exposure from group advertising."

When the coffee was ready, she poured him a cup, added cream, and filled a plate with pecan tarts. "Not exactly breakfast, but they're hard to resist."

He smiled and covered her hand with his as she sat opposite him. "Like some people I know."

The dimples dented her cheeks briefly, and smoothed out.

"Ginny, what is it? You look down. Is it the mortgage? What can I do to help?"

With a squeeze, she released his hand and shook her head, the spirals of her curls moving gently on her shoulders. "It's everything. Doing the accounts always depresses me."

He was pretty sure there was more to it than that. If he knew nothing else about this woman, it was that it took a lot to make that smile fade. Maybe putting her business mind to work on his dilemma would make a good distraction until she was willing to talk about what was really bothering her.

"Remember I said I talked to Dave Petersen about doing the episode of *Shunning Amish*?"

She nodded. "You were going to call him back today with a decision."

"I told him I had to talk to you first, but with all that's been going on, we haven't had a chance."

"So here you are."

"So here I am, no further ahead than I was on Tuesday, despite talking about it with everyone else."

She took a careful sip of hot coffee. "With your... neighbors?"

"Sarah says I shouldn't dwell on the past and present a rebellious nineteen-year-old's view of Amish life. Jesse says there's nothing about said Amish life that couldn't be fixed with fifty grand, and what am I waiting for?"

Ginny made a sound in her throat that might have been a chuckle. "There probably isn't anything in English life that couldn't be fixed with it, either."

"Hence my problem," he confessed. "On one hand, I see those red numbers on your spreadsheet, and the risk of Frith canceling my Christmas pieces, and the wedding coming up, and it seems like a no-brainer."

"And on the other?"

"On the other is the way Paul and Barbara and my sisters and everyone else would feel if I spoke publicly about them."

"Everyone else?"

"Sarah, the Yoders, Priscilla and her family…the ones who have been neighbors to me—and to you, for that matter."

"Hm. But they're all Amish folks. Without televisions. How will they know what you say?"

"It's not even what I'd say. You and I both know how TV people can take a comment on the weather and turn it into a scandal with a little judicious editing."

"Which Amish folks wouldn't know about, either—or care if they did." She put her cup down. "Henry, I love you for thinking about the feelings of…everyone around you…but when it comes down to brass tacks, it really has nothing to do with them or their world. It's *your* world. Your story, that happened decades ago. You have the right to talk about it in any way you want."

"Do I?" There were no answers in his coffee, and he wasn't sure hearing the other side of the argument was an answer, either.

"And to be quite honest, if it means fifty grand and your pieces getting some major recognition—because your pottery will be part of this, Henry, if Frith has anything to say about it—then I think from a practical standpoint alone it's worth doing."

"Sell out my family for money, you mean?"

She recoiled as if he'd struck her. "That is *not* what I mean, and it's cruel of you to make me into the bad guy just because you feel like one."

"Is that what I'm doing?"

She took a deep breath, as though she were praying for patience. "It's what you're trying your hardest not to do. But there's no law that says you have to paint your family in a bad light, or bad-mouth the Amish. If the story is about leaving the church to find yourself as an artist, which was forbidden by the *Ordnung*—well, what's wrong with that? Why shouldn't the focus be on your pottery and not your past?"

He gazed at her. She hadn't pushed him to do the show before—had left the decision mostly up to him, which was why it had been so difficult. Had her sister been talking to her about it while they'd been together? "I'm sorry for what I said. You're right, of course. I just never thought of it that way."

At last the smile that he loved flickered to life, for real this time. "That's why there's two of us. To look at things from both sides."

"This table has one too many sides. Come over here, you." He hugged her, hoping that his embrace would express his apology, too.

Sitting in his lap, she brushed his hair back and kissed his forehead. "I'm glad we can talk about this, Henry," she said softly. "You're about the only person I can tell about the accounts—which is good, since we'll be talking about them often after December. I can't say these things to Venezia because she's the financial wizard in the family and she'd be all over me. And Daddy has no head for business—he's all about people. I didn't want to drag my problems into your decision because that wouldn't be fair...but I can't tell you what this means to me."

He tilted his head back to look into her face, but she buried her nose in the crook of his neck.

"I'm a little scared about that balloon payment," she whispered at last. "I'll do everything I can to bring guests in, but even a portion of that fifty thousand might mean the difference between keeping the place going and having to give it up."

"Is it that bad, Ginny? Really?"

She still couldn't look at him, but he felt her nod against his shoulder. "It's to the point where I'm glad Katie Schrock is getting married. At least I don't have to tell one of the girls I have to let her go. I've cut down on expenses as much as I can, but what we really need is an infusion of real money." At last she raised her head and he saw how troubled her eyes were. "I hate that I can't do this by myself. I hate having to depend on someone else when I've managed on my own this far. I almost feel—" Her voice caught. "Almost ashamed, as though somehow I've failed at something I know I'm good at."

He kissed her firmly and stood. "What did you just finish telling me? This is why there are two of us."

Inside, he felt a little sick, but there was no way that any man worth his salt could look into those eyes and refuse the plea he saw. Scruples were one thing. But so was a roof over one's head and a way to keep it there.

"You're right. I need to stop looking at the past and turn toward the future," he said. "Where's your phone?"

The relief and joy in her eyes were reward enough. If the thought of his family and neighbors came back to bother him in the night, he'd just remember Ginny's face and tell himself he'd done the right thing.

When at last Dave came on the line, he was as genial as if he hadn't just threatened Henry with lawyers three days ago. "Sorry about the wait, Henry—they had to pull me out of the pricing meeting. Not that I'm complaining. So I only have a minute. I take it you've come to a final decision?"

"Yes. I've decided to go along with it, with—"

"Great news! I have to say, Henry, I'm really glad. This will be a terrific experience—one you can tell your grandkids about, eh?"

"I meant to say, with one caveat."

"Oh? And what's that? Want your own trailer and a production assistant to fetch you coffee?"

"No. I want the focus to be on my art. On the pieces I'm doing for Frith. Not on my past or on my family."

Dave hesitated. "Of course, I'm in no position to say what the film crew will or won't do."

"Those are my terms, Dave. I'm telling you up front the same thing I'll tell Matt Alvarez."

"Fine, fine, whatever. I'm sure they'll be happy to spin it however you want. I'll call Matt now and get the contracts on their way. Turns out it won't be Monday—they're wrapping up another episode in Indiana—but next week sometime. Thanks, Henry. I have to go—they're waving at me like they're flagging down a train."

The dial tone sounded in his ear.

Henry's relief at the weight of stress lifting off his shoulders made him so giddy that he whirled Ginny around her office, and then took her out to lunch. By the time the credit card bill arrived, he'd probably have enough of the money in hand to pay the whole thing off.

CHAPTER 24

The Saturday of the *Englisch* Columbus Day long weekend in October was the Amish Market's closing day, marking the end of harvest season. Sarah loved the market when it showed the full bounty of Willow Creek's fields and gardens—and she was clearly not the only one. The place was packed, the parking lot showing license plates from half a dozen states, and even a Canadian province or two, since it was their Thanksgiving holiday. She had some distant relatives in the Amish community outside Aylmer, in Ontario, and when on one of their visits she'd asked why the Canadian version of the holiday was so much earlier, they'd laughed and said it was because winter came sooner farther north.

Evie Troyer was doing a roaring trade in her table runners, place mats, and quilts—and Pris was there, too, presiding over a dwindling stack of pot holders pieced to look like chickens. "I'll take two," Sarah said on one of her breaks from manning her own stall, and Pris had given them to her for half price. Ten dollars was a lot to pay for something she could make herself...but on the other hand, not having to sew them or quilt them was worth it.

When she cashed out and cleaned off the shelves for the

last time until April, she had sold everything but one lonely seed loaf and a couple of bunches of rosemary and thyme. All the teas had gone, and the tinctures and salves she had made had sold mostly to the other Amish stall keepers. And her take-home money after the percentage she paid to the Market totaled four hundred and seventy dollars.

At last, after being in arrears to her in-laws for most of the year's mortgage payments, she would be back on the correct side of the ledger.

What a relief.

The next day being an off Sunday, when Bishop Dan oversaw the service in the neighboring Oakfield district, Sarah sent Caleb over to Henry's before breakfast to fetch Jesse and bring him back for a meal and some quiet time with the extended Yoder family. It was all very well for Henry to allow him to stay there while he recuperated, but a little time to think about God might help with his spiritual recovery, too. She and Corinne had arranged it so that the two families would meet at the older couple's house, and Amanda and Jesse would see each other for the first time since the accident under close supervision.

In Jacob Yoder's front room, they gathered for prayers and reading from the old family Bible, with a chapter from the *Martyrs' Mirror* added for good measure. Sarah couldn't help noticing that Jesse's gaze rarely left Amanda's face, though she kept her eyes on her clasped hands. Probably wise, considering Corinne didn't miss a thing.

Her idea of Jesse moving to the Yoder place for his recovery had been quickly done away with. Sarah didn't know Amanda's feelings, but it was clear that her parents were quite prepared to forbid her to have anything to do with the wayward boy outside a family or church setting.

Poor Amanda. Sarah smothered a sigh and concentrated on her own clasped hands as Simon read the next set of verses, his voice smooth and confident. The one and only time Amanda had gathered up the courage to approach a boy, and the result had been disaster. The episode with Silas earlier in the summer didn't really count, since he had been pursuing Sarah and their relatives had been pushing him every which way. But it certainly had been a disaster, too.

After lunch, Amanda ventured outside for the first time without her crutches, leaning on Jesse's arm as she went slowly down the stairs. But Caleb and Simon went with them, so if there was going to be any conversation, it would have to be the kind that anyone could hear. In Sarah's mind, their faces spoke clearly enough. Amanda would not be accepting any more rides in cars unless they were the big vans that the *Englisch* taxi drivers owned. And Jesse seemed to realize it.

Instead of staying for the afternoon, he walked home with her and the boys. On the path up to the house, he said to Sarah, "Do you want to have a look at me before I go back to Henry's?"

She shook her head. "I don't feel I should practice on Sundays, but I will look if you are in any pain, or you would like me to."

"*Neh*, it's okay. The bruises are yellow now, and my head feels fine, except if I stand up too fast. And sometimes I still feel sick."

Hm. Lingering nausea from the allergy. And she was nearly out of coneflower. "I'll make you something a little different to settle your stomach after I get back from Ruth's on Tuesday and bring it over. Would that be all right?"

"If I'm still here." He kicked a pebble off the walk. "Not

sure how long Henry's going to want me around. Or you folks."

"You could probably stay at Henry's forever if you wedge clay for him," Caleb suggested.

Simon nudged his brother with one shoulder. "Not everyone loves making mud pies like you do."

"They might for a dollar a pound," Caleb said. "I don't have time to now that I'm with Jon, other than Saturdays, but it would be a good way for Jesse to earn his keep."

"That's a good idea," the boy said thoughtfully. "He's going to let me fix up my car in the yard, too. I need to get it running halfway decent and put new tires on it before I'll get any money for it."

"Are you going to sell it?" Sarah asked, hardly daring to hope.

He lifted one shoulder in a shrug. "Might need to. I can't seem to get work with an *Englisch* outfit, so I might have to try Amish, and they won't have a car around, probably. Caleb, I don't suppose Jon Hostetler needs another hand?"

Caleb's nose wrinkled up in regret. "Not so much in the winter. He's letting some of the boys go already."

"You?" Simon asked.

"Not yet, but soon, I'm pretty sure, since I'm so new to the crew. It wouldn't be fair to keep me and not a fellow who's been with him for a couple of seasons."

There was a word in season, and then there was an opportunity as big as a barn door. Sarah took a breath and walked right through it. "You boys might think of something you can all do together this winter. All of you need to be working, and maybe three heads will be better than one."

"Like what, Mamm?" Caleb wanted to know.

"You put your heads together and I'm sure you can come

up with something. What do the other men do in the winter?"

"Dat works on the machinery in the barn," Jesse offered. "He'll fix up the augur, and rig up the lights and the mister for the grass sprouts, and make sure the harrow is working properly so he won't have to do all that in the spring."

"What do you mean, grass sprouts?" Simon said.

By this time they were in the kitchen, and Jesse looked around. "Do you have a pencil and a piece of paper?"

Caleb found him an envelope and something to write with. "We'd fix up a kind of greenhouse in the barn and grow sprouts—you know, to put in the silage feed in the winter," he said, sketching quickly. "Sprouts need a mister and light and plastic all around to keep everything moist, and then you peel the mats of sprouted seeds off the racks and mix it into the cattle feed. It gives them extra nutrients." He looked at the boys' blank faces. "Don't you do that here?"

"No." Simon and Caleb exchanged a glance. "What does Daed use in his feed?"

"Just hay and alfalfa." A note of excitement crept into Caleb's voice. "But if other farmers are doing it, maybe we could introduce it here. Maybe we could hire ourselves out to build these—what do you call them?"

"We just call them sprouting frames, but if we were going to do this, we should call them something better. Something people would remember easily."

"Simon, you're good with stuff like that," Caleb said eagerly. "You think of something."

"All right," Simon said. "But meanwhile, let's draw up a real plan and figure out who we can offer the first one to."

"Why not Daed?" Sarah suggested. "It would be close by,

and he would pay you fairly. And you know how he is about his cows."

"How is he?" Jesse asked.

"If they were children, they wouldn't get treated any better," Simon said, grinning. "And if anyone could do a sales job, it would be Caleb. Come on, let's go upstairs and do some drawing."

"Simon," Sarah said in a tone that brought him up short.

"Oh. *Ja.* Sunday. Well then, tomorrow."

But something about the expression on Jesse's face kept her from letting him go when the boys went out to the barn to hitch up the buggy. The singing that evening was at the Peachey place and they would need to leave a little early in order to get there before the sun began to go down.

"Are you going to go with the boys this afternoon, Jesse? Instead of working on your car?"

"I—I don't know."

She busied herself with the coffeepot and, when that was going, pulled a pan of gingerbread out of the fridge and cut several thick slices. "I'm sure you'd be welcome at Peacheys'. Their boys, Benny and Leon, are around your age and you'd probably have a lot in common."

"But I need to get my car fixed. If we really do get this sprout frame venture off the ground, I'll need it to go around and buy supplies." His face fell for a moment, and he took the piece of gingerbread she offered. "Though what with, I don't know."

"Your customers will give you money for the supplies, I would imagine."

"But if no one's ever used one before, it's like buying a pig in a poke. Unless we had one up and operating, why would anyone take a risk?"

"It's not that much of a risk—some wood, some plastic, some misters, and a water pump. Or did you mean, take a risk on you?"

He swallowed a big bite of gingerbread. "You think I'm messed up, don't you?"

"It doesn't matter what I think—though since you ask, *neh*, I do not. What matters is what God thinks. And what you think."

"I think I'm messed up."

"And I think that whatever rebellious spirit prompted you to buy that car and leave your home and live in a way that no young man should have to...has changed a little. That maybe you're seeing life differently."

"Maybe," he mumbled.

The thing about words in season was that they were like pepper or cinnamon. A very little went a long way toward seasoning the entire dish.

"I think you can choose to be a good influence, like with the sprout frames, or a not so good influence, like with taking girls riding in your car. And you know, God is always ready to help with the first kind."

That was enough seasoning. The coffeepot was making the sound that told her it was ready, so she poured them both a cup and took hers into the front room, where the birthday afghan waited for another few rows of stitches.

And when Jesse went outside to tell the boys about the gingerbread, she heard him say, "Hope you don't plan to give a ride to a girl tonight...I'd like to go with you."

On Monday, Sarah half expected Jesse to turn up, if not to have her look at his bruises, then certainly to begin work on the sprout frame project with Simon. Caleb had gone to work with the crew as usual, and Simon was out in the barn, polishing Dulcie's tack and washing last night's mud off the buggy, staying around the place in case the other boy came over.

When her elder son came in at noon for lunch, he glanced at the empty chairs around the table as he sat down. As soon as grace was over and he'd helped himself to the thick ham and cheese sandwiches she'd made, a dish of applesauce, and some pickles, he said, "I thought we might have seen Jesse by now. Wonder what he's doing?"

"I was wondering that myself. Well, if he doesn't come and see us by tomorrow, I'll go over there and see how he is."

Simon gave her a long look. Took a bite of sandwich. Swallowed. "Jesse's in the house, *ja?* And *Englisch* Henry will probably be out in the barn, in his studio."

"He probably will," she agreed pleasantly. "His hands ought to be nearly healed by now, but he's going to have to change something, so he doesn't wind up with the same problem over again."

She knew very well what Simon was thinking. But it wasn't his place to bring it up—he might be the man of the house, but she was still his mother, and there were certain things that respect taught a young man not to say. But she had a thing or two to say to him, and this seemed like a God-given opportunity.

"You seem concerned about Jesse, and that's *gut*," she told him. "I wish you had as much concern for your friend Joe, after all you've been through together this summer, and after he did so much for you, helping you with your hurt foot."

"Concern for him?" Simon looked honestly lost. "What do you mean, Mamm?"

"I mean Priscilla," she said gently.

He said nothing, only took another big bite of his sandwich. On purpose, it seemed to her. But his face reddened a little, and she took encouragement from a sign that his conscience might be bothering him.

"How do you know about that?" he asked at last.

"I had a little talk with Joe. It's only by God's grace and his own humility that you haven't lost that boy as a friend, Simon. I think you owe him an apology for making free with his girl."

"It was just a little kiss, Mamm. Don't blow it out of proportion."

"Just a little kiss . . . like just a little bit of fabric off the brim of a *Kapp*, like just a little radio under the buggy seat. It's not the size of the sin that matters, it's the attitude and unwillingness behind it. And Simon, you and I both know that you have a little struggle with pride. You thought she'd leave Joe and start dating you, just because you changed your mind and decided you wanted her after all."

"That's not it," he mumbled. "You weren't there."

But Sarah suspected that it was. "Maybe not, but you had no right to step between your friend and the girl he likes. If God has purposed the two of them to be together, you don't want to get in the way of His will."

Simon's cheeks were scarlet now. "The way you keep stepping in between *Englisch* Henry and his Ginny?"

If he had picked up his plate and tossed it across the room, she couldn't have been more shocked. "What? I'm doing no such thing. I'm treating him."

"I've seen how you look at him when you think no one is looking."

And here she thought he wouldn't set foot on forbidden ground. "Have you, now?" Oh, surely she couldn't be the one blushing. Sarah took a long sip from her glass of water.

Simon's tone softened, as though he realized the footing was uncertain. "I've seen the way he looks at you, too. I've seen it... and never liked it, right from the beginning."

"Simon, believe me, no one knows better than I that it's impossible. I'm very much aware that God is not in this—this—in my own struggle. The two cases aren't similar. But the heart is desperately wicked—isn't that what the prophet says? Who can know it? We can only do our best to recognize our sin and ask *der Herr* for help to overcome it."

"Maybe we can help each other do that, Mamm." He rose, bent down to kiss the top of her head, and took his plate over to the sink. "If Jesse comes, I'll be out in the barn."

And he left her there, shaken with the knowledge that her boy had spoken as much truth to her as she had to him. Because hadn't she done all she could to put it in Henry's mind that he was marrying the wrong woman? To step between them in the guise of a friend, saying that it was for the sake of his return to the church, when all along...

Sarah put down her sandwich and went into the bathroom and closed the door, gazing at the reflection in the small mirror over the sink. The reflection of a woman who looked almost like a stranger.

Tuesday morning at breakfast, she passed Caleb a plate of bacon and eggs and said, "Maybe Jesse's busy working on his car. Once I'm back from Ruth's, I'll take his stomach cure over there and see what's going on."

"He seemed all excited about the sprout frame on Sunday," Caleb said through a mouthful of biscuit. "It's funny he wouldn't have come over already. Maybe Henry got in a new crate of clay and he's earning his keep. It would take a couple of days to wedge it all."

Sarah hoped so. The long drive to Ruth's was a relief—with no one to talk to but Dulcie, she could think, and pray, and try to gain the strength to do what she must do, which was to distance herself from Henry. It was all very well to admit that her heart was wicked and to pray, *Lead me not into temptation*, but it was asking a lot of God to do that when she kept running over to it of her own free will.

What kind of example was she to Simon? Had he seen her with Henry and decided that it might just be all right to trifle with Joe's feelings in the way Sarah might be trifling with Ginny's? Oh, how she hoped not. And how glad she was that with truth and openness between them, they had been able to pray together last night without the scent of disturbance that had been hanging over them like wood smoke since his return.

The simple truth was that God had given her a good, useful life. She had everything she needed, a family next door whom she dearly loved, and two strong sons who were her joy. She must put her craving for a man she could not have on the altar of sacrifice and walk away from it forever. She must put her hand in that of the Shepherd, and trust Him to lead her in the way she should go.

There was a relief in having made a choice, she thought as she passed through Whinburg and turned down the county road where the Lehman farm lay. With the sacrifice firmly tied to the altar with strong cords, she could move forward and be grateful for the peace that lay ahead beside the still waters.

When she and Ruth had closeted themselves in Ruth's compiling room, she brought up the subject of Jesse and told her what she wanted to make, which was an easy recipe if you had all the right ingredients. Thank goodness Ruth was well stocked with coneflower.

"Jesse Riehl? Is he one of the Riehls from over west of Strasburg?"

"I think so. I understand that he left his family over getting a driver's license and a car."

Ruth's gray eyebrows rose. "Ah. We heard about the accident—the *gut Gott* surely had our Amanda in the palm of His hand. I know the boy's family. Very conservative. I used to treat Lame Saul Riehl for nerve pain many years ago—I suppose Jesse would have been a baby then. They lived here, you know."

"Are Lame Saul and his wife still living?"

"As far as I know. But I can't see that man having a boy with a car about the place. Jesse would have to get rid of it, put aside his *Englisch* ways, and ask forgiveness before Saul would be convinced to restore the relationship."

This was not unusual, and Sarah would likely hold the same standard if Simon were to do such a thing. But oh, how hard it would be! It would almost be worse than a death to know that sheer unwillingness had driven a wedge between you and the child you loved, and you had to separate yourself from him. This was the purpose of *die Meinding*, after all— to cause the wayward one to realize all that he had lost, and to come back asking to be restored. Many people looked at shunning as punishment, but it wasn't. It was simply to let the person see how much they had given up to take their own way.

Thank you, dear Father, that of all the things You have sent into my life, You have not given this experience to me. But Thy will be done.

Simon's disobedience and rebellion this past summer had done enough to reveal to them both just what the price would be for such a separation. Sarah thanked God that Simon had had a heart soft enough to count the cost of the loss of his family and realize it would be too high to pay. She hoped that now his heart would be generous enough to let him apologize to Joe for what he'd done, and restore the friendship that she knew he valued.

"Nausea still, hey?" Ruth said, pulling down a couple of the bins in which she kept dried leaf. "Let's increase the concentration of one or two ingredients and see what we can do about that."

When Sarah drove home, she had several packets of tea, a couple of bottles of tincture, and an herb journal with five new pages of notes about lowering blood pressure, treating allergies, and two more recipes for the elderberries on the trees along the road now that cold and flu season seemed to have begun.

Simon met her when she drove into the yard, and after he'd carried in her parcels, he took Dulcie into the barn for a well-deserved curry and some oats. It was late—she needed to start supper—but Jesse was stuck in her mind like a burr on the inside of a stocking. Tuesdays were usually a pickup supper anyway, because after driving twelve miles and back to Whinburg, and several hours stuffing her brain full of information, she was usually too tired to start a full meal from scratch.

She took out the half pan of yesterday's casserole and put it in the oven to warm slowly, then put her jacket back on and went out to the barn.

"Simon, I'm going to take this tea mixture over to Jesse. I should be back in a few minutes."

"Want me to come with you?" He turned from Dulcie's glossy flank and leaned companionably on the mare, who braced herself almost as though she were leaning right back.

"*Neh.* I won't be long." And while he might not know of the decision she had made, she was grateful he'd asked. To know he wanted to walk beside her in the valley of temptation. "I've got the casserole warming in the oven."

Because they ate so early, there was still plenty of daylight. The air was still and damp, as though it had just rained, which meant that it carried the scent of the fields around her. Corn stalks, earth, manure. And above the heavy smells of farming, lighter notes—apples fallen under the trees and left for the hens to eat, the crisp scent of laurel hedges and grass, a whiff of mint and lemon from the beds by the back steps.

The moist air also carried sounds—the kind that weren't so easy to identify—as she climbed the hill. Crunching, as though something were being dragged. A metallic buzz that sounded almost like the old generator Henry used to run his kiln. And above it all, a jagged current of voices, slapping against one another, rising and falling.

Sarah crested the hill between her place and Henry's and hurried down the path. There was a van in the yard between the house and barn—and there was another one, along with a big SUV with windows you couldn't see through. The back doors of both vans were open and someone was unloading big black boxes—the source of the crunching sound in the gravel.

Now she could see what was causing the angry voices. Henry stood with his hands on his hips, facing a young man in skinny black jeans whose back was toward her, looking like he was trying to either placate or convince him. Behind them stood a burly man holding a thick coil of cable, waiting patiently for a break in the conversation, if it could be called that.

Sarah hesitated. Everything she'd ever been taught urged her to turn and go home before anyone saw her. Whatever was going on here was worldly, *Englisch* business and none of hers. True, she had come to see Jesse, not Henry—and speaking of, where was the boy in all this? His old car sat with its hood up where it had since the tow truck had dropped it off, and a young man not much older than Simon bent in the driver's side window, showing something to the girl with him, who kept looking anxiously at the man with the cable, as though she didn't want to get caught not doing what she was supposed to. Jesse backed out from under the hood and said something to the young man. He was holding a wrench in one hand and a shop rag in the other.

No matter how she looked at it, this was obviously a bad time to try to treat him. She'd just go home and try again lat—

"Dude! Check out the Amish lady," the girl said.

The young man in the black jeans spun around, his white teeth flashing, and with a jolt, she recognized him. And then she realized what all this was.

A film crew—much bigger than the one that had come to shoot the video. They were here to film *Shunning Amish*.

Her stomach dipped and steadied as her whole body seemed to chill and stiffen. He had decided to do the television show. To put the final barrier between himself and his community.

His marriage to Ginny would separate him forever from Sarah and the church.

But this show would separate him forever from his family.

Oh, Henry, how could you? Father, forgive him. Doesn't he know what this will mean?

Maybe not. Or maybe he did, and he didn't care. Blindly, she turned away, her eyes already welling up with tears.

Chapter 25

S arah!"

Absolutely nothing but the note of relief in Henry's voice at seeing her could have induced Sarah to turn back and venture down into the foreign landscape that the old yard had become. His voice told her two things—one, that he needed help, and two, that he didn't want to ask it of her and drag her into his troubles.

Both those things combined in a moment and she made up her mind. She dashed the tears from her lashes with the heel of her hand. Was this how Moses felt when he walked into the dry path the Lord had made through the Red Sea? Confident that He would provide, yet all too aware of the towering walls of water on either side that could collapse at any moment?

She took a deep breath, skirted the van nearest her, and emerged from behind it to join Henry. "Hallo," she said to him. "I came over to bring Jesse some tea, and saw you had company." She gave Matt a smile and hoped it looked braver than she felt. "Hello, Matt. It is nice to see you again."

"Mrs. Yoder." The young man's smile was every bit as brilliant, but not so wide and sincere as it had been last

time. "Nice to see you, too. I'm afraid we're having a business discussion here. I'm not sure it'll be very interesting
for you."

"It looks very interesting. Henry, did you want to speak
with me?"

"Matt's right," Henry said, raking one hand through his
hair. "I don't know what I was thinking. The last thing I need
to do is drag you into this. Hey!" He raised his voice, and
Matt and Sarah turned to look at a man with a big camera on
his shoulder, aimed at Jesse. Oblivious to it, Jesse was showing the *Englisch* boy something in the wheel well of his car.
The girl now leaned on the rear fender with an air of desperate boredom. "Get that camera away from him," Henry
called. "He's Amish."

"An Amish with a car?" The cameraman grinned. "Trust
me, I've seen enough of these folks to know he's not *that*
Amish."

Henry's lips thinned and he turned back to Matt. "See?
This is exactly what I'm talking about. Intrusion without asking permission. I'm telling you, I can't allow you to send
people to Ohio to film the home place. There's nothing
in this contract"—he waggled the packet of papers in his
hand—"to prevent members of my family from being in
these so-called *establishing shots*."

"No faces or recognizable characteristics, Henry," Matt
told him, sounding as if it wasn't the first time. "We've had
a lot of practice at this, remember. Especially around Sugarcreek. Some of the Amish there even recognize the crew when
it goes by on the highway. They wave."

Henry didn't look as if he'd heard. "I told you how I want
the story slanted. I want it to be about art—with the Amish
focus on community over individuals being the reason I left

the church. About how my art has its roots in a focus on the land."

"That's great. You saw the draft shot summary, right? We'll touch on it, but you know, that's not really what *Shunning Amish* is all about."

"What is it about?" Sarah asked.

"That's right, you've never seen an episode." Matt laughed, though Sarah couldn't see where there was a joke. "Basically, Mrs. Yoder, it's about people becoming who they're meant to be."

"Exactly what I'm trying to convey," Henry said in exasperation.

"But isn't life about becoming who God wants you to be?" Sarah asked of no one in particular.

"That depends on whether you're planning on staying in the church, I guess," Matt said. "The people whose stories we tell or reenact have decided to take their lives into their own hands. The show is about empowerment. Agency, not blind obedience to tradition—no offense. Acting on your own behalf to make a life for yourself. Exactly what we want to show with Henry here."

"That's not what this shot summary says." He pulled a paper from the stack and handed it to Sarah.

Surprised that he would share it with her, and even more surprised that he would think she knew what a shot summary was, she put her basket handle over one arm and took it.

MINUTES: 1–4

BYLER V/O est. shots Willow Creek scenery, buggies, barns, etc. ending at his farm.

Studio, process of making pottery.

PETERSEN D.W. Frith interview and why they chose his work.

MINUTES: 5–18

BYLER V/O on family farm in Ohio. Reasons why he left. Check abusive father?

2 interviews ex-Amish friends. Try for family member?

BYLER life in Denver, tragic death of fiancée. Interview fiancée family members.

MINUTES: 19–22

BYLER V/O driven by his demons back to farm, start over with nothing, underdog makes good.

END BYLER V/O satisfying new life with HOCHSTETLER

CLOSING IMAGE Rose Arbor Inn and wedding.

"*Wedding?*" Sarah didn't understand half the shorthand on the paper, but she did know what that word meant. Her stomach pitched and her skin seemed to prickle as she reluctantly handed the paper back. The urge to rip it into little pieces was not only childish, but futile. There was probably another one in Matt's pocket.

"Great idea, huh?" Matt looked pleased with himself. "Audiences love a happy ending, so every three episodes we give them one. This is perfect—man leaves home and family, loses everything including his first love, then gains it all back in spades. Kinda biblical, even—you know, the whole notion of things coming back to you tenfold. The episode isn't scheduled to air until January, so if we get everything else shot by Thanksgiving and wind up with the wedding, it'll go straight to post-production and be on the air right on time."

"And Ginny has agreed to this?" Sarah asked Henry, amazed. "You, too?"

"Not like this, and that's the whole problem." Sarah got

the distinct impression that if Sadie's farm still had a pig pen, he would have thrown the papers in his hand into it for the pigs to eat. "I can't agree to this contract at all, unless the focus of the episode is changed to something I can live with."

"Not possible." Hands on hips, Matt shook his head regretfully at the ground. "We've already got a second-unit crew scouting the locations in Sugarcreek and Denver."

"Then you're fools," Henry snapped. "I haven't even signed this contract."

"You told Petersen you would. That's why we're here. If we intend to meet that air date, we can't waste any time. I figured I'd save at least four days by bringing the contract in person and doing some preliminary shots at the same time. Waste not, want not."

"I can't," Henry said desperately. "Who told you to include my late fiancée's family? How can I subject them to this?"

"Depends on whether they're fans of the show," Matt said cheerfully.

Henry glared at him in a way that made the smile falter. "Either you change the focus of this episode or you find yourselves another subject," he said with deliberate emphasis. "I'm not a man who issues ultimatums, but I'm at my limit here. This goes against everything I believe in."

Matt took a long breath, as though he was schooling himself to patience. Sarah had done the same thing herself, before she made the mistake of disciplining her boys when she was angry, for instance. But there was no avoiding the fact that Matt was coming to the end of a rope that had never been very long in the first place.

"Henry, first, we have a verbal agreement. You have to stick by it or there will be all kinds of ugly from the network's attorneys. And second, the writers of this show have a lot of practice in giving our audience what it wants. And what it wants is the personal story. They don't care about Art. They leave that to the *New York Times*. What they want is entertainment and the personal side of religion, which this crew delivers week after week. And third—fifty grand. 'Nuff said. Now, once and for all, let's go ahead and sign this contract so my crew can get to work."

Sarah held her breath as Henry's hands tightened on the papers. *Please don't do this*, she begged silently. *It will destroy you, and the repercussions could keep coming back on you for years to come. Don't let worldly ideas about money and recognition blind you to what is most important.*

As though he had heard her silent urging, he lifted his head to look into her eyes. In his own she saw how badly he was torn—like a man holding the reins of Paul Byler's two big Percherons, each horse equally huge and each equally determined to go in a different direction.

"Sarah?" he said quietly. "What's your opinion?"

Goodness. Her opinion meant nothing. Less than nothing. And if there was anything she had learned in the past year, it was that sticking her nose into other people's business invariably led to pain and loss of fellowship.

But you don't have fellowship with Henry. You have friendship.

But that wasn't true, either. For better or worse, she loved this man—and she had made a choice only hours ago to put her love on the altar of sacrifice. The fact that her love could never be acknowledged—could never even be spoken of outside the whispered confines of a prayer—was beside the point. The point was, he needed her help to make a decision that might change his life. As a friend, she could help him.

But it would be he who must decide the actual direction of that change.

She inclined her head, and he followed her off to the edge of Sadie's unkempt, uncared-for old garden. But over there, a clump of Michaelmas daisies bloomed purple and blue on the edge of it, a bright spot of color in what otherwise had been left abandoned. Even amid dead plants and the destruction of order, the daisies showed that there was hope for the future. All was not lost, and maybe they shone all the brighter for the mess that was decomposing around them.

"You don't need my opinion, Henry," she said softly, angling them so that her back was to Matt and his crew—just in case that cameraman got ideas. Her hands tingled with the urge to take his, but she slid her basket up her arm and tucked them under her elbows.

"I wouldn't have asked for it if I didn't." His eyes were haunted, his face drawn, as though he hadn't slept the night before—or the one before that. "You always tell me the truth, even when it might not be strictly in accordance with the *Ordnung*." Her lips tipped up in a smile of acknowledgment. "I need to hear what you think."

"Why aren't you on your phone asking Ginny what she thinks?" she asked. "After all, it's her wedding that they want to film."

"She wouldn't have a problem with it," he sighed. "She's all in favor—for reasons that I can't go into. But no matter what it means for her—for us—I can't do this," he said. "I can't."

"Then that's your answer, isn't it?"

"How can it be? We need that money. I need the commission. I'll lose everything, Sarah. Everything."

"Will you really?" The daisies swayed on the wind, but their roots went deep into the ground. Sarah looked deep inside herself and willed herself to hang on to her composure for one more minute. For his sake. "You have your farm, and you have friends around you who will help when the cupboards get bare and the pipes freeze. You have your two hands and the talent God gave you. D.W. Frith is just one customer, Henry. There are other stores, other people who would buy your pieces. And even if they didn't, there's no shame in making mugs for the Amish Market. It's good, honorable work that fills a need, as any coffee drinker will tell you."

His mouth flickered, as though it wanted to smile, but was dragged down again by the weight of his despair.

It was that despair that made her dig deeper—to say the things that ought not to be said between neighbors. Things she hadn't said when they'd talked before. "Paul and Barbara and your family will forgive you if you bring their names into this filming. But Henry, I'm very much afraid that you won't forgive yourself. That you'll fall into the trap of letting this come between yourself and your family as a way of putting even more distance between yourself and your upbringing. You'll do it—and you'll hate yourself for doing it. I'm not sure that's a road a man can easily come back from."

He stared at her. "Is that what you think I'm doing? What this is all about?"

"What I think doesn't matter. You have to face the consequences of what *you* think, deep in your heart, and ask yourself if you want to be the man who walks that road and has to live with them."

She must not reach out. She must not succumb to the temptation to fall against his chest and wrap her arms around him, in an attempt to give him strength. She must remember the altar. Her body trembled with the force of the control that held her back.

He must have sensed it. His gaze locked on hers and held, as if it were a lifeline holding him against the wind that buffeted him, demanding that he go with it.

And then he seemed to come to a decision. His gaze slid to her mouth, and then to the hands that were locked on her elbows, holding on for dear life.

He nodded, once. Twice.

"*Denki,*" he said.

And then he walked back to where Matt was waiting, the papers slowly crumpling in his hand.

CHAPTER 26

Not for the first time, Henry asked himself how it was possible to have moved in next to one of the few women in the world who would tell you what you *needed* to hear, not what you *wanted* to hear.

Ginny wanted him to be happy, he knew that. But she only saw the man—the individual. Sarah saw him the Amish way—in terms of everyone around him. The decisions he made affected not only his own life, but also the lives of everyone touched by it.

He would see just how far the reach of this decision would go.

Matt hadn't waited for him to finish talking with Sarah— he and the cameraman had gone over to the barn, close to where Jesse was supposed to be working on his car. Matt concluded his conversation as Henry walked up, and gave him an inquiring look. "Well?"

Henry held out the contract. "I can't do it, Matt. I'm sorry you've gone to all this trouble, but I just can't."

Matt didn't reach out to take it. "You heard what I said about the verbal agreement, didn't you?"

"Yes, but that isn't going to change my mind. If you have to bring lawyers into this, then that's up to you. All I know is that I can't subject my neighbors and family to this kind of intrusion, and the sooner you folks go on and find yourselves another subject to film, the better."

Even as he spoke, he had the sensation of a tide going out under his feet, dragging the sand away and leaving him unbalanced. He was going to suffer for this—and so was Ginny—but if all he had to hang on to was the rock of his conviction that doing what all these people wanted was wrong, then that was enough. He wouldn't change his mind.

"I'm sorry you feel that way," Matt said. "We're not trying to be intrusive. Usually our talent wants to have their story told. I thought you did, too, to introduce the world to your art."

"If that were the focus, maybe," Henry said, "but it's clear that it's not."

"Let's not be so hasty." Matt slid an arm around his shoulders and walked him a few steps away, closer to Jesse's car. "Maybe we can negotiate a few points on the shot list, huh?"

"Maybe we could, but there's still no guarantee that the final product will be something I can live with."

"The contract says 'approval of the rough cut.' Didn't you read it?"

"Oh yes. But what happens when you fine-tune the rough cut? Or you run out of time and have to take shortcuts? Matt, I appreciate your wanting to tell my story, but all things considered, I'm happy to let my work do that."

"So that's it? I fly a whole crew out here and rent vans and pay a per diem, just so you can tell me no, I changed my mind? Do you know how much this debacle is going to cost the network?"

The smile was gone, and Matt's dark eyes were no longer

laughing. Maybe now wasn't the right time to remind him that anyone who would mobilize a crew without a signed contract should resist the urge to gamble. Then again, *Shunning Amish* was so popular that maybe Matt simply wasn't in the habit of hearing the word *no*.

"What am I gonna do with all these people?" Matt asked no one in particular, waving an arm to encompass the vans, the packing cases, and Sarah, still standing silently right where he'd left her. Watching.

Praying, probably.

Somehow that thought gave him the strength to stay the course. Not to give in to the threat of Matt's temper and certain legal action.

"Why don't you use me?"

Henry turned at the sound of a young man's voice, which cracked on the last syllable. "Jesse?"

Leaning on a crowbar as though it were a cane, Jesse stood beside his injured car, shaking so hard his pants quivered against his legs. "Would I make a good subject?"

Matt looked at him a little incredulously. "Who are you?"

"J-Jesse Riehl. I'm Amish. Or…I'm on *Rumspringe*, at least. This is my car. My dad kicked me out when I got my driver's license, and when I bought the car with my harvest money, he made my whole family stop talking to me. I've been living in it since the winter."

Matt stared at him, then at the cameraman, who flicked a switch that made a red light turn on. He settled it on his shoulder and began to film.

"An Amish kid, homeless and living in his car?" Matt said thoughtfully.

Without taking his eye from the little screen on the side, the cameraman said, "Episode Twelve: 'Driven Away.'"

"Not quite as good as Episode Twelve: 'Feet of Clay,' but it has possibilities," Matt said.

"Feet of Clay"? Never mind. "No," Henry protested, before this went any further. "Jesse, you can't."

The kid's face reddened. "Why not? I got nothing to lose. And with fifty grand, I could go down to Springfield. Buy a house, maybe. A little one. Or go to Australia."

"But your parents—your family—"

Jesse's mouth hardened. "I can't do any worse in Dat's mind. Car, TV, it's all the same to him. This'll give me a start, at least—and that's just what I haven't got otherwise."

"Jesse, I think we're on to something here," Matt said smoothly. "If Henry doesn't mind us doing a little shooting—"

"No." Henry cut him off at the pass. If he was going to turn this down, he'd turn it down in its entirety. "No filming on my place. You folks make whatever deal you want to with some other farmer, but there'll be no more here. Jesse, is that thing roadworthy?"

"*That thing* is a twenty-five-thousand-dollar collector's item," the cameraman said imperturbably. "Have a little respect."

"No," Jesse said. "I have to pry the front right panel out of the tire and get a new tire first."

"I'm pretty handy with cars," the cameraman said, still squinting through the viewfinder of the running camera. "Maybe Matt will even take the helm for a second while I have a look."

Jesse had been banging away fruitlessly all afternoon, but with one heave by the cameraman and a screech of metal, the panel released its bite on the tire. "We could put the spare from one of the rentals on it."

"There's a repair shop in Whinburg," Jesse said. "We could get a replacement tire there. She ought to make twelve miles."

"Done," Matt said. "We've got reservations at a motel up there anyway. Heidi!" he shouted, and the girl jogged over. "New talent, girlfriend. Take Jesse here out to dinner and listen to his story. I want a shot list by nine tomorrow morning, and a list of locations two minutes after that. You local, son?"

"Sort of," Jesse said. "Over west of Strasburg. Does this mean you're going to do it? With me, I mean?"

"That's what it means, my young Amish friend. You go with Heidi here and she'll get you fixed up with a new contract. And maybe we can advance you a couple of hundred for a new set of tires and a balance."

Jesse's face split in a wide grin. "That'd be great. Just let me wash up."

As efficiently as they'd arrived, the crew loaded up the vans again, swapped out Jesse's ripped tire for a spare, and departed. And as Jesse got into the Falcon with the girl Heidi, Henry gripped the driver's side door. "Are you sure about this?"

Jesse nodded with reckless determination. "I only have one shot, so I'm going to take it. Thanks for everything, Henry."

"Take care of yourself, and let me know how you do." What else could he say? The current of other people's wills had taken Jesse up and was swirling him off with it.

The kid grinned. "Maybe I'll send you a picture of my new house."

"You do that."

And Henry stepped back. The Falcon coughed, wobbled, and finally fired up, and rolled down the lane.

Henry turned in his empty yard to look for Sarah, to share

this fresh disaster—maybe even see if she thought there was a way to stop it.

But nothing moved on the empty hillside except the wind in the grass.

❀

When Ginny opened the door at the Rose Arbor Inn, her eyes widened at the sight of him. "What happened to you?"

"*Shunning Amish*," he said. She went to hug him and it took a moment before his arms went around her to return the hug. The thought of what he was going to have to tell her made it hard to accept something as simple as a hug...when he knew he didn't deserve it.

"Tell me about it." She led him into her sitting room and sat next to him on the comfortable sofa, pulling up her feet under her. Her toenails, he saw, were painted orange.

He told her all of it—or nearly. About the arrival of the crew, about Matt and the lawyers that would probably descend like a swarm of locusts, about Jesse, heading off with them in a direction that would change his life. But he didn't say anything about Sarah. It seemed that every time they talked, Sarah got into the conversation somehow. Besides, those moments when she'd laid his motivations open to him were too private, too raw yet, even to share with Ginny.

"Oh, Henry, you poor man," Ginny said on a long breath, taking his hand. Hers was cold—and Ginny's hands were never cold. "I'm sorry you had to go through that."

"I'm sorry I let it drag on so long." But there was more. "If I'd just known myself well enough to say no when the idea first came up, none of this would have happened. Which is what I told Dave when I called him."

She went very still, and her hand tightened on his. "You didn't."

"Of course I did. I had to. I couldn't let him find out from Matt." Her fingers were starting to hurt. "Ginny? What else would you have had me do?"

She released his hand and knotted her fingers together. "I wish you hadn't. I'm sorry you had to go through this, but...I wish you'd gone after Matt and tried to patch it up. Why didn't you? He offered you a chance—even said they'd change the content. *Why didn't you?*"

He stared at her. "Because I couldn't stand the thought of the intrusion—into our lives, into our neighbors' lives. Believe me, by the time the crew left, they were already on to the next thing and forgetting all about me." Her fingers pressed to her lips, she closed her eyes.

He had to get all this out. To purge himself of it so he could start over. "Anyway. Dave."

"Please tell me that he didn't do what he said he would. That they'd pull the order if you didn't do the show."

Her tone was so tense with dread that it made him feel even worse—but the truth had to be told. "He did. He was furious—I actually had to hold the phone away from my ear because of the shouting. It was almost worse when he finally calmed down, because then it was lawyer this and contract that and..." He sighed. "One thing about Dave. He always does what he says he will. No Christmas order. No catalog shoot, no special section of the website, nothing. On November twenty-seventh, Henry Byler will cease to exist except in the bargain basement—quote, unquote."

Ginny gasped and buried her face in her hands.

"Honey, what is it?" This wasn't right. There was something more going on here than his own poor judgment and humiliation. "This isn't going to affect you or the Inn, I promise. Whatever the lawyers throw at me, it's on me, not you. Even if we have to move the wedding out so you're not affected financially."

When she lifted her head, the corners of her eyes were wet. "It's not that. Or at least, not the way you think. I just bought a nationwide advertising campaign from an innkeepers' co-op. *A Henry Byler mug with each booking. As seen on TNC.*" She groaned. "I don't even want to tell you how much it cost."

His stomach plunged into a deep, cold well, and sweat broke out on his forehead. "Can you cancel it?"

"I'll never get the deposit back—and it was nearly everything I had."

"We'll have a simpler wedding. Cut costs."

"That won't be enough."

"I'll sell the farm."

She got up, her arms moving jerkily as she fought off hands he meant to be comforting, but that she clearly thought were a restraint. "I need to think this through. Think what I'm going to do."

He gave her a few moments to pace across the braided rug and back, biting her lip. Running her hands through her hair. Clutching the top of her head as if she meant to keep it from coming right off.

Until he couldn't stand watching her distress for another second. "Ginny, can you tell me why you would have done such a thing without consulting me first?" he asked quietly.

"Consulting you? I did consult you. We talked about it before, when I told you I had a balloon payment coming up."

"You mentioned it in passing. As an option. Not that you were going to sink your savings into it."

"And what good would it have done anyway?" She stopped pacing and leaned against the door frame as if it would help hold her up. "You're an artist. You haven't been running an inn for years, dealing with banks, dealing with taxes and pay-roll and spreadsheets and everything that goes with it."

"Are you saying I'm not qualified to talk this over with?" Well, maybe he wasn't—not on that level. But he did his taxes every year, just like everyone else. "The only qualification I really have is that I'm going to be your husband, and wives and husbands talk over big decisions."

She sighed. "Right. Like you talked over the show with me before you told them once and for all you wouldn't do it."

She had him there. And who had he talked it over with? Really talked?

Sarah, that was who. The one name he couldn't bring into this conversation at any cost.

"Henry," Ginny finally said when the silence became un-bearable, "this isn't going to work, is it?"

"Of course it is." He couldn't let her give up hope. "I was serious about the farm. I'll sell it, and hopefully it will bring enough to pay off that balloon payment, with a little left over for me to find a studio somewhere."

"I don't mean the money." She took a deep breath. "I mean us."

He gazed at her, feeling as though a rocket had come out of nowhere and hit him in the stomach. "What?"

"Look at the two of us. Each of us went ahead and made a life-changing decision without getting the other person's buy-in."

"We talked—"

"Sure, we did. But not long enough to be sure the other person was a hundred percent good with it. All in. And we did it instinctively, because...well, I don't know why. Because we're used to doing things on our own? Because that's the way we are? Or is it because, deep down, we don't really want to?"

She was losing him. "Don't want to what?"

"Don't want to be a couple. Don't want to give that last little bit that would make us a couple—a unit. One being. Because there's something in each of us that's stopping that from happening, isn't there?"

"I don't—" he began. And then stopped. Because he did know, deep down. In his memory, he heard the echo of Sarah's voice. *You'll fall into the trap of letting this come between yourself and your family as a way of putting even more distance between yourself and your upbringing. You'll do it—and you'll hate yourself for it.*

Was that what he was doing with Ginny, too? Oh, he'd thought about it plenty. Marrying her and leaving the Amish life behind—the whole time thinking what a relief it would be to do something so irrevocable. To close that chapter of his life once and for all and finally be happy.

But from Ginny's point of view, what kind of a reason was that? Didn't she deserve better? Didn't she deserve a man who was marrying her for herself, not for his own selfish reasons? A man who was trying to barge in on happiness—to force his way to contentment, no matter what it meant for her— so that finally, this ache inside would be healed?

But I love her.

Did he, really? *Husbands, love your wives, even as Christ loved the church, and gave Himself for it.* Did he love her with that kind of love? At any time since they'd become engaged, had he given himself for her?

Henry buried his face in his hands and gave it a good

scrub, as if he could make his confused thoughts settle down into some kind of order. "Maybe you're right," he said at last. "Maybe we should postpone, until we've had time to think this through a little more."

"I don't think we need to," she said softly. "I think we know the truth. At least, I do."

"You do? Then please tell me, because I can't see my way to it to save my life."

Her warm brown gaze held sadness, and a growing resolve. "I only know my own truth, Henry. Don't get me wrong— the thought of being your wife made me happy, for a while. But since I went to Philly, it's been coming on slowly that I actually like my life the way it is. I like being able to make the big decisions. Good or bad, it's on me, and there's something satisfying in that."

"There is? What are you saying?"

"I'm saying that postponing the wedding isn't going to help, because there are bigger issues underneath that I don't think even time will resolve. I think we're fundamentally too different to be happy together. We just don't look at life the same way—and don't you think that's necessary for it to work in the long run?"

"But I love you," he said, a little helplessly.

"And I love you, you dear man." When she spoke again, her voice thickened with tears. "But it's not the kind of love that's going to survive these differences, is it? Not the kind of love that's strong enough to keep us together, straining toward one another, the way a husband and wife should be." She cleared her throat. "I don't even know if I have that in me...I'm content and happy to be on my own. I don't know if that's your path, but I'd like to think that if it isn't, I could come to your wedding and be glad that we made this choice."

He couldn't answer. Couldn't think. All he could do was feel the howling emptiness inside as he saw the door to safety closing.

And that, he realized at last, was exactly what she was trying to say.

He got up and held out his arms to her, and she came into them, her curvy body fitting against his so perfectly. But it wasn't the physical side of a relationship they were discussing, was it? That was like the tip of the iceberg, with so much more going on below.

"I'll always care about you, Henry," she whispered against his shirt.

"And I'll always care about you. But you're right. I don't know what's going to happen in the future—but I know you're right."

She walked him to the door and followed him along the path to the rose arbor that draped over the gate. When he turned back for one last look, she wasn't watching him go, but reaching up into the twining vines of the rose, tucking in an unruly shoot, plucking off a dead branch. The little moment of caretaking seemed to lift some of the tension from her face. And already her face looked calmer—the face of a woman who was exactly where she wanted to be, doing what she wanted to do, despite the stresses and decisions that came with it.

Henry walked blindly down the slope of the lawn to the creek, his heart a lead weight in his chest, his mind full of confusion and hurt and desolation. He found no comfort in the sere and gold of the falling poplar leaves and the purling whisper of the water. Unlike Ginny, he didn't see what things would look like next year, when they were in bloom.

On the contrary—everything around him just looked dead.

❁

No matter the state of his personal life, the Thanksgiving pieces for D.W. Frith still had to be finished. Dave Petersen had made it abundantly clear that if the pictorial spread hadn't already gone out in the catalog, the company would have pulled those pieces, too, and demanded the return of the second half of the payment.

As the week passed, Henry found himself wanting to talk to Ginny, though they weren't a couple anymore. Was it so bad to want to make sure she was all right? When four or five days went by and she didn't return the one call he'd had the courage to make, he wondered if she was out of town. Gone home to Philly to be with her family and find comfort there, maybe. Well, outside of calling, there was one source of information close at hand.

On Saturday he'd walked across the road to the Mast place and asked Priscilla if the Inn was open this week. Joe was over there, too, and the two of them looked contented somehow—if it was possible for teenagers to look that way.

"*Ja*, it is," she'd said, giving him a look that said, *Why aren't you asking Ginny?*

"Is everything okay, Henry?" Joe had asked, leaning on one of the posts that held up the verandah. "Your hands all right?"

He'd forgotten his hands had been suffering—they carried small hurts compared to everything else. The cuts had healed and he kept a jar of the balm on the side of the bathroom sink now so he didn't forget to keep the skin flexible and healthy.

"Yes, the balm of Gilead that Sarah had me use did the trick. I wish there was a balm for the rest of me," he added under his breath.

Joe didn't miss it, though. "We'll pray for you, Henry. What you did was *gut*. About the television show."

"Does the whole district know about it?"

"The whole township does, I think," Priscilla told him. "Sarah told us that you sent the television people away. But they haven't left, of course."

Henry turned abruptly from the view of the orderly Mast fields, now turned under and ready for their winter sleep. "What?"

"We've been run off our feet at the Inn—they've been staying there, you know, while they've been filming Jesse and his car."

"Staying at the Rose Arbor Inn?" he repeated incredulously. "Are they filming the Inn, too?"

"Oh, *ja*, and a fine time I've had convincing them that I didn't need to be in the picture. Katie Schrock won't even come to work—but then, with her wedding so close I'm not surprised. They made up some story about Jesse living in the boathouse—you know, where we found Eric Parker when he ran away to come here."

"Good grief."

"They paid Ginny some nice money to be in it, too—said they'd never heard of a black divorced New Order Mennonite and it was just too good to leave out." Priscilla shook her head. "She left the church ages ago. I don't see what it has to do with her now."

Henry sank onto the step. "She's doing it for the advertising. This is all my fault. And how's Jesse handling it?"

"Don't know," Joe said. "We're not really speaking much. Not a lot to say, *nix?*"

"He's doing a proper job of burning his bridges," Henry said with a sigh. "I thought he might go back to church."

"Not now, I don't suppose." And Joe and Pris had looked at each other and by some mutual telepathy decided it was time for Joe to go. "Church is at our place tomorrow," he said, and pointed. "There comes the bench wagon. Dat'll be looking for me and Jake to help set up."

Henry had walked home, deep in thought, and by Sunday morning, like the secondary wave of an earthquake, the shock really began to set in.

He couldn't sit at his wheel—after two mugs had spun off center because he couldn't concentrate, and he'd stretched a bowl nearly into a rectangle trying to control the tension in his hands, he gave up. He needed a walk to clear his head. Needed some time in the cold October morning down in the creek to try and make sense of his life.

Ginny. In despair, he walked the path next to the creek, heading not in the direction of town, lest—Heaven forbid—the film crew was still there, but in the opposite direction. *Aw, Ginny.*

The maples were nearly bare now, their bright, flashy fall colors gone, leaving the branches and the true shape of the trees exposed to view. Was it reasonable of him to even be disturbed? After all, she'd laid out a substantial sum of money because of him when she had debts to pay, and this was a way to ensure her hard-earned cash wasn't wasted. But at what cost? It was hard to imagine there wouldn't be some repercussions for her from the film. He hoped it would all be good. She deserved nothing but the best, laughing Ginny with her crazy earrings and brightly colored pants and her zest for life's smallest gifts, from flowers to sticky buns.

She had a huge capacity for happiness—and for seeing what was right. She and Sarah shared that capacity. But what about him? Where was he to find his happiness now? If not in another person, if not in his work for D.W. Frith, then where?

I will lift up mine eyes unto the hills, from whence cometh my help.

Unbidden, the words sounded in his mind in his father's voice. Dat had loved the Psalms—the poetry and rhythm of them. The sheer love of the Psalmist for his God that came through in the lines. His favorite of all had been Psalm 139.

Though I take the wings of the morning, and fly into the uttermost parts of the sea, Thou art with me.

That's what he himself had done—flown to the uttermost parts of, well, the United States. But God and Aendi Sadie had conspired to bring him back here. And all for what? To be left on the shore, humiliated and hurting, with nothing to show for his life? To never know happiness or a real home? Was that what God meant for him because he'd turned his back on the Amish life so many years ago?

Was it too late to ask God what He had in mind now that He'd brought him to the end of himself, down here in the creek bottom?

In the distance, carrying in the crisp air, came a sound. Long and slow, the way the wind had sounded in the pines and rocks around Boulder.

Music.

The sound of the congregation singing.

He must be just below his cousin Paul Byler's place. Henry climbed the bank and emerged in what had been a soybean field. In the distance was Paul's machinery shed, overlooking the county road.

By the time Henry had crossed the field, his feet moving almost without conscious thought, the congregation had begun the "*Lob Lied,*" the hymn sung second in every Amish service everywhere. Probably even in Colorado.

He came up behind the building, hoping everyone was inside and no one would know he was there. One shoulder leaning on the siding, his hands in the pockets of his jeans, he bowed his head and listened to the melody that was as familiar as the sound of his own name.

Let Thy word in us be confessed
Let us love it with devotion
And live in holy righteousness
Hearkening to Thy Word daily
So we remain undeceived.

I need to be undeceived. Help me, Lord. I've got nothing left. What do You want with me? How can I make my life right—make it worth living again? You've brought me here for a reason. Do You want me to come back to the Amish church? Is that what You want? Because even I can see that I'm not doing very well running the show on my own.

Henry stood there, listening, as the "*Lob Lied*" ended and the next hymn began. And he recognized this one, too, though he hadn't heard it nearly so often. Only twice a year, on the Sundays in October and April when the baptisms were performed.

They were having the baptism today. How many lives would be committed to God this morning? How many heads were at this moment bowed, up there at the front, hands over faces in humility, waiting for the moment when they would feel the trickle of cold water and the bishop would declare them members of the Body together, and welcome them into fellowship?

Despite how I felt when I first moved here, I can't imagine picking up and moving away, either. I feel as though I belong... and yet... there's more You require of me, isn't there? You brought me here on the day of baptism for a reason, didn't You?

I believe it now.

Oh Lord, help Thou mine unbelief.

A tear, hot and bitter, welled up and trickled down his cheek as he closed his eyes and covered his face with one hand. He no longer heard the sounds of passing cars on the road, or the crows in the plowed fields, or felt the brush of the breeze. He merely bowed his head and listened to the slow sound of the *Gmee* singing.

Because of this, the burden of sin
From man may now be lifted
And he may see a ready physician
Christ the healer of all wounds

Could it really be as simple as that—to see Jesus standing at the ready, with oil and wine to bind up his wounds, and to ask Him to come and do what He did better than anyone?

Henry gazed back down the long stretch of memory, trying to see that nineteen-year-old he had been and to understand his reasons for leaving. They had seemed urgent, then.

Urgent enough to leave behind home and family and try to learn how to live in an *Englisch* world for which he'd been completely unprepared.

He couldn't say that taking his own way had been much of a success. Maybe God had had a hand in that, too. Maybe the best years of all were the ones that lay ahead—ahead, where Jesus stood, waiting not for him to give up, but for him to give in.

To give. *Uffgeva.*

To lay his life safely in the hand of the One who would care for it and cherish it—who would heal it and make it whole again.

At the thought of doing that very thing, a wave of relief swept him. *Uffgeva.* The offering up of a life that had only ever belonged to God in the first place.

The tears dripped through Henry's fingers. But this time, they weren't the salty tears of bitterness. They held instead the sweetness of surrender.

And of joy.

CHAPTER 27

Dear Silas,
Thank you for your prompt reply to my letter, which I was happy to receive. I am glad you are going to be in the neighborhood for a visit. Oakfield is not so far away, and maybe there will be a bathroom there for you to renovate ☺ Miriam is very happy with the work you did on hers and loses no opportunity to bless your name.

~~I will be happy to see~~

It will be nice to see you here in church. ~~I wonder how you feel about courting~~

~~About simply being friends~~

~~The feelings in my heart have not changed. There is someone else~~

"I can't do this," Sarah whispered into the sunny silence of her compiling room, and laid down her pen.

She sat at the little white-painted table where so often patients sat across from her. Where Henry had sat across from her, and where he might as well be sitting right now, watching her trying to write a reply to Silas Lapp.

Crumpling up the sad excuse for a letter, she gazed at the empty wooden chair opposite. "This is your fault," she told it.

Thank goodness the boys had left early to go to the singing at the Kanagys' home—early enough, she suspected, for some fun and conversation first. Granted, Caleb was not yet sixteen, but if the younger ones didn't get into trouble and attract too much notice, the older ones often let them join in.

So she had the house to herself, to knit or read or write letters or simply sit here and talk to chairs.

In a while she could start dinner. Or perhaps a better use of her time would be to give it to another. She could walk over to her in-laws' and see how Amanda was doing, give Corinne a hand with dinner, and stay there for the rest of the evening and hope that the warmth and fellowship would raise her spirits.

True to her vow, she hadn't seen Henry since the Tuesday when the film crew had landed in his yard and left just as suddenly. She had stayed just long enough to hear Jesse Riehl volunteer to be the next subject of their film, and had turned on her heel and practically run for home.

That poor boy was going to go the same way as Henry himself had at nineteen, running headlong down a path that would lead him away from his family and church, maybe for good. She could only pray that somewhere down that road he would come to his senses, or that God would step in much as He had with Henry, and lead Jesse back to the green pastures and still waters where he belonged.

Henry might live in the middle of actual green pastures and beside a creek whose waters could only be said to be still when they were really low in the summer, but in a spiritual sense, as far as she knew, he was in a desert and far from the place where he could find nourishment for his soul.

Maybe that was the hardest thing for her to understand about his steadfast refusal to allow God back into his heart. She tried to imagine living right here in this house, so close to her family, and not being Amish. Not going to church every other Sunday, not having the deep fellowship, love, and acceptance that came with each one submitting him- or herself to God's will. Her imagination shuddered away from the picture.

This was what Henry had chosen, and still, in the darkness of the night, her treacherous heart yearned over him, wishing fruitlessly that another woman's man could be hers.

There was a perfectly good man in Lititz who might be yearning for her in the same way, and what was she doing? Trying to write a letter in which she couldn't tell the truth, and couldn't bring herself to tell a kind lie. As she'd found out early in childhood, a lie always came back around to bite you, no matter how good your motives were or how clever you thought yourself in spinning it. And besides, Silas didn't deserve such a thing. If she couldn't be completely honest with him, then at least she ought to make up her mind one way or the other. Be single... or allow his courtship knowing that it might mean marriage.

She wished *der Herr* would send her a sign so that she would know which path He wanted her to take. Because if there was one thing that was completely obvious, she needed His help.

With a groan, she pushed away from the little table, pulled a sweater off the hook in the kitchen, and went outside. Hadn't she found that when she really needed to be close to God, she could do it best in her garden? Simon had turned it over, and her hens were scattered over it like fluffy flowers, pulling worms and eating the seeds that had fallen, especially in the corner where the sunflowers had been planted. The big round heads were drying in the barn now, waiting for Caleb to nail them to the fence post outside the kitchen window, where they could watch the birds eating during the winter.

It was calming, walking between the beds that had held her crazy quilt pattern. And look, here came the silage radishes, responding to the clear weather they'd been having. There was nothing quite so astonishing and hopeful as the sight of the field greening over in October as the radishes came up, and tilling them under in the spring to provide nutrients for the soil. The radishes were hardy, and willing to sacrifice themselves so that other plants could live.

Sacrifice. Is that the lesson You wish me to learn, Lord? If it is, then I pray You will hold me and help me. It is a hard road, and only You can give me the strength to walk it.

Someone called her name, and it took a moment to realize it was not the voice of God, but a very human voice. One she knew as well as those of her sons.

"Henry!" Goodness, he looked terrible. "Are you all right? No, don't come in the dirt. I was just enjoying the chickens enjoying the garden. Can I get you something from the house?" *Maybe some of the trauma tincture?*

He waited for her to join him on the lawn, where she looked up into his face anxiously. "Got anything for terminal idiocy and a broken engagement?"

Oh my. Oh my. Don't react. Be normal. Be a friend, for surely that's what he needs most right now.

"In fact, I do," she said as steadily as she could. "My Sunshine Tea is good for blows to the spirit. Do you want me to put the kettle on and you can tell me about it?"

"No—no. It's one of those days where sitting is the last thing I want to do—and it smells good out here. Your radishes are coming up, I see. Where are the boys?"

"They're at the singing, over at Kanagys'. I suspect there might be something more interesting to Simon over there than singing and snacks, since they've gone so early."

"Ah. Isn't there a dark-haired girl Priscilla is friends with? Well, at least they won't have far to come home."

"I had hoped Jesse Riehl might have been with them, but I suppose all hope of that is gone?"

"I think Jesse is committed to his path now. Did you hear the crew had been filming at the Rose Arbor Inn?"

"*Ja*, I did." Sarah strolled beside him. "Everyone did. But I don't understand it. How can they film Ginny if you haven't agreed to do the show?"

"The crew were staying at the Inn, and somehow they involved her in Jesse's story. Priscilla told me that they were spinning it as though he was living in her boathouse while his car was being repaired, but that's a little far-fetched. More likely he was bunking on the sitting room sofa. At least, I hope so. I haven't heard." He gazed up into the maple trees, as though looking at the last of the red leaves. "I can't blame her. If both of them got something out of it, then all the more power to them."

"But I still don't understand," Sarah said after a moment of trying to work this through in her head. "If you were adamantly against the filming, and she is to be your wife, then how could she have gone ahead with something you didn't approve of and had already refused to do?"

"Trust you to hit the nail on the head." He met her gaze.

"Remember what I said a minute ago about the broken engagement?"

She hadn't believed it. Thought it might be some kind of dark joke. Could it be possible? "Oh, Henry...no..."

"Not because of the show. Ginny's a businesswoman and she has every right to choose to be on it if she wants to. She also has every right to choose a guy who knows what he wants out of life—which used to be me—or even no guy at all."

"Used to be?" She wished for a moment she had a cup of Sunshine Tea herself, to calm the bumping of her heart against her ribs.

"Last church Sunday, I couldn't work, so I took a little walk. Went the opposite way along the creek and wound up below Paul's place."

"Church was there that morning."

"I heard it. The singing. So I climbed up the bank and leaned on the back of the shed to listen."

"We had the baptism."

"So I realized, when you began singing number 108. That was always the one my dad chose."

"He was a minister?"

"Yes. And you know the verse about man being able to see the Physician ready for him? Why is that even in there?"

"Our ancestors had good reasons for everything they included in the old hymns. But I often think of the parallel— you know, how we bathe a wound before we dress it. It's like the cleansing of the baptism, washing everything away so we can start new."

In silence, he paced beside her. At this rate, they would have to open the gate and go into the fields.

"Is that what God is doing to me? Washing away my

whole life so I can start new?" He huffed out a laugh. "The Lord giveth and the Lord taketh away."

"*Ja*, He does," Sarah said quietly. And like the breeze in the trees, the words came in a rush. "He gives his Son in sacrifice so He can take away all our sin. So we can stand in front of Him not because we're worthy, but because His Son has stood in our place before." His gaze didn't falter, nor did he make a joke or turn away or change the subject. So she plunged on. "Maybe it looks as though everything is being taken away. Your prospects. Your contract. Ginny. My heart hurts for you, truly, because I think the love between you was real."

"There you're wrong, Sarah, much as it surprises me to say it."

"I'm wrong all the time. Just ask Linda Peachey. Or my mother-in-law. She just loves me enough to overlook it."

"Well, Ginny might overlook a lot, but when it came to marrying a man who wasn't a hundred percent committed to her, she drew the line."

"What do you mean?"

"We had a long talk. An honest one—probably the first really honest one we'd ever had. She cut through all my self-delusions and held the truth up to me so I had to face it. She knew it wasn't going to work but she was the only one with the guts to say it. And she was right. Love has to be whole. When it's divided, half isn't enough to live on."

Even Ginny could see that God wanted Henry for His own. What would it take for this stubborn man to see that for himself? "Come with me. I have to put the chickens in, and I don't want to wait to hear the rest."

"I don't know if there's any more to tell."

"Maybe not with words." They crossed the lawn to the

henhouse, where Sarah gently encouraged the last few stragglers to stop hunting in the grass and take refuge in its safety and warmth. When she closed the door and heard the sounds of settling for the night, she smiled up at him. "Come out to the orchard with me."

"Picking apples on a Sunday?"

"No. But you said you liked the way it smells out here. It's even better out there—and as you say, walking helps a person think."

"Who's thinking?" He fell in beside her. "You or me?" With a deep breath of the scented, cold air, he said, "You're right. There's something about the way an orchard smells in the autumn, isn't there?"

"Every tree contributes."

He chuckled. "To the sweet-smelling savor, you mean? I suppose it does. Is that what you're saying I can do?"

"Even if I was, I'm not the one to listen to. Listen to the still, small voice, Henry. What is it telling you?"

He was silent, the branches rustling as they passed. "It's saying, *You're home. Your family is here. Your church is here. Love is here. All you have to do is let yourself be healed, and reach out and become a part of it.*"

Sarah's throat closed and she could not have spoken if she'd tried.

And then their hands bumped accidentally as they passed under the last of the apple trees and reached the wagon track. The poplars that Michael's great-grandfather had planted as a windbreak lined this track on the north side of his fields. She would have jerked away, lest Henry think she was being forward and trying to attract his attention at a serious moment like this, but before she could, he entwined his fingers with hers.

It had been a very long time since a man had held her hand. She could feel the strength in those potter's fingers as they walked slowly along the windbreak. In the silence—as she teetered between the warmth that her heart craved and the knowledge that this was forbidden—the poplars rustled, the golden leaves whispering even as the last of them fluttered down on the track in front of them.

"My love wasn't divided because I was lost between being worldly and being Amish," Henry said quietly. "At least, that was only part of it. It was divided...because of you."

"Me?" Now her heart really would stop—if it didn't bump right out of her chest first.

"Yes, you. My gray-eyed friend who never hesitates to tell the truth, even when it's hard to hear. Who cares more for others than she does for herself. Who would never admit to loving outside the faith...but who does anyway."

He was silent while she struggled to find words to say, but they seemed to have left her and were up there in the poplars, whispering to themselves and being no help whatsoever.

"Am I right? Or have I made a huge mistake and I'm in this by myself?"

He was still holding her hand. And she would bet he wouldn't let it go—as long as she held on, too.

"You're not," she whispered at last. "In it by yourself. But Henry, we can't. It's wrong. You must give your heart to God before you share it with me—you know it and I know it...and God knows it."

He squeezed her fingers in acknowledgment. "Do you think Bishop Dan is home this evening?"

She gasped—more because she'd been holding her breath than anything. "Why?"

"Since the baptism was this month, that means classes will

start after Christmas for the spring baptism. I suppose if I drove the car over there to ask him to include me, that would send the wrong message, wouldn't it?"

She had her breath back now. "Henry, don't tease me."

"I'm not teasing. I'm dead serious. The problem is, I don't have a buggy and it's too far to walk."

There was just enough light to see his mouth twitching as he tried not to smile. "Oh, Sarah, the look on your face. Come here."

He pulled her into the circle of his arms while she tried to read his eyes in the fading light. "Do you mean it?" she whispered. "You're going to let God finish His work?"

He tipped his forehead against hers and linked his arms at the small of her back, where her apron was pinned. "He's gone to a lot of trouble to bring me here, and waited patiently for me to come to the end of myself. And it worked. I've got nothing to offer you, Sarah. A rundown farm. Probably a bunch of lawsuits. Only my heart—and I'm not even sure what condition it's in."

"The Great Physician will take care of that, once it's in His care. And don't forget your hands," she said softly. "Give your heart to God, and those hands to His service, and He will bless you. You'll see."

"And you? Will you accept them, too?"

A poplar leaf fell like a coin of gold. Then another, and another as the breeze caught them. A shower of gold, like a blessing, showing her the way she should go.

"At the baptism in the spring," she said against his warm cheek, "the old man will be put away, and a new one will be born. While I like the old one very much, and find him talented and smart and even rather good-looking, I know it will be safe to give the new one my love. To accept him no matter what God brings our way. And so will Caleb, and Simon, and my family."

"Good-looking, huh?" He grinned, and she had to laugh.

"A woman looks on the beauty of the inner man," she said primly.

"Ah, but can she kiss him?"

And that was a very good question.

But she couldn't answer it, because he proceeded to prove beyond a doubt that she could indeed.

EPILOGUE

On the second Thursday in May, the buggies began rolling into Jacob Yoder's yard before the sun had a chance to clear the tops of the hills. Though it was to be a small wedding, there was still more room over there than there was at Sarah's place, so the decision had been made to reserve her yard for the *Englisch* taxis and for those who were helping with the food. Small, to the Amish, was a relative term.

The service began at eight o'clock. To Sarah, though she had been married before and had been to dozens of weddings over the years, it still seemed as though she were walking in a dream.

She had put on a new blue dress that she'd made herself, even though sewing was far from her strong suit. Over it went the traditional white organdy cape and apron, and her *Kapp* was brand new and crisp with starch. Even her shoes were new, and her underthings, signifying a fresh start to her new life. Beside her for the preaching was Amanda, her *Newesitzer*, and across from them sat Henry, with Simon as his supporter. She had thought he would choose one of his cousin Paul's boys, but he had shaken his head and given her the smile he kept for her alone.

"We're going to be a family now," he'd said. "I can't think of anyone I'd rather have at my side than the young man who's going to be my son. It will be like your Michael being there, in a way. I'll make my promises to you in front of the *Gmee*, but at the same time, I'll make a few to him."

"What promises?" she'd teased.

But he'd grown serious. "That I'll love you for as long as God gives us together. That I'll look after you with everything I've got. And while I can never be the father he was to them, I hope I can be a good influence and an example to your boys, at least. And a friend."

Besides Sarah and Henry themselves, the happiest person in the congregation packed into the house was Caleb, who insisted on telling everyone he had seen this coming for months, and in fact was the person who had brought the couple together.

They let him think so, though Sarah knew who it had really been. God had had something special in mind for both of them, after their losses and trials. It had just taken a little time to soften their hearts and change their directions so they could walk together on the same road, both guided by His hand.

Across the space between the men's side and the women's, Henry caught Sarah's eye. It would never do to smile, but she saw it in his gaze. He wore a blue shirt that matched the color of her dress, but Corinne had made his wedding suit as a gift. "You'll be making his pants and shirts from now on," she'd said when she brought it over the week before, "but at least there's no blood from needle pricks on these ones."

Since he'd had no Amish clothes, the women of the family had discreetly pitched in to help her fill that need, until finally they had taken the *Englisch* clothes to the Goodwill in Whinburg and donated the lot.

And then it was time. Sarah rose to stand next to her bridegroom before everyone—the Willow Creek church; Henry's little sister Lizzie, who had brought her four children and the good wishes of all the relatives in Ohio; all of Sarah's sisters, their husbands, and children, who filled two *Englisch* vans and had to leave at four in the morning to make it from Mifflin County in time; Ruth and Isaac Lehman and their daughter, Amelia, and son-in-law, Eli Fischer, with their children; and at the back of the living room, Sarah saw a face that filled her with even more happiness, if that were possible.

Ginny Hochstetler sat next to the budding young potter Eric Parker, whose father had brought him from Connecticut for the weekend so he could be part of the celebration. Ginny's face held nothing but beaming happiness for them, and the last little corner of Sarah's heart filled with peace.

Henry's voice was soft as he made his confession, and then it was her turn.

"Can you confess, sister, that you accept this our brother, and that you will not leave him until death separates you?" asked Bishop Dan Troyer. "Do you believe this is from God, and you have come so far by faith and prayer?"

"*Ja*," she said softly. Oh, yes. Nothing less than faith and prayer had brought them to this moment.

They vowed their loyalty and their care for each other through sickness, health, and adversity of both the natural and the spiritual kind, and then it was done.

She was no longer Michael's Sarah Yoder, but "*Englisch* Henry's" Sarah Byler.

The next several hours passed in a blur of well-wishes and food and laughter—especially when Carrie Weaver's little girl and Amelia Fischer's little boy somehow got mixed up with a cake and a decorative tablecloth and pulled it over on themselves.

"Now, there's a match made in Heaven," Henry said, doing his manful best not to laugh as the blushing mothers set their children to rights and several others whisked away the evidence and cleaned up the floor.

"We'll see what happens sixteen years from now." Sarah smiled into his eyes from her place next to him at the *Eck*, the corner table reserved for the bride and groom and their supporters. "If it's God's will."

Wasn't that the lesson they'd both had to learn before God was able to bring them together in the way He had planned? Henry had to learn to surrender his own will to that of the One who knew better than he did what he needed most. And Sarah had had to learn to broaden her understanding of who exactly was the family God wanted her to care for. Her own, certainly. But more than that, His family and beloved children, of whom Henry and Joe were the very newest members.

There was nowhere as safe as the place where God wanted you, and Sarah's soul rejoiced that Henry could share it with her.

Later that evening, after everything had been cleaned up and the guests had gone back to farms and milking, and after they'd had a big family supper at Isaac and Corinne's before the out-of-town visitors went to find their beds for the night, Henry tucked Sarah's hand into the crook of his arm.

"*Kumme mit, mei Fraa,*" he said softly. "Let's go home."

Were there any sweeter words a man could say? Because her home was his now. Her acres had become their acres, and her yard his yard. And that was just as it should be.

But the garden was still hers, she thought with a smile.

They walked together along the well-worn path between the two properties, the smell of the freshly mown lawn and Corinne's roses heavy in the soft night air. Fireflies danced all around them, their light warm and liquid compared to the frost of the stars over their heads. Sarah extended a hand to brush the delicate heads of the Queen Anne's lace as she passed; since she didn't cut her hill, it had grown above her knees now.

"I have some news," Henry said, breathing deeply of the scent of the meadow.

"You saw Simon sitting with Rosanne Kanagy at supper? I put them together on purpose, you know. Bride's privilege."

"Son of the bride's request, you mean," Henry said wisely. "I know how these things work. No, I meant other news. About the farm."

She drew a breath of anticipation. "Lizzie likes it?"

His sister and her family were staying at the old place until Monday.

"More than likes it. I don't know what it is—she seems to have far clearer memories of Aendie Sadie and Onkel Jeremiah than I do, even though she's two years younger. She says she's always loved the place and she's going to talk to her husband about moving as soon as she gets back. I hope it will stay in the family." He squeezed her hand.

"Oh, I hope he agrees."

"It will be *gut* to have her here. Lizzie and I always got on much better than Anne and I ever did. Not that I don't love her, but Lizzie holds a special place in my heart. And she has a good man. They'll be able to make a success of it again, and with their boys just coming into their teens, there will be lots of work to keep them busy."

They crossed the log bridge over the creek and walked across the lawn. On one side was Sarah's quilt garden, with the peas already climbing their trellises and the tomatoes as high as her knee. The smell of her herbs was strong at night—lemon balm, verbena, elderflower, and calendula. On the other side, behind the orchard and nestled under the hill that divided their two properties, the bones of his new studio rose from their foundations. It would be spacious and airy, yet snug, for Henry had given Jon Hostetler explicit instructions about drafts and storage and temperature control when it came to green ware.

Henry had acquired a couple of clients since the debacle with D.W. Frith... people who seemed quite happy to adjust themselves to the schedule of a man who put his family and his church first before commerce.

Sarah slowed at the edge of the lawn, under the maples, and Henry stopped beside her, gazing at the house. Before they'd gone over to Paul and Barbara's for the night, Caleb and Simon had lit the lamps, the golden light shining out to welcome and guide the newly married couple across the fields.

"*Kumme mit, mei Herr,*" Sarah whispered, echoing Henry's earlier words. His hand was warm around hers as they climbed the steps together. "We're home."

Glossary

Aendi: auntie

Ausbund: Amish hymnbook

Bischt du kalt?: Are you cold?

Bob: bun; hairstyle worn by Amish girls and women

Bobblin: babies

Bohnesupp: bean soup, often served at lunch after church

Daadi Haus: "grandfather house"—a separate home for the older folks

Daed, Daadi: grandpa

Dat: dad, father

Deitsch: Pennsylvania Dutch language

Demut: humble

Denki: thank you

Die Botschaft: Amish weekly newspaper

Dochder: daughter

Dokterfraa: female healer

Englisch: non–Amish people

Fraa: woman, wife

Gelassenheit: humility, submission

Gott: God

Gmee: church community in a district

Grummbeere: potatoes

Guder mariye: good morning

Gut: good

Herr, der: the Lord

Hinkel: hens

Ischt du okay?: Are you okay?

Ischt gut: It's good.

Ischt krank: Is sick.

Ja: yes

Kapp: prayer covering worn by plain women

Kinner: children

Kumme mit, [mei Herr, mei Fraa]: Come with me, [my husband, my wife].

Liewi: dear, darling

Maedel, Maedeln: young girl, girls

Mamm, Memm: mother, mom

Mann: husband, man

Maud: maid, household helper

Meinding, die: the shunning

Neh: no

Newesitzer: lit. "side sitter," or the bride or groom's supporter

Nichts?/Nix?: Is it not so?

Ordnung: discipline, or standard of behavior and dress unique to each community

Rumspringe: "running around"—the season of freedom for Amish youth between sixteen and the time they marry or choose not to marry

Uffgeva: giving up of one's will, submission

Verhuddelt: confused, mixed-up

Was duschde hier?: What are you doing here?

Was ischt?: What is it?

Wie geht's?: How goes it?

Youngie: young people

READING GROUP GUIDE

1. Have you enjoyed getting to know Sarah Yoder and her family?
2. Do you think Sarah has grown as a person and as a child of God as she treats the members of her community?
3. What do you think Henry's greatest difficulty was in this book? Have his conflicts changed since we met him in *Herb of Grace*?
4. One of the themes in *Balm of Gilead* is that real friends tell each other the truth, even when it might not be what the other person wants to hear. This is based on Psalm 51: *Behold, thou desirest truth in the inward parts: and in the hidden part thou shalt make me to know wisdom.* Have you ever been in a position to do this? What kind of experience did you have?
5. Do you think that friendship is a balm that can heal life's hurts? Can you share a time when you experienced this for yourself?
6. In the unwritten period between the last chapter and the Epilogue, when Henry was taking baptism classes and before he joined church, do you think that Sarah allowed their relationship to be public?
7. Do you think it's wrong to put conditions on love?
8. Amanda Yoder has had a hard time in the relationship department. What do you think she'll do now?

9. If Silas Lapp comes to visit his friends in Oakfield, and decides to court Amanda, do you think it's right that Amanda should settle for being second best, if it means having a home and family of her own?

10. Has God been able to speak to you through books, nature, and reading about the Amish? What lessons have you appreciated the most?

The Healing Grace Series

Herb of Grace
Book One

To help make ends meet, Amish widow Sarah Yoder becomes an herbal healer using the plants she grows in her garden. As Sarah compiles her herbs, she awaits God's healing in the life of a man who rues a decision he made years ago, and in Henry Byler, a lonely prodigal with whom she shares a budding—and forbidden—attraction.

Keys of Heaven
Book Two

While treating a woman for infertility, Amish herbalist Sarah Yoder does her best to accept that Henry Byler will never return to the Amish church—in fact, he has taken a pottery commission that will ensure plenty of worldly recognition. But what happens when Sarah and Henry are called upon to help a runaway *Englisch* boy—and it unexpectedly brings them closer together?

Available now in print and electronic formats from FaithWords wherever books are sold.

Visit the neighboring community of Whinburg, Pennsylvania
in the Amish Quilt Series

The Wounded Heart
Book One

Widowed with two young children, Amelia Beiler struggles to run her late husband's business until Eli Fischer buys it. Eli has a personal interest in her, but when she's diagnosed with multiple sclerosis, Amelia feels she must keep her distance in order to protect him.

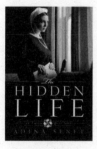

The Hidden Life
Book Two

Thirty-year-old Emma Stolzfus cares for her elderly mother by day and secretly writes stories by night, her hidden life shared only with close friends. But when a New York literary agent approaches her about her work, it will change her life in unexpected ways.

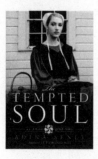

The Tempted Soul
Book Three

After years of marriage, Carrie and Melvin Miller fear they'll never be blessed with children. Carrie is intrigued by the medical options available to the *Englisch* in the same situation, but her husband objects. Is God revealing a different path to motherhood, or is Carrie's longing for a child tempting her to stray from her Amish beliefs?

**Available now in print and electronic formats from FaithWords
wherever books are sold.**